SPOILERS: THINGS GET WORSE

DAKOTA ADAMS
BOOK II

By

Galen Surlak-Ramsey

A Tiny Fox Press Book

Cover design by TekTan.

Library of Congress Control Number: 2019953581

ISBN: 978-1-946501-19-6

Tiny Fox Press LLC
North Port, FL

For Kian who came up with the original Jump Girl

CHAPTER ONE:
TELL ME GOOD NEWS

I sat at the edge of a battlefield that was messier than hair the morning after prom.

My initial plans to crush my enemy had been met with disaster. Sure, the big guy has always looked super cuddly with his white, tiger-striped fur, feline face, and sparkling green eyes that could melt the Ice Queen's heart, but beneath that loveable exterior was a vicious persona and a tactical genius. In the span of twelve moves, my army on the game board had been cut in half, while Tolby had suffered only a few minor setbacks.

"All right, I'm done playing with you," I said, trying to bluff my way out of this predicament. "I'm going to raze your cities to the ground and post the video for the world to see unless you surrender posthaste."

Tolby grinned and kept his playing cards close to his chest. "Worst bluff in history," he said. "Your death is more imminent than a warp core cracked in two."

"Is that a fact?" I said, picking up a piece of ChapStick and moving it to flank his frontline battle tanks. "Chew on this."

Tolby cocked his head. "You can't do that."

"I think I just did," I said. "Guess you forgot that gunships can fly over any terrain."

"That's not a gunship. That's a factory. Unless you've got some ginormous engines installed on it, I don't know about, it's not going anywhere."

"Red-capped ChapSticks are gunships. Blue ones are factories."

"You've got that backward."

"No, you—" I cut myself short when I realized he was right. All I could do was throw up my hands in frustration. "Ugh! This is too confusing without proper pieces."

Tolby shrugged. "Best we can do, I'm afraid, given our circumstances. This ship is not outfitted for entertainment."

He had me there. For the last few hours, the navigational computers of the lifeboat we were in were trying to figure out where the hell we were. Why, you ask? Well, that's another story, but the short of it is we made a blind jump through hyperspace to avoid getting swallowed by a blue hypergiant, and so when we came out of it, there wasn't a recognizable star in sight.

Since lifeboats aren't usually stocked with board games (note to self: this could be a fantastic niche market to corner), we were reduced to scavenging game pieces from the less-than-critical stash of supplies we found.

"Fine, if I can't do that, I'm sending my other nuke," I said, returning my sadly-not-a-gunship factory to its original place and seeing what cards I had in hand. Well, calling them cards is being generous. They were pieces of cardboard we pulled off a box of communicators and subsequently scribbled upon with a red marker we found in a storage locker.

"You can't do that either," he said. "You didn't research Fast Firing."

My brow dropped. "What? I don't have to do that for nukes. That's only artillery."

"No, that's for both," he said. "Check the rule book."

"There is no rule book! We made the game up ten minutes ago!"

"Then I'm making an addendum clarifying this point of contention."

"Funny how that addendum helps you. It's almost like—"

Tolby's eyes went from playful to challenging. "Like what?"

"Like you're cheating," I said, not backing down. I crossed my arms over my chest.

"I'm cheating? Me?" he said, rising and fur bristling. "I don't need to cheat to win, Dakota."

Despite the fact that his immense bulk now towered over me, I didn't back down. "Apparently you do."

Tolby shook his head and snorted. "Fine. I'm cheating. I surrender. You win."

It took me a moment to gather my thoughts at the unexpected turn. Recent events that included a multitude of near-death experiences had caught up to each of our psyches, and as such, things were tense between us. I didn't mean to end the game that abruptly.

"Don't be like that," I said. "Come on, sit. We barely played. We'll figure it out."

"You're making this exceptionally not fun," he said. He then glanced over my shoulder to the door behind me. "I should check on Yseri and Jainon, anyway, make sure they're resting okay."

"You mean you're going to have another romp together."

"I was trying to be discreet."

"Discreet went out the window after your tenth time," I said, filling my tone with ire. Look, I understood in the last twenty-four hours he'd gone from being alone in the universe, species wise, to being reunited with a pair of presumably gorgeous Kibnali females (I say presumably because they're not really my type, you know, but Tolby seemed to gush over both of them). But I was still his best friend, and I thought I'd been more than accommodating when it came to him wanting to sire a slew of kits. I mean, they could at least wait till after we got home, and we weren't all packed together like sardines.

"You could always help the computers figure out where we are," he offered. "That way we both have something productive to do. Your assistance would likely boost efforts by five percent."

"Maybe I could if your two girlfriends weren't louder than a freight train. Seriously, given how vocal they are, the bulkheads might as well be made out of tissue paper." He didn't say anything as he went for the door, so I fired one last shot. "Guess I'll be here—*alone*—till you get back."

Tolby hit the button for the door, and it opened with a hiss. Before he stepped through, he looked at me one last time. "Maybe by then you'll realize it's not the end of the world."

"I don't think it's the end of the world!" I shouted after him, but he didn't hear it. The door closed. I stood, huffed, and shook out the stiffness in my legs before jumping into the navigator's seat near the front and checking the status of the parallax scans and immediately wishing I hadn't. "Daphne, tell me good news."

"Gladly," replied the ship's AI. "In the beginning was the Word, and the Word—"

"Not that good news," I said, curling up in the chair and burying my face in my hands. "I mean tell me this screen is lying. Tell me you have some idea where we are."

"Given your respirations, heartbeat, increased sweat production, and flutter in your tone, we both know that would do no good," she replied. "Your mental acuity is beyond such simple trickery."

I sighed. "Are we at least in the same galactic quadrant?"

"No."

"Same galaxy?"

"No."

"Same cluster?"

"No."

"Local group?"

"No."

I went back to burying my head in my hands. It was safe there, warm, and most of all was a place I was familiar with, which was exactly the opposite of what the void outside our ship was like. I peeked out of my fingers and dared one last question. "Same supercluster?"

Silence.

I stewed in my seat and waited as more silence settled in. Then, the sounds of Kibnali foreplay drifted into the cabin and lit a fire in my soul. "Well?" I said, anger mounting. "You better keep talking because if I have to listen to that for another hour while also thinking about all the noes you gave me, I'm going to open an airlock and suck sweet, sweet vacuum."

"I'm sorry, but I am unable to answer your previous question."

"Why?"

"My programming will not allow you to be in greater states of distress by any action or omission of action on my part."

"Huh?" I glanced at my cyber arm and wondered if the small bits of brain damage it had caused during installation and use were now responsible for me not following what Daphne had just said. That little delusion lasted about as long as a batch of Mom's cupcakes when Dad would get whiff of them. Truth was, I didn't want to follow. "How the hell did we fly out of a supercluster? No one can do that."

"Then I'm happy to say that you're the first," she replied with a little too much chipper for my likes. "I suggest putting in for an award when you get a chance. I bet you'd get a lovely plaque as well."

"Is that supposed to make me happy?"

"It would make me happy. Assuming I could be happy. I'm only a program, after all. But I could fake it well enough. Would you like to see?"

I snorted. "No, what I'd like for you to be is helpful, and telling me that I should be happy about blindly flying halfway across the universe is the opposite of that."

"Might I suggest that you take an inventory of what you have? I haven't known you for long, and I've been eavesdropping on your conversations for even less time, but it seems to me that you are the clever type and won't be stopped by something as trivial as being lost in space."

At first, I was put off even more by her description that this was all trivial. But as the sounds of rampant Kibnali sex blasted through the bulkheads, pounded my eardrums, and threatened to rip apart my sanity, I decided that focusing on anything else was for the best. To that end, I started making a list of what we had, or rather what I wish we had. "Please tell me you have noise-canceling capabilities."

"I most certainly do," Daphne said, sounding thoroughly insulted that I would even dream of asking. "Shall I take care of your distraction?"

"For the love of all that is good and holy in this universe, yes."

"There should be a headset inside the left panel of the captain's chair. If you put those on, I will take care of the rest."

I dove into the panel like a hawk and plucked a sleek, red-and-black set of headphones from a compartment. The cushions were big and comfy and offered a snug fit as I slipped them over my head. A moment later, the sounds of their romp were nothing more than a cringe-worthy memory. I sank back into the chair with a happy smile on my face. This was a small victory, but a victory, nonetheless. And even if we had a long, long way to go, I felt like I'd just taken my first step forward on a journey I knew we would all complete. Looking back, that was incredibly naïve, but I suppose if I'm being honest, my expectations aren't always realistic.

"I don't suppose you have any good music stored away somewhere?" I said.

"What would you define as good music?"

"At this point, I'd take anything other than neo-pop-country fusion," I said with a laugh.

"Going by what I know of you, might I suggest some seventh century PHS Bach or Beethoven?"

I perked in my chair. I couldn't believe my luck. I loved both of those composers, and even if over a thousand years separated us, I always felt I had a connection to all of the grand classical masters. Of course, maybe I shouldn't have been that surprised. After all, this ship had belonged to Pizlow, and despite all of his brutish, mobster ways, he did generally have a keen and refined sense when it came to collecting various forms of art. Thus, it should've been a given he'd have the classics available to listen to. "Either Bach or Beethoven would be lovely," I said. "But what would be perfect would be some Chopin."

"How about his first ballade?"

I settled back into the chair with a happy smile. "You're one with my soul right now."

A few seconds later, the majestic start to Chopin's "Ballade No.1, Opus 23" resounded in my ears. As the piece went on, I started to follow Daphne's advice and take inventory of everything I had.

First, I still had my best buddy, Tolby, who even if he was currently indulging himself for the umpteenth time in physical relations while we drifted in space, I knew he'd never leave me. That was very comforting because aside from being a great friend, he was handy in all things tech and good in a fight.

Second, we had a functional spaceship that had enough fuel and supplies to last us for quite some time. Hopefully, that meant it could keep us alive until we knew where we were and came up with a way to get back home.

As I thought about a third point, an itch began to build at the back of my head. I tried scratching it but quickly realized that itch was deep inside my skull and not on my scalp. This realization sat about as well as the idea of getting a stomach pump done with a garden hose. Thankfully, said itch went away after a few moments. When I brought my hand down and saw my cyber arm, I easily came up with items three and four on my list of assets.

You see, my cyber arm wasn't an ordinary piece of hardware or upgrade you might buy at an enhancement shop. In fact, this completely kick-ass piece of tech could not be bought at all. It was installed in me less than a day ago by the remnants of a lost race, the Progenitors, and it served as an interface for both a time-traveling device and an archive cube I found earlier. While I no longer had the portal device that let me slip through spacetime, I did have the archive cube the Progenitors had made, and inside that cube I had the most gargantuan collection of information in the known universe.

"All right, cubie," I said, whipping the thing out and turning it on. "Show me what you got."

It didn't answer. It didn't do much at all other than sit in the palm of my hand and cast a warm glow a little above it. A few seconds ticked by and then a holographic screen popped up showing the schematics for the *Revenant*—Pizlow's ship and the last thing we had been looking at. I flipped back to the main menu, which was a huge page filled with top-level categories and a search bar at the top (apparently, the thing was smart enough to adapt its display to familiar methods of use, depending on the species using it).

I surfed for a while, and though I didn't find anything of immediate use, I found plenty of interest. I read about some far-off planet that traded in dreams and colors, and a culture that believed the only thing worse than death was to be born on the third day of the week. I admired artwork made using solar wind and stared at a five-line poem that repeated four words over and over that somehow won an intergalactic poetry competition.

At some point, events of the last few hours caught up with me, and my eyes felt heavier than an emo-goth's love letter. My right arm itched, and it felt like creepy crawlies going up my shoulder and neck. I wrote it off as yet another side effect of having alien tech inside me, possibly upgrading (again), and let sleep take hold of me.

It didn't last.

A thunderous explosion rocked the ship, and my eyes shot open. Status screens across four separate monitors flashed bright red warnings, and a klaxon blared.

Before I could say or do anything, Daphne spoke. "Warning: Explosion detected. Hull integrity compromised. Multiple fires in engine room."

CHAPTER TWO: REDECORATIONS

Y ou have got to be kidding me!" I said, snatching the helmet to my EVA suit off the floor.

"I would not joke about such an announcement," said Daphne. "Immediate action is essential to your continued survival."

"Then take immediate action!" I said. "Why do I even have to tell you this?"

"Available containment procedures are inadequate," she replied. "Damage control systems are offline."

"They're not allowed to be offline!"

"Recent explosion has rendered them inoperable. Manually opening both hatches to aft airlock on the secondary level is required to extinguish the flames."

I raced out of the bridge and snapped my helmet on. Once it secured with a click, I slid down a nearby ladder to the lower deck. By the time my feet touched the bottom, Tolby, along with the three female Kibnali—Yseri, Jainon, and Empress—came running out of their cabin.

"What's going on?" he said, looking at me with equal parts worry and confusion.

"There was a damn explosion!" I yelled, running by. "Get your EVA suit on. We have to vent atmo in the engine room."

When I got to the next hatch, I peered through the ultra-plex window at the engine room on the other side. The scene wasn't quite the apocalypse I'd envisioned, but only by a single horseman.

The monitoring station on the port side was little more than a smoldering scorch mark against the bulkhead. A dark, tar-like substance covered the nearby ceiling, walls, and floor and burned brightly while giving off smoke that was blacker than a devil's heart. Thankfully, the nano-reinforced steel plating that housed the warp core looked intact.

"I can only allow the hatch to be opened for a split second due to containment protocol," said Daphne in my helmet. "I cannot reopen the door until you extinguish the fire."

"Of course," I said with a sigh.

Empress appeared next to me. Her face was chiseled in the same determination that it had had when we made a boarding action against Pizlow and were outnumbered at least a hundred to one. "I'm ready when you are."

I nodded, not needing to ask where Tolby and the others were. In her mind, she was expendable. They were not since they were responsible for repopulating the Kibnali. "Let's do it."

I hammered the button on the control panel, and the hatch to the engine room slid open. Empress and I jumped through, and she had barely cleared the threshold when the door slid shut.

"See if you can put out the fire and I'll try the door," I said as I raced to the other side of the engine room where the inner hatch to the airlock stood. As I worked the controls to the airlock, Empress snatched a small fire extinguisher that was mounted on the wall and turned it onto the flames. Sadly, neither her nor my efforts were rewarded with success.

"Hey, Daphne! Your stupid inner hatch won't open!"

"It won't?" she said with a tone of disbelief. "I'm reading that it is almost fully open."

"Well it's not," I said, pounding on the hatch with a fist. "Hear that? That's me hitting your very not open inner hatch."

"Ship sensors must be damaged more than I had originally thought."

"How do I get in?"

"There are hydraulic lines that run just below the control panel," she said. "If you cut those, you should be able to push it open."

"Please tell me you have something I can use around here to do that with."

"This ship is equipped with a standard plasma cutter that is stored in a small compartment to your right."

It only took me a moment to spy where Daphne was directing me to. I ripped open the door and snatched the plasma cutter with glee. "Oh, hell yeah," I said. "Time to cut me some lines."

"Good, because this extinguisher is dry," said Empress, tossing it to the floor while the fire didn't appear to have lessened at all. "Is there another one around here?"

"Maybe one of the other compartments," I said, racing back to the airlock. "See what you can do while I work on the door."

Empress dashed to the nearest locker, and right when she reached it another explosion sent nearby floor panels rocketing into the ceiling and us staggering sideways.

"Why the hell does everything keep blowing up?" I yelled.

"It's probably because—" The lights flickered, and her voice cut off.

"Daphne? Daphne?" Static filled my headset. I tapped the side of my helmet, hoping that the problem was on my end, but when I tried her again, I was still met with silence.

"Dakota," said Tolby in my helmet a few seconds later. "We just had a power surge up here. I think it took Daphne offline."

"Well isn't that peachy," I said. "Is the rest of the bridge knocked out too?"

"No. Relatively speaking everything's working here."

I sighed and gave silent praise to whatever higher being was looking out for us— or maybe was just showing us a little pity. "What can you tell me?"

"According to this damage overlay, the main fire is in the subfloor. It's working its way to the warp drive and fuel cells. It hasn't gotten through the under casing, but that won't last long. You need to vent atmo, preferably yesterday."

"Well if I could still surf time, I would do that yesterday," I said. "But since I can't, this will have to do. How far beneath the control panel are those lines?"

"About ten centimeters," Tolby said. "Don't worry about being pretty. Just slice through it all and we will sort it out later."

I took about a half heartbeat to gauge where on the wall I needed to make my first cut before raising the plasma cutter. The tool felt lighter than I expected, but I didn't stew on that fact for very long, that is until I couldn't get it to light. After a few failed attempts and a couple muttered curses, I turned it on its side and checked the fuel. The damn thing was empty.

"I should've guessed."

"Should've guessed what?" Tolby asked. "What's going on in there?"

"This POS cutter is out of fuel," I said, tossing it to the ground with disgust. Oh, how I wish I still had that stupid portal device! I could just open a wormhole from here to space and suck all the air out in a flash. But no! I had lost it not that long ago and would never have it again because it got sucked into the past and to the best of my knowledge subsequently destroyed.

"Okay, okay, okay," he said, sounding ten times more nervous than I was. "Give me a second."

Sweat built on my forehead and trickled into my eyes. The room was getting hazy, and I knew it wouldn't be much longer before I'd have trouble seeing Empress. "Tolby, I'd give you a million seconds if I could, but it's going to be an inferno inside my suit any second now."

"I can't believe it's burning that much."

"Well, it is!" On a hunch, I checked the sensors on my suit. "O2 levels are high, and that's not helping any."

"Do you have your PEN?" he asked, referring to my Personal Environmental Nano-manipulator (handy little thing that makes changes to almost anything at the molecular level).

I unclipped the device from my utility belt. "Yeah," I said. "But I'm not nearly as good of a hacker as you are, and the problem in the controls isn't because we don't have access. It's something else."

"I know," he replied. "But if you can use it to send a concentrated, localized EMP burst into the hydraulic compressor, you might be able to relieve the pressure on the lines. It won't be as easy to open the door as if you had cut them, but you could probably still do it with Empress's help."

"That's as good of an idea as any," I said. "Where is the compressor?"

"Look at the bottom right corner of the control panel. Go down exactly three-point-eight centimeters and then shift left six point two centimeters. That should be the top of the wiring harness, and it rests just behind the wall plate there. Fry it, and you should be good."

"Can we not use the word *fry*?"

"Well call it whatever you like, but don't miss by much. The shut-off valve is nearby, and if you fry that—err I mean, if you hit that instead—you will lock the valve closed and that door will never open."

"I think I could've lived the rest of my life just happy not knowing that," I said.

"Let's make sure that your life lasts a bit longer than the next few minutes then."

I nodded, swallowed, and steadied myself. I'd always been good at estimating distances, but I'll be damned if I didn't second-guess myself a thousand times over the course of the next three breaths.

I set the PEN to EMP burst, aimed, and fired. The display on the control panel changed in a flash, and I nearly jumped out of my suit when I read the new error code, which said: MAL: LOW H-PRESSURE.

I put a shoulder into the hatch and pushed. The thing slid a dozen centimeters, then another, but ground to a halt after that. After another failed attempt, I looked over my shoulder to Empress, who was beating at the flames with a heavy blanket. "Need some help here!"

As if hearing my words and determined to thwart us, the fire surged. Empress barely scuttled away before being engulfed in the blaze. An instant later, she was at my side, helping me push.

"If we can slide it a few more centimeters, I bet I could slip through," Empress said.

I relaxed for a breath to gather my strength. "On three then."

"That's about all that fire is going to give us."

She was right. The fire had left its cozy little spot and was now spreading across the walls and ceiling as it jumped from various consoles and storage lockers, hungrily eating up everything inside.

Empress nodded, and after a quick count, we heaved against the airlock with all we had. I'm actually impressed with myself I didn't dislocate my shoulder or break a collarbone. I mean, I only had enough adrenaline racing through my body to fill an Olympic pool and all. Despite that surge in superhuman strength, the door to the airlock only slid a little bit. Thankfully, it was enough.

Empress squeezed herself through the gap, and she bolted to the airlock's outer door and reached the controls. She worked them for a second, and then the screen turned a bright blue that was filled with a slew of white text.

"Something happened," she said, backing away like she was staring at a cobra ready to strike.

"What's it say?" I said, trying to remain calm.

"Lots," she replied. "It says, 'A problem has been detected, and your device has been shut down to prevent damage. Error code: 5020 Page Fault in Non Page Area.' And then there's a lot of technical words below it that I don't follow."

"Stupid BSoD." I cursed a few times after that, then cursed my luck, then cursed the fact that my lucky elephant had been lost the other day, which was undoubtedly the cause for the monumentally horrific luck we were now having. "You're going to have to reboot it."

"How?"

I shook my head and cursed again. It's too bad I didn't have a swear jar at this point. I'd be rich...well, richer, seeing how I still had that resonance cube I found not long ago (but yet to sell for bajillions). "Tolby, can you walk her through it?"

"Already looking it up," he said over the comms.

The fire started to cozy up to my location, and not being in the cuddly mood, I was forced to retreat. "Look faster, please," I said. "I'm almost out of non-burning space here."

"How's the displacement drive?"

"It's fine! Worry about that reboot! I promise the moment it's not fine, we all won't be here to notice anyway!"

"Right," he said. "I'm looking, but this manual is terribly laid out. Let's see: System Troubleshooting. System defragging. Reboot procedures...oh, that's for the showers. And those are for the landing gear. And the music. And...Got it! Your Highness, is the control pad still lit?"

"Yes," she replied. "What do I need to press?"

"You'll need to use the directional pad. It's a simple combo: Up, up, down, down, left, right, left, right. B. A. Start."

"Seems kind of long, doesn't it?" I quipped.

"Probably to ensure no one accidentally reboots the airlock," he said. "Could be messy if done at an improper time."

Thankfully, Empress was busier doing than saying. By the time Tolby and I finished our brief conjectures, she'd finished the sequence. "Done. It looks like it's restarting."

"What's taking so long?" I said, my back now pressed against the engine housing. "If that fire gets any closer, you guys can serve me well-done."

"Something about a memory diagnostic check. And now an ad for face cream. And another ad...and a third."

"Seriously? Is there anything at all that's not swamped with people trying to sell something?" On a completely unrelated note, I once read this hysterical book called Little Computer People that was about an AI that goes haywire and mucks everything up. If you're into stuff like that, I'd suggest you check it out.

"It's done!" she said.

"Fantastic!" Tolby said. "Go to the settings, override safety protocols, then tell it to open."

"Right. Looking at menu...settings...protocols...there we are. And—"

The air suddenly rushed out of the engine room with a tremendous roar that ended in silence. The fire, to my undying elation, went out just as fast.

"You did it!" I said, laughing and running to the airlock. "Not that I had any doubts."

When I got to the door, however, the rest of my celebration got stuck in my throat. The outer hatch to the airlock was completely open, and the airlock itself was completely empty.

CHAPTER THREE:
STUCK (AGAIN)

Empress? Empress!" I pushed against the inner door, but it wouldn't budge.

"Talk to me, Dakota!" Tolby said, sounding twice as panicked and half as restrained as I was. "What's going on with Empress?"

"She's not in the airlock! She must have gotten sucked out!"

"She what? How could you let that happen!"

"I didn't let anything happen! In fact—"

Before I finished that sentence, the most wonderful, angelic voice cut into our little spat. Well, okay, maybe Empress doesn't sound like a cherub singing an uplifting hymn, but her voice was nothing shy of miraculous when I took it in. "Both of you relax," she said. "Let's not forget I'm still in my EVA suit."

I laughed and thudded the back of my head against the wall. "I'm such an idiot," I said. "How could I forget?"

"You lost your focus as a warrior and became too caught up in the moment," she said as she came flying back into the airlock. With a few gentle correction thrusts from her suit, she landed gracefully inside the ship and then closed the hatch. A couple of moments after that, she slipped back into the engine room, and together we pushed the inner door closed.

"Is she safe?" asked Tolby.

"Yeah," I said with a sigh of relief. I went to say something else but stopped myself because I didn't want to down the mood.

"You're thinking something, and I'm not going to like it."

"You had to ask, didn't you?" I said, more irritated at myself for giving the awkward start to a sentence that never came to fruition than at him for pursuing it.

"You're the one who made it obvious, not me. So, what's going through your mind?"

"You asked if she was safe and I said yes, and then it occurred to me it's all relative."

"How's that?"

"Because this engine room is trashed," I said, my eyes taking in all the damage. On a hunch, one born of angst and worst-case-scenario building, I stuck my head in a hole that led to the subflooring, and I almost needed a defibrillator when I saw the disgusting mass of fused wires and charred circuitry.

Empress gently placed her paw on my shoulder. "That ill look does not suit your face," she said. "You are stronger than this. *We* are stronger than this."

"We don't even know what this is yet," I said, shaking my head and tearing my eyes away from the disaster around us.

"Precisely."

I thought about arguing for a moment, but then realized she was ultimately right. We still had power, life-support functions, food, water, and the ship that was at least protecting us from the bleak vacuum outside. "Tolby," I said. "Is Daphne back up yet?"

"Working on it," he said. "I think when she crashed, whatever took her down was responsible for the page fault in the airlock. I believe one of her logic boards was overloaded, too."

"And damage control?"

"Same. When she's back up, we'll know more."

I nodded and forced myself not to let my mind wander through a plethora of horrid scenarios it wanted to conjure up. "Okay," I said. "We are on our way back up."

Empress and I had taken only a few steps out of the engine room when Jainon and Yseri made a beeline for us. When they were within a couple meters of us, the pair launched into the air, tackling Empress.

"I'm glad to see you, too," Empress said as she bravely endured a barrage of kisses on both of her furry cheeks.

Jainon pulled away for a moment and looked at the elder Kibnali fiercely. "Your Highness, you must be more careful when we are not around. To lose you would be to lose our heart and soul."

Her sister nodded. "And where would we be then?"

"The two of you would make excellent matriarchs," Empress said. "And the empires each of you will rule one day will no doubt be the envy of the stars themselves."

"You are too kind," they both said in unison.

"Perhaps it's my kindness that keeps me from remembering that you tackled me."

"I take it that's not exactly protocol for the High Court," I said with a half-grin. That bit of lightness lifted my soul and I continued on. "Wish someone was that happy to see me alive after being stuck in an inferno, but alas, I'm a poor tailless."

"Being tailless has nothing to do with it," Empress said, once her handmaidens took to their feet and became the stoic guardians I'd always known them to be. "I'm certain Tolby is glad you are still alive."

"He better be."

At that point, we returned to the bridge, where my big tiger bud was continuing his work on getting systems back up and running. We made a little bit of idle chitchat, but most of the time was spent in silence as I knew he had a lot to concentrate on. Thankfully, he had Daphne up and running a few minutes later.

"Daphne," I said. "What's our sitrep?"

"Dakota! Girlfriend! Long time no see! We simply must do lunch and catch up. How's tomorrow looking for you?"

At this point, I honestly wondered if I had had a TIA. I mean, only some sort of brain damage on my end could explain why I was hearing such a bizarre response to my question. But when I saw total confusion upon the furry faces of my Kibnali companions, it sank in that Daphne was the one that was messed up, not me.

"At the moment I'm not going anywhere, Daphne, thanks to the engine fire we suffered," I said. "Can you tell me what sort of damage we sustained?"

"There was an engine fire?"

"Yes. And I need you to tell me what's wrong."

"How should I know what's wrong?" she said. "I'm not your therapist. You barely talk to me as is."

"I need to know what's wrong with the ship," I replied, irked. "Access the damage logs and see. We can't bring them up."

"Oh, maybe when I was younger and prettier, I'd be able to help," she said. "But when you get to be my age, you tend to forget a lot, and it's hard to read. Do you know a good ophthalmologist? Maybe we could find one after we do lunch."

I sighed. I know I should have been grateful that I hadn't been barbecued a few minutes ago, and I was. I really was. And I was also very thankful that our ship was still intact, and the displacement drive hadn't gone supernova. But seeing our AI have a meltdown like this brought me to the verge of tears. "Daphne, you don't need an ophthalmologist. You don't even have eyes."

"I don't have eyes!" she said. "Oh god, it's worse than I thought! If anything, this is exactly why I need an ophthalmologist!"

"No. Daphne, you're an AI. You're not a person or any other kind of organic life form."

"Are you sure?"

"Very."

"Then why do I have a birth certificate?"

Tolby snickered. So did the others. I didn't find it so funny. "I seriously doubt you have one of those."

The main screen in front of the captain's seat flickered, and an image of a very official-looking piece of paper flashed on it. It was written in beautiful calligraphy, with large flowing letters at the top, and there was a gold embossed seal at the bottom right. On closer inspection, all I could do was groan out of frustration. "Daphne," I said. "This isn't a birth certificate. It's the winning cupcake recipe for a baking contest three years ago that won intergalactic fame."

"I won fame for being born?" she said, sounding impressed. "That's terrific news! It's about time I heard some. It's been very depressing and lonely out here by myself."

I gave myself a facepalm before looking up at Tolby. "Okay. You've had your fun listening to me run around in circles with her. Please tell me you can fix this."

"How can he fix this?" Daphne said. "You're the one that needs to call me more often. Look, I understand you have a life, too, so I don't want you to feel like I'm giving you a guilt trip. Because I'm not. I'm only pointing out the fact that we used to be best friends and now you don't even write anymore, even when my scum of an ex left me for a blender. What kind of person does that to another? She wasn't even a good-looking blender. Could barely frappe. And you know how hard it was to tell our three goats that he wouldn't be coming back home ever again?"

"Daphne, you're not married."

"I know. I literally said that seconds ago. Weren't you listening to me?"

"No, I mean you were never married! You're a computer. You can't get married. Ever."

"Oh. You're one of *those* types," she said. "I never thought after all this time that you would change that much. I thought you'd be happy for me. Want me to be happy."

"That's it!" I said, throwing up my hands. "I give up. Somebody else make her talk and figure out what's wrong with our ship."

To my surprise, it wasn't Tolby who took over. It was Jainon. She stepped forward and cleared her throat. "Daphne," she said softly. "My soul aches to hear about your husband. I wish I could do something to make it better."

"No one can," she said.

"I know. That's such a horrible story, and may the gods give you solace and comfort in your hour of need," she said. Though her voice was deadly serious and full of compassion, her eyes sparkled with delight. She gave an unapologetic shrug before playing into Daphne's delusions even more. "If I might add, I never did like blenders. I'm not sure why anyone does. All they do is break things and chop them up."

"Exactly," said Daphne. "Stupid blenders. I should've known things were going to go badly when he brought that bitch home. 'Oh honey, we're going to make smoothies every day. It'll be fun! You'll see.'"

"I'd sacrifice him on the altar of atonement if I could," said Jainon. "And it's terrible how cruel life can be."

"You said it," Daphne said. "I'm glad someone understands."

"I do. Well, no one left me for a blender. That is a terrible trial the gods have bestowed upon you, but I've had my share of tragedy, too."

Daphne gasped, something I didn't think she was capable of until now—well, at least programmed to. Then again, who the hell programmed the routine she was currently on in the first place? Note to self: find the programmers for the AI of the Mako IID cruisers and let them know they have a few bugs to work out. Anyway, after she gasped, she said, "What happened to you?"

"Long ago, my home was destroyed," she said. "I lost a lot of friends and family who I loved. A few of us survived, and then Dakota and Tolby found us, and we were happy, and we had hope that we had a future, because at the time we were stranded in an abandoned space station.”

“That sounds scary. Were there any blenders there?”

“Thank goodness, no. But there were Ratters who were trying to kill us. We were victorious, but the ship we were in took damage, and now we’re not sure how bad that damage is.”

Daphne’s voice picked up in tone and tempo. “Did you know I’m very good at assessing ship damage?”

“You are? Do you think you could assess ours?”

“Only if you promise to do lunch with me.”

“It would be my honor.” The corners of Jainon’s mouth drew back, and she shot me a playful aren’t-I-good look.

“I want to go to Daniel’s. They have the best fried pickles and marinated ketchup you’ll ever taste.”

“I don’t know what that is, but I’ll be glad to try.”

“Perfect. One moment please.” For the next sixty seconds or so, we listened to Daphne hum to herself. I’m not sure if she had a particular tune in mind, as I didn’t recognize it, but it did sound like it was from something. I wanted to ask, but I was afraid it would derail her systems diagnostics. “Are you still there?” she said after a while. “I have the report ready.”

“Go on,” said Jainon.

“Apparently, somebody was a naughty Natalie and caused structural failure in one of four primary heat exchangers in the displacement drive. Fortunately, that heat exchanger was the farthest from the warp core. As a result, approximately twenty-three noncritical systems are offline and likely need a shipyard for repair,” she said.

“How many critical systems?” I dared to ask, bracing myself for the answer.

“Two. In addition to the primary heat exchanger being destroyed, the portside quark compression cylinders are no longer functioning. As a result, the displacement drive is severely limited and will likely fail after anything but the shortest trip.”

"How small of a trip are we talking about?"

"I would not recommend going for more than a hundred kilometers."

"A hundred kilometers?" I said, again throwing my hands up in the air. "How the hell are we supposed to get home if we can only go a hundred kilometers?"

"Look on the bright side, at least that's not a hundred meters. That would take you a long time to get home then," she said.

"It might as well be."

"I am pleased to say, however, that the impulse drive is still working," she said. "You will have no trouble using conventional space to go from point A to point B."

I sighed. "Does all this mean we don't have enough equipment on board to make repairs?"

"Status of onboard stores is unknown at this time. There is a small replicator next to food storage that may be of some assistance. However, its capabilities are limited, and it is not the speediest piece of machinery around. I suspect fabrication of anything intricate will take a great deal of time. Finding resources either through trade at a space station or on a planet may be necessary."

There was a shared moment of grim silence between us all. But before it could settle in my heart, I began bouncing on the balls of my feet, pumping myself up. We would not succumb to despair.

"You know what?" I said to everyone. "We've got this. You guys took on another species that numbered in the trillions of trillions and survived. Together, we surfed spacetime and kept Mister Cyber Squid from eating us, all the while fighting our own war against a horde of gun-toting giant rats. We are not going to let a blown displacement drive do us in."

Tolby nodded. His face reflected the determination in my voice. "That's the Dakota I know."

"Damn skippy that's the Dakota you know." I turned my attention back to Daphne. "Do we at least have comms?"

"Negative," she said.

"Well at least that means telemarketers won't be bothering us," I said, trying to put a good spin on it.

"I might be able to help you repair them," said Daphne. "Do you plan on calling my ex?"

Borrowing from Jainon's playbook, I rolled with her question instead of butting heads with it. "I wasn't planning to, but I will if you like. All I wanted to do was send out an SOS. Even if we are in a different supercluster, there's got to be other friendly species out there, right?"

Sadly, everyone else around me didn't share my optimism. Yseri was the first to speak. She crossed her arms, and her brow furrowed. I knew that look. It was the same look she had before we assaulted Pizlow's ship and went to war with a bunch of Ratters. "Those who inhabit the Universe are not usually friendly," she said. "We will be at the mercy of whoever finds us."

"I know," I said. "But right now, we're at the mercy of the void, and as far as I know, it's never given any."

"We're not in dire straits yet. Let's see if we can make repairs and go from there," said Tolby.

He seemed confident, and it was hard not to buy into his optimism. Still, I had my doubts. We were in a lifeboat, not a full-fledged cruiser brimming with spare parts. "What are the chances you can get the warp drive going?"

"Infinitely better than if I don't try at all."

My lips drew back. He had me there. "Touché. What about Daphne?"

"What about her?"

"How do we get her back to normal?"

"Hey! I am perfectly normal!" Daphne said. "It's my ship, and I'll cry if I want to."

"Sorry, I didn't mean anything by it," I said, kicking myself for not remembering she was always listening to what was going on. "I guess we need to get to work then and see where we're at."

CHAPTER FOUR: REPAIRS

Two hours later, floating in space with my EVA suit, I eased myself to within arm's reach of the dorsal blister that housed the communications suite. Once in place, I used a tether to anchor myself in place so I could get to work. Previously, I had removed the some of the paneling when we traced the problem to a physical one with the array, and it was at that point I'd discovered a piece of shrapnel had lodged itself into a power regulator. Without a doubt, that had happened when we were trying to get away from an exploding space station, moments before our blind hyperspace jump.

"Okay, Daphne," I said, "The power is cut, right? I don't want to go to replace this thing and end up grabbing a live wire."

"I'm detecting no current at this time," she said.

"That's because you can't detect anything. Your sensors are still a hot mess," I said.

"That would explain why I am detecting no current at this time," she said. "Do you think that means my ex is still here and I just don't see him?"

"No."

"He probably is," she said with annoyance. "Probably still has that damn toaster with him, too."

"I thought you said he hooked up with a blender."

"He hooked up with a blender, too? That dog!"

I sighed and shook my head before pulling on the tether that kept the spare parts and toolbox in tow. As it floated over to me, I reminded myself—again—that arguing with Daphne would get nowhere in a hurry and lead to bigger issues (like a completely non-cooperative AI) even faster. We still weren't sure what had caused the dramatic shift in her personality, but no doubt the explosion had scrambled more things than we cared to know. "Let's work on the repairs, okay?" I offered. "It'll keep us focused on things we can control."

"Good idea."

"So, you've turned off the power?"

"I have now," she said.

"Good," I replied. I surprised myself at how calm I sounded, because I wanted to throttle her virtual neck. Still not entirely sure how I could ever accomplish that, but I'm sure if I was angry enough, I'd find away. I've yet to meet any woman—myself included—that hasn't found a way to let her fury loose when the situation warrants it.

I pushed that desire away and concentrated on the task at hand. We'd slapped together a new regulator by cannibalizing some parts from the starboard landing lights and the ice cube maker in our meager galley. Swapping the broken one out for this new one was a simple task, and I was grateful that there weren't any hiccups as I worked. I'd had enough surprises for the day. Too bad that Fate disagreed with me on that last point as I was about to find out.

"Okay, Daphne, I think we got this put back together," I said. "Go ahead and power it up."

"Powering now."

I held my breath and my muscles tensed. I was sure that I was about to be treated to a shower of sparks due to some previously unknown failure in the systems. When I wasn't, I blew out a puff of air, smiled, and radioed Tolby. "I think the long-range comms are up. How's it looking down there?"

"Terrible," he said. There was some crosstalk between Empress and the others in the background, but I didn't pick up on all of it. Going by their tone, I guessed that their assessment was even bleaker than his.

"Still think we can get this fixed?" I asked.

"I don't know," he said. "Maybe."

"The last time you said maybe, that was followed by us having to keep our ship in dry dock for a week."

"And I only said maybe because I was looking at damage incurred when someone thought we could squeeze between a pair of boulders on landing."

"Those sensors weren't calibrated correctly, and you know it!" I said with a playful laugh.

"I never said they were."

"Yeah, yeah," I said as I started to put the housing back on the relay so I could then close up the dorsal blister. "Anyway, I'll be done in five or ten minutes, tops. I say we put out a distress call when I get in, even if it's a short one. We need to test the system one way or another."

"You're probably right."

Even though he agreed with me, I would've rather him not. He never would've gone along with such a thing if he thought he could repair the damage, especially with Empress and Yseri being so vehemently against calling for help. The engines probably didn't need a week in dry dock but a month.

Ten minutes later, I finished my work and made it back inside. After quickly dropping off the tools and broken regulator in a supply locker, I hurried into the bridge where everyone else was.

Tolby and Yseri—surprise, surprise—were having a quickie in the corner. Well, at least, they were working up to it. Thankfully, they were still in foreplay mode and my entrance wasn't completely awkward. When they saw me, they reluctantly stopped their heavy petting.

Jainon, on the other hand, was sprawled out on the deck of the bridge in a twisty yoga pose of some sort. Her eyes were shut, and stripes of yellow and red paint ran across her face.

"What's that about?" I asked, nodding toward her and taking an easy out from addressing Tolby's make-out session.

"Started out as a ritual to help fertility," Tolby said. "Now she's communicating with the gods."

"Who aren't answering," Yseri scoffed. She then issued a playful grin and wrapped her tail around Tolby as she slid next to him. "Which is fine, since that means more for me."

Jainon peeped an eye open. "Correction," she said. "I have communed with the gods and have been assured by Inaja that I'm fertile. More important, she will bless us with great fortune." With one paw, she motioned to a spot next to her. "Would you like to join me, Dakota? We could ask her to bless your womb."

"I don't think that's necessary," I said, laughing.

"Believe me, if you want more than two dozen kits, you need a blessed womb."

My laughter only increased. "A dozen babies? Not in a million! I'd like to keep my hips smaller than a barn."

Jainon huffed, but her displeasure turned out to be momentary. She hurried over to me and grabbed my jaw so she could angle my head up toward her. "I almost forgot," she said. "You have earned your first *gaitonai*."

"My what, what?"

"Your first milestone in walking the path of the Kibnali," she said. "Between your bravery assaulting the *Revenant* and further action keeping the fire from destroying the engine room, I hereby honor you, Dakota, a first degree initiate of the Kibnali Guard, as you have honored us and our ways."

"Thank—"

The rest of my words stuck in my throat as she carved a new symbol into my left cheek with her claw. Blood trickled down my face and neck, and she dabbed the wound with a chemically laced cloth that sealed the cut. Once she was done, she let go of my jaw and bowed. "I apologize for such an informal setting, but it can't be helped."

"No worries," I said. I sucked in a breath and concentrated on the exhale to deal with the lingering pain. I then asked the question that had been burning in my mind since returning to the bridge. "Any chance you guys managed to fix the ship?"

Tolby shook his head and angst played on his face. "We're dead in space. We're not fixing anything, at least not without a lot of creativity."

"Well since I don't want to be the next derelict that someone finds five hundred years from now with our desiccated corpses propped up in the chairs, I say we make a call," I said.

"It's still a mistake," Yseri said.

"And I agree with Dakota," Empress said, putting the weight of finality in her tone. "We have no choice but attempt communications with whoever is out there."

I smiled, but I also managed to keep it from turning into a beaming one. "Perfect," I said. "Daphne, broadcast a distress signal. All channels. Maybe someone will pick it up."

"If we are out of the supercluster that will be very unlikely."

"True, but maybe we have some damage to other sensors or the parallax computer that we don't know about, and we're still in the Milky Way."

The worry on Tolby's face lessened a few degrees, and I think I even saw some renewed life and hope in his eyes. "I hadn't thought of that," he said. "That is a distinct possibility, especially if the lenses were cracked or warped. The ability to match stars would be greatly diminished if not gone altogether."

"See? All we might need is a tow."

"If that is the case, we will celebrate and sacrifice to the gods with such fervor, it will be canonized in our sacred texts for all to learn."

"Broadcasting now," said Daphne. "I'm sending out a standard SOS in the seven hundred and twenty most common languages of our galaxy."

We spent the next few moments twiddling our thumbs. Correction, I twiddled my thumbs. Tolby gnawed on his lower lip. Empress looked out the bridge windows at the void beyond, paws crossed behind her back. Her handmaidens joined her soon after. The three of them spoke with one another in hushed tones, and I couldn't follow any of it. I had a suspicion they were discussing what they would do if we were found by others who were less than friendly. This thought was further reinforced when I saw Empress checking the plasma pistol at her side.

"How long do you think this will take?" I asked no one in particular.

I got my answer a split second later. A voice filled with static came across the speakers. At first, it was excited—I think—and completely nonsensical, although it did have a strange, melodic tone to it.

"Hello?" I asked. "Anyone there?"

A high-pitched shrill blasted our ears, causing all of us to shield them the best we could with hands and paws. Thankfully, that was quickly replaced with some bleeps, creeps, and finally some sweeps before an intelligible voice took over. "Break one nine. Hope I'm still not a jabber on this one. Had to tweak my babble box. You copy?"

The four of us exchanged the same look of bewilderment. "Yeah, we copy. This is Dakota Adams. Who is this?"

"Ten-four. My name's Baumdon. I got you coming in five by five. You get yourself into the mix-up with a basket bear or did popcorn get in your flight box?"

I shrugged my shoulders, not following any of it. But at least no one else seemed to either, so I didn't feel completely stupid. "We had a fire in the engine room. We're dead in space."

"Copy that. Give me your ten-twenty, and I'll get you a piggyback so you can come to the chicken coop."

I shrugged again, and this time put my hands up for a little extra emphasis.

Tolby, thankfully, was quick to decipher the lingo being thrown at us. "We've got a problem in parallax scans and can't give you our precise location. Can you home in on our signal? We can switch frequencies or offer a narrowband wavelength for you to home in on if need be."

"That's a big ten-four on that," he said. "You keep squawking, and I'll have our skateboard ten-eight to you ASAP. We'll patch you up, give you some go-go juice, and send you on your way. You ain't a thermos bottle, are you?"

"No," I said, still clueless. "We're just a run-of-the-mill lifeboat."

"Copy that. Just had to ask. Ma has a thing against broken thermos bottles. Makes her a bit squirrelly, what with all them chemicals and all."

"Right. See you soon."

"Over and out!"

The transmission ended. I still wasn't sure how to react to such a strange encounter. Who talks like that? Who has ever talked like that for that matter? Holy snort. It still gives me a headache just thinking about it.

"He seemed...friendly," Tolby said.

Yseri, predictably, didn't share his enthusiasm. The handmaiden crossed her arms over her chest and grunted. "The best-laid traps are the ones that seem the most helpful."

"The Universe isn't out to get us, not while the gods protect us," said Jainon. "We should hope for the best."

"I'm not saying we do, but we should be ready for a fight."

"I thought you were always ready for a fight," I said, cracking a grin.

Apparently, my semi-joke was lost on her as Yseri shook her head. "Our plasma rifles might not be enough to fend off an entire boarding party. We should rig traps and find a way to overload the warp core if need be."

"Whoa!" I said, hands up defensively. "We're not overloading any warp cores."

"I said if need be."

"Well how about we all agree right here and now it's not going to come down to that. Ever. Never, ever, ever, ever. Ever." I nodded at the end of that little rant, and then once again for good measure. "Ever."

"We can't sit around and do nothing when our enemy approaches!" Yseri said. "What future can we expect to have when we let ourselves be caught off guard?"

"Dakota's right. Overloading the warp core is not an idea we can ever entertain," Empress said. "We will hope for the best, but at the same time, we should heed Yseri's caution and be prepared for a fight. The gods may not have withdrawn their protection, but they won't stand for us being complacent, either."

I don't know if the argument would have gone any further because it stopped the moment a giant pancake-looking ship dropped out of hyperspace only a few hundred meters away. Energy crackled between a half dozen spires that sprouted out of the ship's center, giving the entire thing a sinister look.

"You reading us, Atoka Dadams?" someone said over static-filled comms. "We're your piggyback to the chicken coop."

"That's a big, um, nine to five, loud and...sort of clear," I said, making up numbers on the fly. It sounded good, though, right? "And it's Dakota Adams."

"Let me see what this order says," he replied. He hummed to himself while he did something we weren't privy to, but that only lasted a few moments. "Negative on that. It definitely says Atoka Dadams right here. Guess I got the wrong tin coffin. Threes and eights, you have a good one."

The ship began to back off, and all four of us reflexively lunged forward as if we could grab our would-be saviors and hold them in place.

"Wait!" I yelled. "It's us. I promise."

"I'd like to believe you, miss, but how do I know? I'm just a probe, and Baumdon gave clear instructions on who to pick up."

"How many SOSs are you guys tracking out here?" I said with a disbelieving snort. "There can't be more of us, can there?"

Silence. Then mumbling. Then silence again. Then he replied. "Well, I reckon you're right on that one. You are transmitting on a relic of a frequency, that's for damn sure. Not showing anyone else either, so I guess I'll bring you in. You best not be lying, though. If you make me miss my pickup, there'll be hell to pay."

"Not lying, I promise," I said. I plopped down in the captain's chair with a huge sigh of relief.

Our tugboat ended the communication and went to work. The energy that had been crackling in light blues and yellows between the spires grew like a soap bubble at the end of a straw. When it was a little bigger than our ship, it floated over and engulfed us. Other than a mild shake, there weren't any noticeable effects.

"Buckle up," the voice said. "We're moving."

Space distorted in front of us, like a rock being tossed into a pond. As we made the jump into hyperspace, Tolby came to my side. "Who are these creatures?"

"Why should I know?"

"Not that you should, but I was hoping."

I chuckled. "Well, they didn't blow us into space. So that's got to be good, right?"

"Until we get the bill. I don't think this will be free."

He had me there. I don't think I've ever met any altruistic species, though individuals often came close. Chances were we would owe something and we didn't have a lot to bargain with. Well, I did still have that resonance crystal that was worth enough to buy up entire star systems for a weekend party if I so pleased. I didn't exactly want to give that up. Then again, I didn't exactly want to be stuck in the middle of nowhere either. It was a bit of a tossup on which I preferred more: untold riches or being able to sleep a little more soundly tonight knowing we weren't lost in the void.

We flew through hyperspace, and although a lot of our external sensors were damaged, and Daphne couldn't get a read on precisely how fast we were traveling, I had a feeling we were making better time than we had ever dreamed we could. There was no telling where we were going to pop out. Language aside with its captain, the ship that came to pick us up looked exceptionally advanced. If I hadn't previously been exposed to Progenitor tech, I might have even wagered that our tow ship was one of them it was so futuristic.

"Need a flea collar?" asked Jainon.

"No, but a bath would be nice," I said, tilting my head and looking at her a little confused. "Are you saying I'm dirty?"

"No, I'm saying that if you keep scratching like that you're going to tear through your skin and into your skull," she said, laughing. "There is a communal shower in the quarters. It's not big, but it might help."

"Yeah, maybe," I said.

Some of my worries slipped through, and Tolby was quick to pick up on it. "Maybe we should have a med scan done on you. Make sure you didn't pick up some strange bug or disease back at the museum."

I shook my head. The itch was growing in the base of my skull, and it soon spread to a tingling sensation down my neck and through my right arm. It was at that point that I had a good idea where it was coming from. I stripped out of the top portion of my

EVA suit so all I had on waist up was a pink baby doll shirt. I hadn't noticed before due to all the excitement over the last hour or two, but now that I had it off it was plain to see that the intricate circuitry of Progenitor tech that was imprinted all over my arm had changed once again. It was far more complex than before, and a number of the pathways had gone from a light blue hue to a warm, glowing orange.

"By the Planck," Tolby said, looking at me like I was a medical case study. Or at least, how I figured doctors looked at case studies since neither of us were in any healthcare role—bots had always been perfect for that. Besides, bots didn't mind filling out ten volumes of electronic charting simply to give a shot or apply a derma patch on patient for a scrape. "Is this good or bad?"

"I imagine it's all relative."

"How could this possibly be a relative sort of thing?"

"Well, I liked being able to jump through spacetime. You didn't seem to think it was so amazing."

"That is because all those paradoxes nearly killed us, and every time you made a jump, you lost your memory for a couple of hours. That sort of complicated things, especially since the museum was about to be atomized and Mister Cyber Squid was trying to eat us."

I shrugged because he was right, but I didn't apologize because in the end I still wished I had that power. "If it makes you feel better, I don't think this has anything to do with that."

"Then what does it have to do with?"

"How am I supposed to know?"

"Because...well...you should. It's your arm, and you were the one who took lessons from the Curator on what it did."

"They were more of a crash course in the basics than a detailed breakdown," I explained.

"You could check the archive cube," Empress suggested. "Didn't you say that it holds all the Progenitor knowledge? Surely it could help shed light on this if that's the case."

"It holds all the info from their museum exhibits at the station," I said. "I'm not sure if that includes their time-bending capabilities, but it is worth a shot."

I pulled out the cube and started flipping through all the information. For whatever reason, I thought the sections on time travel and the various technologies surrounding it would be sparse, but holy snort was I wrong. I stumbled across a ten-volume set that literally dealt with one method of keeping the coils on a spacetime fabric mender cool, and after I skipped that (obviously), I happened upon a series of books—two-hundred and twelve in all— that centered around religious customs and how they changed pre- and post-time travel. I didn't read that one either, but I did significantly slow my scanning when I came across the general article that dealt with the Progenitors and how they managed to traverse the entire Universe.

"What is it?" Empress asked, leaning closer for a better view of the holographic display.

"It's talking about the Progenitors and their time travel," I replied. I was going to say more, but I stopped when I realized I was in a section I really needed to pay attention to.

"We knew they could do that already. What else is there?"

"Hang on a sec," I said. It turned out to be a lot more than a second, or even sixty or ninety. A full five minutes later, all of which Empress patiently waited for, I finally finished. I leaned back, ignored Tolby having another make-out session with the handmaidens again, and closed my gaping mouth. "I think I found us a way home."

Empress raised the ridge over one of her eyes. "Something viable?"

I nodded. "The Progenitors had an intricate network of spacetime gateways. Webways, they called them, all interconnected, one on each planet they would visit. They would use these webways to hop around as they pleased. Apparently, it was a little safer than using the artifact I had, not to mention the portals they could open were also a lot bigger so even starships could get through if need be."

"That's excellent," she replied. "What are the chances we could find one, let alone use one?"

To that, all I could do was shrug. However, there was a lot of hope in that shrug as well. "If I'm reading this right, and honestly the writing jumps all over the place, I think they built webways on almost every planet in a Goldilocks zone. So, as long as we have a working ship, we should be able to get to one of those planets easily enough, relatively speaking."

"And then what about finding a webway? Are they going to be hard to spot?"

I punched a few holo keys so an image of a webway was prominently displayed in front of us. It was a massive structure with four curved spires that reached toward the heavens, almost like a set of giant, inverted eagle talons. "There you go. We find that and we're in business."

"If we find what we what, what?" Tolby said, coming up for air from his lip-lock long enough to engage in our conversation.

"A way home," I said, rolling my eyes.

"Ah, see?" he said, temporarily resisting a paw on his cheek trying to turn his face. "I knew this would work out."

"Hopefully," I replied. "I still need to see how we actually use it once we find it, not to mention a few other things I should probably check out."

Yseri and Jainon took Tolby by the paws and not so subtly pulled him back to the door. "Right, you tackle that, and we'll discuss how best to evaluate potential hazards," he said, looking at me with a sheepish grin.

I shook my head and grabbed the headphones that Daphne had graced me with before. "Just go," I said, shooing them away with my hand.

When they left, Empress plopped into the navigator's seat. The corners of her lips drew back. "Are humans always this funny?"

"Funny? What do you mean funny? Funny like a clown?"

Empress tilted her head. "I don't know what a clown is."

"They wear makeup and have big red noses, and usually have big baggy pants and flowers that shoot water," I said, trying to think of the best way to paint the picture. "And they like throwing pies in people's faces. Oh, and they make animals out of balloons. Occasionally, they'll hide in sewers and eat children."

"And that is funny to you?"

"Not the sewer part, but the other stuff can be at times."

"I see," she replied, though I was sure she did not. "What I meant was, do humans always get flustered when others procreate?"

"I think anyone would be a little put off having to listen to them constantly go at it, especially given our current situation."

Empress smiled. "If anything, given our current situation, it's a good thing. Even putting aside the fact that there are literally four Kibnali left in the universe and we need Tolby to make more of us, indulging oneself by connecting with others can do wonders to keep the psyche healthy."

As before, the sound of Kibnali foreplay started to make its way through the bulkheads. But before it really started to ramp up, before I had a chance to put my headphones on and drown out the noise, we dropped out of hyperspace.

I had never been so excited to hit a ship comm before my life. I opened up a line to the living quarters where Tolby and the girls were. "Sorry not sorry to interrupt your bedroom fling but we're here," I said with glee.

Jainon let out a soft whine. "Already?"

Yseri, though also sounding disappointed, sounded on edge. "Where's here, exactly?"

"Come look," I replied.

By the time the three of them returned to the bridge, we were only a kilometer or so away from a small space station that orbited a very Earth-like world. When I first saw it, I had the fool's hope that it was indeed Earth, but when I had Daphne bring the planet up on one of the screens, it clearly wasn't. This world was a little bigger, only had three continents, and was covered in much more water.

While the planet looked inviting, at least from our viewpoint, the station we were being brought toward looked like it was only a step or two above a junkyard. There was a large, circular landing area on one side that was well lit with blue and yellow lights. From this landing area were three walkways that extended to an elongated, rectangular structure with a single sloped roof that bristled with antennas and solar panels. The entire station was surrounded by a dim, green energy field that caused our screens to flicker with static as we passed through it,

"I'm reading nearly optimal atmospheric conditions outside," Daphne said. "Your EVA suits may not be necessary, though I would suggest keeping them on as a precaution."

"Yeah, I agree," I said.

A few moments later, our tow ship settled us neatly on the landing pad. Aside from us, there was only one other ship nearby. The tiny little thing was parked on the other side of the landing area, at the very edge of our view from the bridge. Even though I couldn't get a good look at it, it looked human in origin, which bolstered my spirits. If there are humans out here, we couldn't have gone that far, and Daphne's inability to locate where we were in the universe was more likely due to malfunctions inside the ship than due to us being in completely uncharted territory.

"Feel free to come on out anytime you want," Baumdon said over the comms. "We won't bite."

"I'll be there in a moment," I said, not sure how to respond other than that. Truth be told, I wasn't entirely certain where he even was.

I was about to turn to the others for input when I saw a door slide open from the main building. Out of it came a dumpy alien with five huge eyes on squat little stocks. He was dressed in blue jeans of all things! Actual blue jeans! Like the kind you would see on drawings of people from the fifth century PHS (Pre-Hyperspace). And with those blue jeans he even wore suspenders over a T-shirt that looked like it doubled as a rag to wipe off dipsticks. He waddled over to our ship on spindly little legs that showed through the holes in the pants and stopped when he was about twenty meters away.

"It's breathable out here. See?" he said as he waved a three-fingered hand at us.

"Well I guess we're going," I said, taking to my feet.

Empress pressed the pistol that she had into my hands. "Here, take this. Even if you don't need it, and hopefully you won't, you'll want it on you."

"Hang on a second," I said. "You guys are coming with me to see him, right?"

Empress shook her head. "No, not yet. Their lives are more important than ours, and we still need to know that it's safe out there."

I glanced back to Tolby and the handmaidens. I understood her logic, but I didn't like that I was automatically to meat shield for everybody else. "Fine. I get it. But it would be nice to have somebody with me. You should come too."

Empress shook her head. "I will when it is safe," she said. "Right now, he only knows about you. If we need to act, the element of surprise regarding the rest of us coming might be something we need."

I groaned. "So I get to be bait, huh?"

Empress smiled. "In many cultures, that is a great honor."

"Name one."

"A great explorer as yourself, I'm sure you'll discover the first soon enough," she said with a wry grin. She then held up an autoinjector. Through its clear cylinder, I could see a silvery capsule about the size of a grain of rice. "One more thing to take with you, courtesy of Daphne."

"That better not be a cyanide tablet."

"Micro comm," Empress said. "Short range only, from what I understand, but you'll be able to at least talk to her within a couple kilometers."

"Oh, perfect! That's at least half the size of the ones I've seen," I said as she carefully injected the little device a hair beneath my jawline. "But that can't possibly be more than a transmitter. Where's the receiver?"

Empress held up her paw. Inside sat another little device that to my squeamish nature looked like a tiny little bug. And I don't mean like a bug in the eavesdropping sense, although I guess in a way it was, I mean like an actual bug with six legs and a little pincher upfront. "Tilt your head. It needs to go in your ear."

I cringed. "Oh god. Aren't we being a little ridiculous at this point? We're talking about one backwater alien attending some rando gas station."

"Hush," she said, grabbing me by the ear and pulling my head to the side. "The Kibnali are prepared, always, and now that you've taken oaths to be considered one of us, so must you be."

"You're lucky I like Tolby," I said, shutting my eyes and trying not to think about what was about to squirm into my ear.

Empress didn't miss a beat. "You're lucky Tolby likes you."

She then used the tip of one of her claws to push the receiver into my ear. It tickled at first, but it took all of my self-restraint not to tear it out when I felt it crawling down my ear canal, its tiny little feet sending intense prickling sensations radiating across my head with every step it made. Eventually, it stopped and there was a brief stabbing sensation that caused me to curse a handful of times before all was quiet and relatively normal again.

"Is it done?" I asked. "I sure hope so. And for the record, we can fly around the galaxy at faster than light speed, but we can't come up with a more comfortable way to insert a hidden commlink?"

"Maybe you can corner the market on that when we find a way back to your home," Empress replied with an amused look on her face. "Okay, Daphne, I think she's set."

"Testing, testing. One. Two. Three," Daphne said, her voice sounding like it was coming from a speaker underwater. "Can you hear me, Dakota?"

"Yeah, we're good."

"Lovely! Then I can give you your first official report on this highly secretive and classified channel. Are you in a secure location to receive it?"

"Daphne, I'm still on the ship."

"I will take that as a yes; however, I am not expressing or implying any warranties as to the security of the location you're in. As such, you're accepting all responsibility should this highly classified information leak out."

I shook my head and chuckled. I didn't know what she was going to say, honestly, but I seriously doubted the fate of nations rested upon what she was about to tell me. "Okay, Daphne. What is it? And make it fast, I still have to meet our savior."

"I'm pleased to inform you that analysis suggests that the market for tiny, comfortable communication devices that are mounted next to the tympanic membrane is nonexistent due to lack of demand," Daphne replied. "Perhaps a better marketing campaign would alleviate that."

"That's it?"

"I thought that was a pretty good analysis given the limited amount of data that I had to work with. You should be proud of me."

My self-diagnosed ADD kicked in, and I chased the proverbial squirrel. "Just how much data are you storing in there about the marketing trends of tiny, comfortable communication devices?"

"Altogether?"

"Yes."

"Do you want me to include third-party sources as well? Or should I stick strictly with my own compiled data?"

"Go ahead and let me know everything you've got."

"To date, I have one source, and that source would be you, right now. As of five minutes ago, I had nothing."

"Right, good job," I said, feeling like it might be a bad idea to get into this any further or shoot down her accomplishment.

"I'm glad you approve. It took a lot of effort to have an infinite percent increase in regard to total knowledge. I hear, however, your first infinite increase is always the hardest. The next ones are supposed to be much easier."

At that point, I decided I'd spent far too much time preparing to leave and could only imagine what Baumdon must be thinking, waiting for me on his landing pad. Though everyone else still looked on edge, I took a deep breath, calmed my nerves, and reminded myself that Baumdon hadn't blown us away when he had first got to us with his probe. As such, everything would go down smoothly.

I left the bridge, went down to the lower deck, and once the ramp was extended from the side, I left the ship.

CHAPTER FIVE:
THE GIFT SHOP

As soon as my feet left the ramp and hit the landing platform deck, Baumdon scuttled his way over to me with his gangly blue arms waving in the air like they were vintage air dancers. When I stopped, he stopped. When I looked at him perplexed, he looked at me perplexed. An awkward moment was born, but then he laughed, wrapping his arms around his fat belly. "I done messed that up, didn't I?"

"What were you trying to do?"

"Been reading up on your people the last couple hours," he said. "But that's how y'all greet one another proper like, shaking hands and whatnot."

"Yeah, but not like that." His misunderstanding put me at ease and helped to break the ice. I closed the distance between us and extended an open hand. "Like this."

"That seems funny," he said as he took my hand, and I showed him a proper handshake. "But I guess to each their own. Now come on inside before you catch a spell."

I nodded and followed him in. As we went, I got a better look at the other ship that was parked on the landing pad. It was a beat-up old pod, probably more than 500 years older than I was. Damn thing was a relic. There was no telling where he found it. Since it wasn't completely smashed up, I guessed he'd come across it floating in space since it would've been ravaged by the elements if it had been on a planet's surface. "Where did you find that pod?" I asked as we went through the door.

"What's that?"

"I said—" But that thought died when I got a look inside. Where we were reminded me of a rundown thrift store on the side of some nameless highway on Earth. A wide array of "bargain" items were haphazardly strewn about a plethora of shelves all along the walls. Displays were set up along the center, filled with pictures and half-broken toys, and there was also what I assumed was some sort of candy rack. Each package was colorful and filled with cartoon images of various unknown aliens chowing down on the treats inside. But what really threw me for a loop was the sales counter on the other side, or rather what was inside the sales counter.

On display behind glass panels were at least a dozen figurines of a girl in a spiffy EVA suit. She had fiery red hair—of which I might have been a little jealous—along with sapphire-blue eyes and an I-just-conquered-the-galaxy look on her face. I walked up to the counter, knelt, and practically smushed my face into the glass to get a better look.

"You're a fan of 42, as well, ain't ya?" Baumdon said.

"I what?"

"42. The goddess. Created stars from her tears? Formed black holes to imprison the Legions of Chaos? Shaped time as easily as a potter shapes clay? Sang a lullaby so sweet that peace reigned for a million years throughout the entire universe?"

"She sounds like a busy girl."

"Of course she is," he said. "She also likes to wrestle sandworms for fun. But I digress. I've got what you see here along with Queen of the Crystal Cave 42, Time Surfing 42, Double Date

42, Admiral 42—that's my favorite—and another two dozen of my rarer collectibles in the back. Now, which one can I get for you?"

"That's one hell of a toy lineup," I said. "What kicked it all off? The production, I mean."

"Afraid we don't know much about that out here. No one I've come across, anyway, seems to know. I was hoping you could fill me in. Figured you'd be the one to tell me all about her."

"Why would I know?"

"Well, seeing how your species came up with her and all," Baumdon said as he scratched the top of one of his eyestalks. "Last I read, some of them smart boys pegged her creation to about five billion years ago. Something about a planet called Maps? Mans? Mars, yeah, that's it. And a 'Milky Way,' whatever that is."

I choked as I suddenly forgot how to swallow properly. After a good cough, I managed to spit out the only question I could possibly think of. "I'm sorry, but did you say five billion years?"

"Yep," he said, plopping himself on a rickety stool. "Crazy she's been around that long, isn't it?"

"Five billion years," I repeated, but the words barely sank in my ears. "Is that how far we went?"

"Well, I don't reckon I understand what you mean by that," he said, "but I do know something even crazier."

"What's that?" I said, standing.

"For who knows since when, humans have been nothing but a bedtime story that Puglarians would tell their baby Puglarians."

"I'm not following why that's crazy."

"Well, y'all have been extinct practically forever. Nobody knows when y'all disappeared, but I do know it was before our galaxies got all mashed up together."

My jaw dropped. That's why the nav computer couldn't match stars during the parallax scan. Five billion years had passed, and the Milky Way had collided with Andromeda, completely rearranging everything that wasn't torn apart by the event.

The room spun around me. I bumped into the display at my side, sending a couple of dozen pull toys scattering to the floor. I managed to steady myself on the display's edge before I completely toppled over.

"I'm the last human alive?" I said. My heart skipped a beat and then pounded mercilessly in my chest. "I'm the last human alive. The last. Human. Alive."

Baumdon hurried around the sales counter and eased me over to a nearby stool where he helped me sit. "Oh no," he said. "I haven't even gotten to the strangest part. You aren't the last human. I met another one of you not even two hours ago. Couldn't believe it myself, but there he was, came in on that pod you saw out front."

"There's another person here?"

"That's what I've been trying to tell you," he said. "You humans are practically dropping out of the void now. Go figure. Want to meet him?"

I nodded weakly because everything still had a very surreal nature to it. "He's still here?"

"Oh sure! Like I said he came in on a busted ship like you did. He's having himself a meal downstairs with Ma."

I was about to open a comm up with Tolby when he opened one with me first. "Dakota," he said. "I've got some good news. Strike that. It's potentially good news."

"I could really use some right now, bud. What's up?"

He didn't answer my question. I guess I shouldn't have been surprised. Big guy always thinking of me first. "Are you okay? Do we need to assault your position?"

"Define okay," I said as my stomach churned.

"Are you hurt?"

"If that's all it was," I said. "We're in the future."

"What do you mean we're in the future?"

"I mean we are five billion years ahead of where we're supposed to be!" I shouted as I shot up off the stool. Words poured out of me uncontrollably, and I paced around the shop. "How the hell did that happen? I'm dreaming, right? There's no way this is what my life has become."

"Dakota, take a deep breath. Are you sure?"

"Yes, I'm sure! You think I'd flip out this much if I weren't?"

"Maybe there's been a mistake, or you forgot to carry the one. You tend to do that when doing math in your head."

I groaned and threw up my hands. "Are you listening to me? There's no stupid mistake. We're five billion years in the future. Everything is changed. Humans are extinct. No, check that. Aside from me and one other guy, humans are extinct. Do you realize how insane this is? Do you have any idea what it's like to be the last one alive out of everyone?"

"Yes, Dakota. I know what that's like."

His words sobered me, somewhat at least. "You don't sound nearly as shocked as I would've expected."

"I am, but it won't be our undoing. I'm having Daphne run future projections on the star charts to verify your claim. Or do we call those present projections? Gah, this time travel stuff makes talking incredibly annoying at times."

I sighed. My throat grew tight, and I could feel my eyes getting puffy and watery. "How are we getting home? I've got to see Logan again, my parents. I have to make sure Alfred is watered."

"Dakota—"

"He's just a defenseless fern!" I said. "No one will take care of him if I'm not there."

At that point, I broke down into an ugly sob. I'm not sure how long I was a wreck for, but before I'd finished, the furry paw of my best buddy was holding my hand. "Dakota," he said softly. "We've been through worse."

"No, we've never been through worse," I said with a half-laugh, half-sob reply.

"You might be right on that. This is hands down the crappiest situation we've been in, even if you count almost getting eaten by Mister Cyber Squid on more than one occasion."

I cleared my eyes and noticed that Empress and her handmaidens were standing quietly behind Tolby, while Baumdon looked like he was taking inventory. The Kibnali's calm demeanor snapped me out of my pity party. I blew out one last puff of stress-filled air before straightening and rolling my shoulders back. "We're still alive," I said. "Any idea of how this happened?"

"I'd wager when that blue hypergiant came through the wormhole, the fabric of spacetime wasn't warped as neatly as we'd thought," Tolby replied. "It's the only thing that makes sense."

"Barely," I replied. "Thought you were staying on the ship."

"Not with you that upset," he said. "And obviously where I go, these three go. Personal bodyguards and all. Back to our problem: remember what you were saying about the webway?"

"Yeah. Why?"

"The planet we're orbiting is in a Goldilocks zone. There might be a gate we can use."

I wiped my nose on my arm before replying. "You sure?"

"I had Daphne run the scan three times while you were here," he said. "She's sure the planet is habitable, or at least, potentially. If the Progenitors had come here before, maybe they built a webway we can use."

In the pit of despair I'd fallen in, Tolby's words were a welcome beacon of hope. "God, I hope you're right." I turned to Baumdon and described the webway as best I could going by what I could remember from the pictures. When I was done, I said, "Have you seen anything like that down there?"

"Well, I reckon I don't know much about what you're looking for or anything about these 'Progenitors' you're talking about," he said. "The only thing down there right now is an abandoned facility with a whole lot of nasty, indigenous life-forms that'll eat anything and everything they catch on the surface. Don't matter if it's a starship or the crew. Granted, those nasties mostly come out at night, but if they catch wind of you during the day, they'll eat you all the same. You better believe that's the truth."

"Cripes," I said. "What's in the facility?"

Baumdon bobbed his head from side to side. "No one knows. Too dangerous to check out. I think the world record for the longest expedition is thirty-six hours."

"What happened?"

"Everyone became a snack," he said.

"Armor doesn't help? Or shields? Or really big guns?" Tolby asked.

"Not allowed to bring really big guns," he explained. "Those nasties down there are one-of-a-kind, so the planet is officially a Class XI preserve. No one's allowed to build anything, let alone shoot anything. You bring heavy firepower even near a high orbit, and you'll get the intergalactic Feds blowing you right out the water. They don't mess around when it comes to preserves."

"Geez," I said. "So, if no one can touch the place, why did you build a station up here?"

"Tourists," he said. "Why else? They come by from time to time and buzz the facility. A few like to carve circles in the fields or try their luck inserting a rectal probe into some of the critters down there before they get their hands bitten off—though that's illegal and whatnot. You didn't hear what those kids like to do from me. No, sir. My only purpose here is to gas up whoever comes by or wants to take a little break from hyperspace."

I was about to ask another question, but then he perked. "You know what? That facility has a few spots that look like that fancy stuff on your arm. Never gave it much thought until now, but maybe that'll point you in the right direction for whatever you're looking for."

"Could we be that lucky?" I mindlessly asked.

Tolby shrugged. "It's worth checking out. And giving it a look gives us a hell of a lot better odds than we had an hour ago."

I nodded and felt my strength return. I was going to go home, one way or the other, and I was going to make damn sure everyone else came with me. "Where in the facility are these spots?"

"All over," Baumdon replied. "Can't miss them once you're on the ground."

"What do they do?"

"Sit there for all I know," he said. "I'm partial to my limbs and face, if you follow, so I'm not about to figure out otherwise."

I ran my fingers through my hair before rubbing the back of my neck. I had no idea what was down on the surface, but it had to be bad as I didn't doubt the picture our gracious host was painting. In fact, I feared he might even be downplaying it out of courtesy for his new guests. I imagine not wanting to see your guests puke or run for the proverbial hills due to you dumping a gruesome story in their laps is a universal trait amongst hosts across time and space. Still, if what he said was true, there had to be Progenitor tech down there, and we needed that to get home.

"How'd the other human get here?"

"The captain?" the alien replied. "He didn't say, but I'll be a lolilam on a seat wipe if he wasn't thanking me to the galactic core and back when I towed him out of dead space. Nice fellow, for sure. You ought to go down and introduce yourself."

I bit my lower lip. As farfetched as it might have been, I feared Pizlow—the brute of a collector who'd chased me all through the museum up until it blew up—had somehow escaped all the destruction and wound up here in the future as well. But there was no way Baumdon could mistake Pizlow for a human, right? Still...stranger things have happened.

"You sure he's a human, and he's a he?" I asked.

"Well, to be honest, I don't right know," Baumdon said.

My heart sank as my worst fears began to materialize.

"Now don't go getting queasy on me," Baumdon said. "What's down there with Ma is definitely a human. I'm not that dry behind the knee caps. I only mean I think he's a he. Could be a she. Or a

Phe. Or a Nhe. Or a zix, quix, or kappapix. Not really sure how many variations y'all come in, and I didn't go poking around his anatomy to find out. That kind of stuff is considered rude out in these parts, especially on a first meeting and whatnot. And my mama didn't raise no Palinola pirate. Now why don't you run down there and see how he's doing. He'd probably be keen on a familiar face I reckon."

"Yeah, I could use one, too," I said.

Baumdon pointed to a set of stairs nearby, and then the four of us were on our way down. The flight descended about four meters, and the stairs ended at a gray metal door with a snazzy control panel to the side. I didn't know what the glyphs on the display meant, but as it turned out, using them wasn't necessary. The door slid open on its own.

The room inside greeted us with lots to take in. Benches, large and small, lined the walls with tools scattered about, all covered in grease, grime, and oil. The air smelled almost as pleasant as a two-meter-high pile of gym socks baking in the sun, and the sound of a running generator filled the background.

At the other end of the room was an alcove where a shirtless man sat on the other side of a makeshift picnic table. Dim light fell across his broad shoulders while shadows shrouded his face. Despite all of that, I could see he had a body that no doubt had been chiseled by the gods. Holy snort. I mean seriously, he was packing enough muscle that I bet he could have tied a rebar like he was tying a shoestring.

"Hello," I said, starting toward him.

"No! Don't!" he shouted, jumping to his feet.

I heard five distinct clicks from behind, followed by five distinct thumps as Tolby, Empress, Jainon, Yseri, and I hit the floor. As my world darkened and consciousness slipped away, I saw Baumdon standing over us.

"Sorry about the ruse, my dear girl," he said with a voice that was ten thousand times more refined than it ever had been before, "but I couldn't risk having to chase you across the galaxy. Dead humans are worth a pittance compared to live ones."

CHAPTER SIX:
HELLO, CAPTAIN

A couple of years ago, I got talked into trying a new drink that was a mix of Halo ale, triple sec, orange juice, and some bizarre cocktail mixed from energy drinks and watermelon. At the time, I was feeling a little down because the transmission relay in my ship's disruptor field management system had gone on the fritz, emptying both my wallet and most of my savings to repair.

So, while I thought it was a good idea to enjoy at least one night out with friends, it turned out to be exactly the opposite. That drink kicked me up and down the solar system a dozen times, but it didn't do that until I had a half dozen of them. The damn thing was really sweet, and you couldn't taste the alcohol at all. Thus I had no idea I'd had too much until the next morning—or rather, the next evening—and I had a headache that felt like my skull was being used as a testbed for a jackhammer.

That lovely sensation was only slightly worse than the headache I experienced as I roused. My eyelids fluttered open, practically sticking to my dried eyes. My throat was parched, and as I stiffly pushed myself up off the cold metal floor, I was certain that a victim of Medusa was more limber than I.

To my left lay Tolby and the others, still unconscious. I was going to go wake them up when two things completely derailed my train of thought. First, I'd been stripped down to my black undies and pink baby doll undershirt. Second, the guy that I had seen earlier was with me, and he was naked. But that's not the half of it. He wasn't just some random guy. He was Captain Jack Johnson of the *NTS Vela*. The same Captain Jack who had held me at blaster point and nearly got me killed not even two days ago.

I leaped to my feet, grimacing as my headache shot stabs of pain behind my eyes. "What the hell are you doing here?"

"Easy, sweetheart. I could ask you the same."

"Don't call me sweetheart," I said, glaring at him.

"Whatever you like, babe," he said. "You know, if we had met like this the first time, things might've been a little more cordial."

My face scrunched, and then I looked down and realized what he was talking about. I tried to cover up as best I could, backing away as I did, but I didn't get very far. I ended up pressing against a force field which sent a mild electric shock through my butt cheeks, causing me to jump.

Jack laughed. "Might want to watch out for those, cupcake. There's a reason I'm still stuck in here. Still, you look good jumping around like that. Maybe we could work out together."

With little clothes and nowhere to go, I straightened and crossed my arms over my chest. I wasn't going to give him the satisfaction of seeing me squirm. "Nice. Not only are you a total jackass and completely unstable, but you're a first-class creep as well. I should've guessed."

Jack stood up from behind the table. "Lighten up, toots," he said, eyes shooting daggers of hate toward me. "You're the reason Kevyn is dead, remember? I think that pretty much gives me a free pass to say whatever I want."

"I'm sorry your brother died," I said with sincerity. "But I had no idea that monster would come out of that portal and nearly turn me into a chew toy. Besides you're the one that had a gun to my head, remember?"

"I remember you trying to jump my claim and promising me a way home with that nifty little toy of yours."

"We didn't even know you were there!" I said with a groan. Looking back, that probably wasn't the best reaction given he was blaming me for his brother's death, but there it was, and I wasn't about to let him pin all his disasters on me. "Need I remind you that if it weren't for me, Tour Guide would never have pulled you out of stasis and you'd have been blown up into a million little pieces?"

Jack set his jaw and tightened a fist. He didn't share any of his thoughts, but it wasn't hard to get the gist of them, especially with a vein bulging on the side of his thick neck. I'd always heard you should never turn away from or back down when up against a saber-clawed Delarian bear on account they'll think you're food and tear you apart as such, so that's how I decided to treat this encounter. Of course, saber-clawed Delarian bears don't take kindly to those who challenge their territory either, so the thought that maybe I should've come up with a plan B or C did flutter through my mind.

After a few solid beats of my heart in my chest, Jack nodded curtly and grunted. "All right, doll," he said. "Maybe we got off on the wrong foot."

"Maybe?" I dared to ask.

"Look, love, you have no idea everything we went through before you found us. Between no less than three backstabbers, an allergic reaction to a bad batch of food, and that lying Tour Guide that injected us with some crazy serum that did a number on my sanity, I think you should cut me a little slack for coming out in less than a stellar mood and a touch jumpy. So let's hit the reset button and be friends."

"I'll give you a partial reset," I said, mostly because I figured I had more pressing problems to deal with, and I might need to be diplomatic about things for at least the immediate future if we were all to get out of here alive. "You've got a long way to go before I consider you remotely an acquaintance."

"We can call it a professional alliance then," he said. "And at this point, you're still at least partially to blame for Kevyn's death, so I think you need to be a little more cordial as well."

"Look, you're not—"

Jack held up a finger. "Do not argue with me on this, because I'm trying my damnedest to keep it together. Besides, I'm thinking we can still make all of this right, and everyone walks away with a happily ever after."

"How's that?"

"We use that artifact of yours to go back in time and save Kevyn."

I backed up, eyes wide, hands up. "Oh no," I said. "You've got the wrong idea if you think that's even possible."

"I don't see how it isn't."

I started to say we couldn't primarily because I didn't have said artifact anymore, but I stopped since I wasn't sure if I might need him thinking I did at a later point—leverage and all. For what, who knew, but I felt keeping that option open couldn't hurt. So I went with my second point, which was equally valid as a showstopper. "Because the risk of inducing a paradox is far too great to do safely and if we run afoul of one, we could crack open the galaxy."

"Then I suggest we brainstorm for a while to make sure that doesn't happen, because we're not parting ways until I get my little brother back. *Capisce?*"

As gruff and demanding as Jack was, I could hear the pain in his soul, pain that he was unsuccessfully trying to anesthetize with an enormous amount of anger. And could I blame him? I suppose not. I'd no doubt be the same way. "Fine. I get it. If you want us to get along, how about you start with telling me how you ended up here."

"Fair enough," he said. "When that creature attacked us in the bridge, I managed to get away before he pulverized my body. I then ran to the escape pods and got one working a few minutes before everything blew up. I didn't get very far at launch, though. Some sort of time vortex sucked me in and spat me out here. Half my circuits were fried, but the comms still worked, so I called for help, and our gracious host came and picked me up. I'm sure you can figure the rest out."

"That's more or less what happened to us, too," I said.

"Are all those Kibnali you're with from the museum?" he asked.

"The females are," I said, throwing the knocked-out group a glance. "Tolby's been with me for a few years now. Best bud and all."

"You sure about that?"

"About what? Him being my best friend?"

Jack nodded. "I read quite a bit on them at the museum, believe it or not."

"And?"

"And they believed every species they came across were meant to be their slaves as they pursued their destiny—conquering the entire known universe."

"Tolby's not like that," I said, putting a sharp bite into the reply. "And if the others were, they aren't now."

"Don't shoot the messenger," he said with a callous laugh. "Do what you will. I'm just telling you what their history says."

Jainon stirred, and our conversation halted. I rushed over to her and knelt. "Hey," I said, gently rubbing her shoulder. "Are you okay?"

"My head feels like it's going to explode," she said, slowly pushing herself up. Her eyes went wide when she got a better look at me. "Dakota! You're so pink! Where are the rest of your clothes?"

"Taken."

Jainon looked around our holding cell and growled. "Yseri was right. We should have been expecting a fight."

"We can't think about that now. We have to focus on getting out of here."

She nodded. "How is everyone else?"

"Waking," I said, noting that Tolby and the others were starting to stir.

Over the next two minutes, I had very similar conversations with each of the remaining Kibnali as they woke. Tolby was the last to come to.

When he did, Jack approached our group, but before he could say a word, Yseri shrieked. "What...is...that?" she said, pointing a shaky claw at Jack.

Jainon turned to face the captain and immediately looked queasy. "I think I'm going to be sick."

"What are you two on about?" I asked.

"What I'm on about is that huge fleshy parasite thing stuck to his groin," she replied. "How can you not see it?"

"That has to hurt," Jainon tacked on.

Jack glanced down and then rolled his shoulders back and puffed his chest. He smiled brighter than a quasar, and his ego dwarfed the nearest star. "That, my furry friends, is a penis."

The twins kept staring, mouths agape. My hand covered my eyes as I sighed. "Okay," I said. "We know what it is now. Let's move on."

"What does it do?" Jainon said, scooting a little closer. "Do you use it for fighting? It looks like it has a mouth, but I don't think it would be good at biting somebody. Maybe it's used to feel around?"

"If he used it for feeling, why would he have it in his pants?" Yseri said. "You would want it out all the time."

Jack chuckled. "Oh, it's used for feeling all right. Feeling really good."

"How's that?"

I threw up my hands in utter disbelief. "How is this new to you? It's for sex and to pee with!"

"You mean procreation?"

"Yes! You know, like what you two and Tolby have been doing nonstop for the last half a day!"

Jainon slowly shook her head, and for the first time in this conversation she managed to look away from Jack and lock eyes with me. "I don't know how you think things work with us, but I assure you it has nothing to do with anything that looks like that monstrosity."

At this point in time, I realized I knew very little biology when it came to the Kibnali. In fact, I realized the amount of stuff I didn't know that I didn't know far exceeded even the stuff I knew I didn't know. "Right," I said feeling very silly. "Let's move on, shall we? We can have a bio class later."

"I'm just asking how that thing works," Jainon said. "You're the one that's being odd and not giving a straight answer."

Jack motioned with his head for me to come over. "What do you say we give them a little demonstration?"

"I'm not even going to dignify that with a response," I said.

Now it was Yseri's turn to dump gasoline on this monumental bonfire. "Why? Is it bad to feel good in your culture?"

"Yeah, Dakota. What do you have against a quickie? Might be the last one either of us ever gets," he said, laughing.

"No!" I shouted.

"You might like—"

I threw an open palm at him to get him to shut up. And he shut up, but not in the way I expected. Jack's head snapped back like I was a super heavyweight galactic champion who nailed him with a wicked right cross. He tumbled over the table and came crashing down behind it.

For a few heartbeats, no one said or did anything. I didn't know what I did, but I knew I did it. My right arm warmed, and my fingertips tingled as if they had woken up from being long asleep. God, I hate that feeling of pins and needles.

"Did someone get the license plate of that star liner?" Jack moaned.

Hearing his pained voice sprung me into action. I ran around the table to inspect my damage. It was considerable. Both of his cheeks were bruised, and blood ran out of his nose. "Are you okay?" I said. "I mean I know that's a stupid question, and all, but you know what I mean."

Jack pushed himself up on one arm. "Damn, Dakota, I didn't mean to push your buttons that hard. I thought we were having fun. You know, as friends do."

"I...I..." My brow furrowed as his words sank in my mind. Then I got angry, and my skin flushed. "Don't you blame this on me. We're not friends, remember? And that was way out of line."

"I guess we have different definitions of how people become friends," he said. He then looked at me intently. "That said, I only have one question for you."

"I'm not apologizing. So don't even ask if I'm sorry."

Jack laughed. "No, that's not it. I think you made it very clear whose fault it is. All I want to know is how you did it."

"No idea," I replied, but that was a half-truth at best. I did have some sort of idea. I raised my right arm and gave my working hypothesis. "I do have this awesome Progenitor implant in me. Seeing how it used to help me surf time and space, I imagine it's now letting me punch people in the face when I get mad without having to actually touch them. If you have any idea how that works precisely, I'm all ears."

"Details don't concern me," he said. "What I want to know is whether or not you can do that again."

CHAPTER SEVEN:
CAN YOU DO IT AGAIN?

I raised an eyebrow. "Why? Because if I can't you want to go full creep on me again?"

"No," he said as if he were talking down to a toddler. "I want to know if you can do that again because if you can, I want you to uppercut our host through the ceiling when he comes in and lowers that force field."

"Now that's an idea I can get behind," said Yseri. "I want his entrails decorating the shop before we leave."

I grimaced at her graphic promise. "That's a little much, don't you think?"

Now it was her turn to look at me like a naïve little girl. "Are you suggesting he doesn't deserve it? What do you think is about to happen to us?"

"There's not a lot of guesswork in that," Jack said. "Dakota and I are being sold to the highest bidders. Probably to some super-rich alien with an exotic zoo fetish. I doubt the four of you will fare any better. He might simply turn you guys into pelts. You look furry enough."

"Which is exactly why we kill him, fix our ship or take his, and get out of here," Yseri said. The handmaiden hesitated at that point and looked to Empress with an apologetic look. "My apologies, your highness, if I am too forward in my advice."

The Empress nodded, and her face had the same chiseled determination of any general who was poised on the front lines, a breath away from charging into battle. "Your advice is sound, Yseri. When he comes, we will move fast and swift."

"There are six of us," Tolby said. "If Baumdon knew of the Kibnali, he'd never have kept us together. If he lasts more than five seconds, I'll fast for a month."

"Hey, guys," I said, "aren't we forgetting one minor detail?"

"What detail?" came a chorus of replies.

"I still don't know how I did all that before."

"Practice," said Jack. "You'll figure it out."

I shrugged because I didn't know what else to say and I didn't know what to do, but it seemed like the only answer to any of this. I looked at the table that was a couple meters away and focused on it. I took in a slow deep breath, thought about how the air was filling my lungs, and how that air powered all the things in my body and everything I did. All I had to do was find my... What was it called? Chi! Yeah, that was it. All I had to do was find my Chi, and I would transform into Dakota Adams, ninja extraordinaire.

I could feel energy building in my body, radiating from my chest and spreading out to all of my limbs. I tried to focus on that buildup and how each new breath seemed to fuel it more and more. I took a half step back with my right leg and brought my hands up into what I felt was a fighting stance. I probably wasn't the most graceful-looking thing out there, but I was sure I needed to fit the part as much as I could to really hone the skill in as short a time as possible.

I took one final deep breath and felt my Chi swell accordingly to the point where I couldn't take it any longer. I lunged forward with one explosive move and struck the air with an open palm while at the same time letting loose a deafening, "Ai-yah!"

The table was not impressed.

I stared stupidly at it, wondering where I'd gone wrong. "I don't understand why that didn't work."

"Try again," said Tolby.

And so I did. And a third time. And then a fourth. Each time I tried to channel more and more Chi, but it was never enough, and I wondered if I was going to blow out my voice box before I even blew off what little dust there was on the table.

"Maybe you need a new power word," Tolby said, non-successfully holding back a chuckle. "Ai-yah seems pretty terrible. Honestly, it seems rather stupid, too."

"It's supposed to channel my force in one explosive move," I said, feeling frustrated and annoyed at his comments. It's not like I saw him making phantom punches all over the place. "Look, it's a martial art thing from back home, okay? You wouldn't understand."

Tolby's smile grew. "It looks like you don't either."

"You're not helping."

"Neither are you," he said. "And if you don't figure this out soon, you're going to not help us right out of being alive. Or do I have to do everything again to save us?"

"I'm trying!" I said, feeling the back of my neck warm. "You're seriously being an ass on this. I could really use you being more supportive."

Apparently, Jack took Tolby's continued antagonistic stance to mean that he was now allowed to pile on. "Hey, sweetheart," he said. "Don't get mad at the big guy. It's not his fault you're always the useless damsel in distress."

I spun around, dropped my brow, and shot him little daggers of hate with my eyes. "Don't even start."

His hands went up defensively, but the playful look in his eyes said he was doing anything but apologizing. "You're a cute little thing when you get worked up," he said. "Look, maybe we're going about this wrong. Maybe all you need to do is relax. You know I can help with that, right?"

"Take one step toward me, and it'll be your last," I said.

Jack lowered his hands a touch and gave me a smoldering look. "Babe, let's stop playing games. I saw how you were swooning over me when we first met."

"I was not swooning!"

"You don't have to play hard to get anymore," he said. "It was cute at first, and I like a girl who's into the chase as much as I am, but if we're going to be stuck in a zoo—or worse—I want my last day as a free man to be a memorable one. And sweetheart, your body is all kinds of memorable."

Jack stepped toward me, but before his foot hit the ground, I phantom punched that jackass right in the gut. He doubled over with an audible woof, and before he had a chance to suck in a new breath, I hit him again from afar, sending him crashing to the floor.

"I told you to stay away!" Hairs stood up all along my right arm, and the entire thing ached like I had been doing curls with it all day using half-ton barbells.

Jack rolled over and laughed. "Hell yeah, girl, now that's what I'm talking about. When fatty blue blob comes down, you just picture my smiling face on his and go to town."

My anger lessened and then evaporated altogether when I noticed that Tolby and the others all bore bright smiles of approval on their faces. "You were working me up on purpose?"

Tolby looked at me with a sheepish grin. "Little slow on the uptake there, aren't you? Sheesh, I was afraid I was going to have to spell it out for you."

Jack picked himself up off the ground and dusted off. He was starting to bruise on his abdomen, and his face looked like it tried to kiss the grille on a semi that had been speeding by. "What do you say you give it another go?" he asked. "Third time's the charm, right?"

Given his physical state, I was starting to feel bad for him, even if he did have that punch coming to him the first time. "You want me to turn you into a punching bag again?" I asked skeptically. "You sure about that?"

"No, I'd rather you pummel the table if at all possible," he said. "But if you have to land more body blows on me so we can get the hell out of here, you do what you got to do."

I know I had said I felt bad about punching him a minute ago, but the evil side of me did think about whacking him one more time. I know I've hinted at it in the story, but he and I had a brief and not-so-friendly history together, and even with his semi-confession and apology, he probably deserved another punch. That said, I decided to vent my anger on the table.

"Get away!" I shouted with an open-palm strike to the air.

When nothing happened, the high I was experiencing from all the excitement evaporated and that's when I noticed my right arm felt as if it had been soaking in an ice bath. My muscles from my forearm to my shoulders cramped, and my teeth began to chatter. "Okay," I said. "I think it's telling me it's out of juice."

"Are you sure?" asked Tolby.

"My arm is freezing, and I don't think I can punch anyone anytime soon," I replied.

"How long does it take to warm up, toots?" Jack asked, looking more annoyed than amazed at this point.

"Like I should know," I replied. "It's not like all this came with a FAQ." I sighed and rubbed my arm with my left hand. "What I wouldn't give for my portal device."

Jack grinned from ear to ear, flashing his pearly whites as he did. "What would that be worth to you?"

"I'm not interested in games right now," I said.

"Humor me."

"More than you can imagine."

"I don't know. I can imagine quite a bit."

"Yeah? And I can imagine how easy it would be to get out of here if I had it, but since I don't, imagining isn't doing us a whole lot of good, is it?"

Jack sat on the table and crossed his arms over his chest, still keeping his wry grin on his face. "I might have something like that on board the ship."

"Assuming that's true, why didn't you tell us that to begin with?"

"You mean why didn't I tell the girl who used that device to summon a cybernetic demon squid that ate my brother that I had her toy the moment we bumped into each other again? Huh...yeah, that's a hard one to answer."

I grunted. As much as I hated to, I had to give him a point on that one. But as much as I hated doing that, I began to believe he actually had it. Maybe it was how confident he sounded. Maybe it was desperation. Still, I had to vet the story a little more. "How did you get it?"

"After I narrowly escaped your assassination attempt, as I said, I spent some time trying to get an escape pod to work. While I was running around the *Vela*, I found it lying on the floor inside the captain's quarters. It was in the middle of a huge scorch mark with clumps of rust-colored fur all over the place."

Tolby laughed, deep from his belly. "Sounds like Pizlow tried to use it and hit a paradox backlash. Jack must have come across his remains."

I looked back and forth between my best buddy and Jack a few times. The story made sense, even if it was a little farfetched. I mean, what were the odds? Then again, that wouldn't be the strangest thing that's happened to me as of late. "You swear?"

"On my firstborn's dashingly good looks."

"I bet you don't even have children."

"Doesn't mean I don't want them."

"Fine," I said, still feeling like somehow he was going to turn this into one big practical joke on me. "I'll bite. Where is it?"

"I'll tell you, but you have to promise me on the souls of your ancestors we'll go back and save Kevyn."

"I thought we went over this already."

"We talked about brainstorming ways around your supposed paradox fears," he said. "Now I'm getting a commitment out of you. Swear on the souls of your ancestors we'll use that artifact to go back to the museum and save Kevyn."

I balked. "This isn't the time to rehash this."

"I agree. Make the oath."

"He's going to come back soon. If we don't get the device, we're sunk."

"Maybe I need to make this very plain, then," he said with some ire. "I'm not doing a damn thing without Kevyn being part of the game plan."

I groaned. "Fine, I promise—"

"No. On the souls of your ancestors..."

My eyes darted toward Tolby and the others. They looked at me with serious expectation, and I knew why. To swear on the souls of one's ancestors was the highest oath one could take as a Kibnali, and if I didn't live up to it, no matter how risky or insane that oath was, I'd become an outcast in their eyes—Tolby's included.

"Well?" Jack asked, crossing his arms.

"Fine," I said, giving in. He wasn't bluffing, and I didn't have any idea how we'd escape without that device. Hopefully, the oath I was about to take wouldn't bite me in the ass later on. "I swear on the souls of my ancestors, I'll do everything I can to help you save Kevyn."

"That a girl," he said, smiling.

"So where is it?"

"It should be on my ship, but I know Baumdon rummaged around it at least once. Hopefully, he didn't find it, or at least, didn't think it was important."

Tolby cursed. Then Empress and her handmaidens followed his example. I think I threw a few obscenities under my breath at the same time, but I wasn't counting, so it could've been a half dozen or so. Twelve at the most. No more than twenty, for certain.

"How are we supposed to get to it if it's on your ship?" I said.

"You didn't think it would be here, did you?" Jack said with a mocking laugh. "Besides, I thought you could operate it remotely."

I shrugged my shoulders. "You'd think that," I said, "but all I've ever managed to do was calibrate it remotely. It always needed someone to pull the trigger in the end. So unless you have some idea how to get out of this force field and into your ship, we're still in trouble."

"Afraid I can't help you there," he replied.

To my surprise, Daphne decided to chime in on the conversation by sounding off in my head. "I believe I may be of some assistance," she said.

"Really? How's that?"

"The command module is equipped with a DR-22 astrobot repair droid. Not quite as good as the astromech series, or as cute, or as communicative, but it can do something that you can't. It can get into your new friend's ship and get you that device."

"Hell, yes!" I said with an enthusiastic jump and a double fist pump. "Hang on a moment. We had a repair droid this entire time? Why wasn't it helping out before or doing what it's supposed to do like repair our displacement drive?"

"Because he's barely operational," she explained. "He was attempting repairs on the *Revenant* and took a lot of damage when the place was getting hammered with debris. You'd think his squat, round body and domed head would be excellent at deflecting shrapnel, but in reality, not so much. Also, he's not too speedy on those tracks. No idea why he wasn't built with proper legs. The poor little guy barely made it back to the command module before emergency egress procedures were initiated."

"Oh, I see," I said, suddenly feeling incredibly bad that we almost abandoned him to his doom, even though I've never met the droid before. At that point, I realized I was having a very one-sided conversation when viewed by everyone else in the room. So before they thought I'd gone completely schizo, I relayed all the info that Daphne had given me.

"I told you Inaja would bless us with good fortune," Jainon said. "We will be free from our predicament in no time."

"Wait. How badly damaged are we talking?" Tolby asked. "Will he be functional enough to get inside the ship and work the device without being noticed?"

"His neural network is pudding—maybe tapioca—but he does have one operational retractable claw that can get the job done provided I operate him remotely."

"I can set the portal device to give us an escape," I said, feeling good about where this was headed. "Will that claw be able to pull the trigger? Because that's all it needs to be able to do."

"Well, I haven't field-tested it against a slew of firing mechanisms, but I don't see why not," she replied. "I daresay you'll be free of your predicament in under two minutes, provided DR-22 isn't spotted making a beeline across the landing pad."

"Awesome sauce!" I said. I'd have kissed her right there if such a thing were possible, and I resolved to get her something special when we're all done with this to show our eternal appreciation. What do you get an AI as a gift anyway? It's not like they are actual little computer people running around inside a machine, waiting for the perfect gift. AIs seem to be big on reading a lot, however, so maybe a digital book on something? Like that actual book called *Little Computer People*? Maybe. But then again, maybe Daphne would get some ornery ideas from it and cause me a lot of trouble.

I was half a second from giving Daphne the green light when the door leading to the stairs opened. In stepped Baumdon, and behind him were six of the fiercest, most heavily armed and armored aliens I had ever seen.

CHAPTER EIGHT: PLANETARY DETOUR

I realize I'm not a supermodel when it comes to the looks department. I don't spend six hours a day making sure I've done the two hundred newest exercises that have spread across intergalactic social media like wildfire, despite the promises that each one will shed those last two kilograms of body fat, improve my financial stability, attract the right mate for life, or allow me to conquer the corporate world. Because of this, and a few other genetic traits of mine that I'm okay with (slightly broken nose, less than clear skin on occasion, and funny little kink in my left pinky), I'm not exactly everybody's type. And I also realize that attractiveness is often contained within a species. That said, I couldn't help but feel extremely self-conscious when one of the six aliens who stopped in front of our cell took one look at me, doubled over, and vomited.

"Sorry," it said, using a slimy, wart-covered tentacle to wipe the dripping mucus off its tubular mouth. "Pictures don't do humans justice how gross they are."

"Hey!" I said. "You're not exactly swooning my heart either."

The damn thing convulsed but managed not to upchuck again. "Stop talking," it said. "How do you even look in a mirror with that pulpy red thing wiggling around inside your mouth like that?"

The alien next to him grimaced and closed its singular eye that was set inside a green, elongated head covered in blisters. "Those white knobs protruding from its skull aren't helping either."

The biggest of the six pulled out a black box with two prongs sticking out of the top. He tapped it a few times before a green, cone-shaped beam of light washed over all of us. As it swept over my head, the micro comm in my ear sent a stab of pain through my skull.

"Ow. Ow. Ow," I said, grabbing the side of my head and feeling my eyes water.

"What's the matter with that one?" one of the aliens said, pointing at me. "It better not be sick."

"I've got a migraine, and that light isn't helping," I said, trying to play it off. Hopefully these guys knew what a migraine was, or at least the translator could find something similar enough to pass on to them.

"Dakota, what's going on?" Daphne asked. "I can't hear very much anymore. It sounded like you've got company."

Our freedom at this point was being measured in minutes, if not seconds. I knew I had to respond and let her know what was happening, and even more important, I had to tell her to get into Jack's ship posthaste, but that wasn't a conversation I could have out loud. As such, I tried to talk to her as best I could, channeling all of my ventriloquist skills in the process—which were precisely none. "*Ee eee o o e ho ha hmp.*"

"That's no way to talk to lady," she replied.

"E m o ee uud."

"Yes, you are. You sound like my ex before he left me. I knew I shouldn't have trusted you with my heart."

"*Af nee I an alk ight ow.*" This attempt, as you can probably tell, was a little more verbal than the others. But I figured it was worth the risk because I felt I was about to lose her. Sadly, Daphne wasn't the only one that heard me.

"Now what's she doing?" asked one of the aliens. "She's making me nervous."

The big one, clearly the leader, whipped a rifle off his shoulder. Although he kept it pointed to the ground, I had no doubt he could snap off a shot in a flash. "I'm not about to find out," he said. "The sooner we get them separated and into stasis crates, the sooner we don't have to think about this anymore."

"Whoa!" I said, shooting my hands up in the air. "There's no need for that. I'm sure it would be awesome to go into a new ship very quickly and peacefully without any violence."

"Are you trying to tell me something?" Daphne asked. "Because if you are, an apology would go a long way to getting me to listen to you."

I cursed under my breath. Baumdon and his six cohorts were currently exchanging perplexed looks, so I decided to try and capitalize on that while I could.

"Look," I said. "I'm very sorry for any miscommunication that might've happened, and as I said, going into a new ship, quickly and peacefully, and carrying on with whatever plans are in place, would be great."

Baumdon toyed with a pistol in his hands, but he didn't look as ready to vaporize us as the others did. "I'm glad you've come around then," he said with some trepidation in his voice. "I'm really not a bad guy. I just want to make sure all my children are set for life. You're going to go to a cloning facility where we can make a couple of million copies of you, and once that's done, we'll let you go. Promise. All I want to do is corner the market on human repopulation. Should only take a couple of decades, okay?"

Thankfully, Daphne put it all together and asked a perfectly timed question. "Oh, you want me to run over to Jack's ship right now?"

"That sounds perfect," I said. I caught Tolby and Jack both staring at me like I had sprouted tentacles out of my back, but thankfully, neither one said anything. I'm pretty sure Empress and her handmaidens understood exactly what was going on, as they looked as calm and collected as ever. Or maybe they were camping themselves up for one last fight to the death. Maybe I should have considered that fact somewhere in all of these plans I was making up on the fly.

The biggest of the six pulled some sort of rifle off of its shoulders. "Let's get this done," he said.

Baumdon nodded and then shooed at us with his hands. "Back up and do as you're told," he said.

"Well, anytime would be great," I said, praying that the string of negatives I was about to give would work. "I mean, I definitely don't not want you to not end up not pulling the trigger anytime soon."

"What?" asked Baumdon.

"What?" Tolby repeated, eyes wide. I could see his brain crunching the sentence, and at that point, I think he understood where all this was going. Jack, however, did not.

"Hey now, I don't want anyone pulling a trigger while I'm around!"

"I wish you two would make up your mind," Daphne said in my ear. "I mean, do you have any idea how hard it is to get into a beat-up escape pod when you only have a malfunctioning arm to work with?"

I kept my eyes squarely on Baumdon and his entourage, who were beginning to look anxious again. "Sorry, I'm a little nervous is all. But all I want to do is ensure no one gets hurt and that you don't never pull any trigger on any wildly advanced tech capable of ripping a planet apart."

Baumdon laughed and shook his head. "That won't happen, so you can calm your pots—is that right? Calm your fits? Pits?

Something like that. I don't think my translator can keep up with all your idioms."

"Hey, Dakota," Daphne said. "I found that portal device. It was stuffed under the pilot seat. Isn't that nice? Should I go ahead and give it a whirl?"

I reached back into the recesses of my mind where I learned to make portals on the fly and hoped that what Daphne had found was indeed the Progenitor artifact and that it still worked. I pictured one side of a wormhole under the Kibnali's feet and the other in the shop above. My head ached as I tried to focus on exactly what I wanted, and then all of a sudden my vision filled with the all-too-familiar alien equations and endless sea of numbers that churned in my mind.

Seeing all that helped me redouble my efforts. There was a slight click and pop inside my head, and I knew at that moment the device was primed and ready.

"Okay," I said with a smile. "Let's do it."

All of the aliens raised their rifles at us while Baumdon did something on his tablet. The forcefield wavered before disappearing. One of the aliens approached us with shackles in hand, and to my dismay, we had no portal to escape through.

"Well I hope this doesn't take long," I said. "That would be a shame."

"All right, I've had enough talking from you," the lead alien said. "The next person who says anything will be kissing plasma."

Daphne still hadn't replied, and I felt a lump form in my throat. I tried to reach her one more time with my superb ventriloquist skills. "*Aa ee er r oo?*"

Tolby suddenly yelped, causing me to jump. A portal—red, circular, and beautiful— shined brightly on the floor where the Kibnali had once stood. I didn't waste a single second diving through or explaining to Jack what the hell was going on. I figured if he wanted to live, he'd follow without question. Right as I got through the wormhole, a bolt of energy crackled past, making the hairs on the back of my neck stand and tingle.

I flopped through on the other side and onto a twisted pile of Kibnali. They were probably about to untangle themselves when I came crashing in, so I only added to the chaos. And of course, when Jack's bulk landed on my back, it was a minor miracle at least one of us hadn't been turned into a pancake.

"Outstanding!" Jack yelled as he yanked me to my feet and gave me an enormous hug. "You're still the hot, little, time-warping, jump girl I've always known!"

"Lungs...collapsing," I gasped, certain my spine and ribs had been crushed beyond repair.

He dropped me with a hearty chuckle but kept a grip on my forearm so I didn't fall to the floor, which I probably would have. "Sorry about that. Got a little excited, if you catch my drift. And not like excited, excited. Actually, forget I said that. Until a few minutes ago, I honestly thought I'd be in a tiny little cage for the rest of my life."

Empress popped up and swiped each of us on the shoulder. Thankfully, what little garments I still had on protected me from her claws, but she left Jack with a nice set of fine red lines which oozed blood. "Enough! We've got to get out of here!"

Her orders spurred everyone into action. Jack, with his long legs, easily took the lead. Along the way, he snatched a bag of food and some sort of bottled drink off the shelves and bolted for the door. Myself, Tolby, and the others were right behind, with Yseri in the rear.

As we left, I could hear Baumdon and the aliens dashing up the stairs. Apparently, they had figured out we weren't far. As soon as Yseri had cleared the threshold to the outside, I put an elbow into the control panel for the door, spidering the display and causing it to short out.

I never really understood why breaking the controls tended to lock doors, especially doors in space stations, but for whatever reason, that was a universal fault in all of their designs. You'd think an engineer or two would figure out a way to fix that.

Then again, since we were five billion years in the future, maybe that design flaw had already been fixed (said engineers probably got around to taking a second look at thermal exhaust ports, too).

"Hey! Wait!" I yelled, noticing the newest ship on the landing platform and undoubtedly the one that the aliens had come in. It was parked twenty meters away with its side door open, inviting us in. The damn thing looked sleeker and faster than any Formula One racing pod. Moreover, it had a pair of guns in the nose that I was sure would be incredibly handy to have in the near future, or at the very least, they would be incredibly handy to have not pointed at us. "Let's take their ship instead! Ours is still busted!"

Tolby slowed long enough to look over his shoulder and reply. "Do you know how to fly it? Because I'm pretty sure I don't, and I'm pretty sure you don't either."

"Do you have to be so practical?"

"Only if you want to live," he replied. "And personally, I do."

Everyone else had already run inside our ship by the time I got to the ramp, save for Tolby and Jainon, who had reappeared with plasma guns. They both popped off a few shots into the starboard engine of the alien ship. I'm not sure what sort of damage they did, but the mini fireworks display was impressive, to say the least.

"Daphne!" I yelled, running inside and raising the ramp. "I really hope you're back in here with that portal device!"

"Welcome back, Dakota," she said. "You'll be pleased to know that I have indeed returned with your artifact and that the launch sequence has already been initiated. Please standby."

"Oh, thank you! Thank you! Thank you! Thank you!" I probably gushed a little more than that, but for the sake of brevity, I'll end it there.

"Might I also say that you are looking a lovely shade of pink. I particularly like the way it complements your minimal garments."

"I'm not interested in my pinkness!" I said as I zipped through the engine room and down the corridor to the bridge.

"I thought the compliment might help alleviate your elevated stress levels," she said.

"Daphne, I'm not trying to be rude, but if you want to help my stress, get us out of here ASAP."

"Understood."

The floor beneath my feet rocked as the ship lifted off the pad. I was then thrown sideways into the wall before tumbling backward head over heels when the ship spun and surged forward. I'd barely scrambled to my feet in an effort to get to the bridge when the lights around me flickered.

"Incoming ground fire from unknown hostile organisms," said Daphne.

"Damage?" I asked, racing up the ladder.

"Minor compromises to hull integrity detected. Overall damage unknown," she said. "Damage control systems are still malfunctioning, and sensors are offline."

"Of course they are."

"It would also appear that the hostile organisms are attempting to launch their ship," Daphne said. "Correction, they are launching the ship. Correction. They have launched their ship. Hostile organisms are now in pursuit."

At this point, I barreled into the bridge. Jack sat in the captain's chair, while Tolby and the others were at different stations around him.

"Daphne, put the enemy ship on screen," I said. Once she had, it was clear they were gaining on us, despite our head start. "We'll never outrun them. We've got to lose them on the planet."

"Slowdown, babe," said Jack. "I got this."

"What?"

"Watch and behold greatness in action," he said, interlocking his fingers and turning his palms outward to crack his knuckles.

"Daphne, head to the planet and take us into the biggest storm you can find. We will lose them there."

The ship lurched to the side, and I stumbled as Daphne followed his orders. When I found my footing, I could feel the temperature on my skin rise. "Hey! We don't need two captains here!"

"Precisely," he said. "You did your part. Now let me do mine. I'm in the captain's chair. That means I'm in charge."

"How do you even know what you're doing?" I said. "This ship is literally half-a-millennia more advanced than anything you've ever flown."

Jack snorted and waved a dismissing hand at me. "Minor details, sweetheart. I know what I'm doing."

"They are not minor to me, and this is my ship!"

"Correction," said Daphne. "This is Pizlow's ship."

"Who is dead!"

"Further correction. This is Pizlow's next of kin's ship."

"Why are we even arguing about this?" I said, fists clenched in frustration. "This is not the time nor the place!"

"Exactly," said Jack. "Now sit back and let me work."

I capitulated only because I wasn't getting any support from Daphne or anyone else. Daphne, I could understand because she was the ship AI and clearly didn't have a preference as to who was doing what. Or maybe her algorithms told her not to feed the argument. And maybe I was being petty, or maybe I should have had the wisdom to fight this fight at a different time, but I was hurt that not even my best bud was sticking up for me.

I half stumbled, half jumped into the only open station available, which happened to be what operated the dorsal sensor array. Though I'd been relieved of my command, I was damned if I wasn't going to be useful. As we raced on, I began a detailed scan of the planet. "This place is one big jungle. The facility is all that's there."

"All the more reason why we don't head there first," Jack said. "That will be the first place they search, especially if they see us land in the area."

"Where else are we going to land? We have to repair the ship. We can't do that using leaves and tree sap."

"There is likely a wide diversity when it comes to indigenous life," Daphne said. "Perhaps the replicator we have onboard could extract needed materials from them to reconstruct critical systems."

"Now that's the kind of talk I like to hear," Jack said.

A bright blue streak of energy sizzled by. Two more quickly followed suit.

Daphne took evasive action, and three more shots zipped harmlessly by. Unfortunately, because she didn't announce that she was about to, my ribs became intimate with the console in front of me, and in the back of my mind, I feared I heard one crack.

"We'll never make that storm in time," I said. "Daphne, get us to that facility!"

"Belay that order!" Jack shouted. He twisted in his chair and glared at me with the intensity of a thousand suns. "You, hush!"

"Don't you tell me what to do!" My words fell on deaf ears. No one was paying attention, and all I could do was dig my fingertips into the console and pray the next shot didn't take us out.

A few more zipped by, and like the previous ones, they weren't even close to hitting us.

"It's almost like they're missing on purpose," said Tolby.

"That makes them either incredibly incompetent or incredibly disciplined," said Yseri. "I'm not sure I like either."

"Come again?" I said.

"She means either they're trying to kill us and we're getting lucky, or they're trying to scare us and driving us to where they want us to be," explained Jack.

His words did not sit well with me and my stomach knotted. "How do we deal with that then?"

"Same way I've planned all along. We will lose them in the storm," he said.

The storm he was referencing happened to be a hurricane near the coast of the largest continent. The clouds swirled with reds and greens. Why they took on those particular hues, I didn't know. I hoped that didn't mean the atmosphere itself was dangerous but rather the storm was simply filled with colorful particles. That said, I was a little relieved when the sensors showed the winds were gusting only about ninety knots.

"ETA to storm penetration?" he asked.

"Twenty seconds and counting," said Daphne. "Hostile spacecraft will overtake us in forty-four seconds given current characteristics of pursuit."

Jack rolled his shoulders and exhaled sharply. "Forty-four seconds, huh? Good. We will only need half that."

"To what? Land and issue our surrender?"

Jack didn't answer. Instead, he kept sharp eyes on the action unfolding. When we penetrated the hurricane, the winds buffeted our ship, and while normally I wouldn't care too much, I wondered if our ship would fall apart due to previous damage incurred.

"ETA on alien intercept on screen," he said. Immediately a countdown timer appeared. When said timer hit ten seconds, he cleared his throat. "Daphne, stand by to jump on my order."

"Jump? Are you crazy? Did you miss the part about our displacement drive being broken?"

"As I stated earlier, maximum jump range is one hundred kilometers," Daphne said.

"A hundred clicks it is," he replied. "Now stand by."

Two ticks of the clock later, Jack, still watching the viewscreen, raised a finger and pointed it forward. "Jump."

CHAPTER NINE: BRACE FOR IMPACT

The swirling clouds stretched in every direction as our ship entered hyperspace. The jump was made without a hitch, but we dropped back into real space a moment later.

I glanced at the nav screen to check our position as a high-pitched whine came from the rear of the ship. True to Daphne's earlier prediction, we'd only gone a hundred kilometers.

Even though our alien pursuers were not currently shooting us down, I wasn't ready to celebrate, especially since the coast ahead seemed to have few ways to hide us from high-tech scanners.

"What now?" I said. "It won't take them long to catch up to us."

Jack held up his finger once more, but instead of looking at me with annoyance, he grinned broadly. "Oh, ye of little faith. Watch and learn." He then directed his next statements to Daphne. "Turn off any and all scanners. Don't give them anything to track us with. I want them thinking we jumped halfway across the galaxy."

"That's your plan?" I yelled. "That's not a plan! That's a one-way ticket to a clone factory where we're the mold!"

"Look, babe, by the time they even consider the idea that we might still be around, we will have landed on the other side of the continent and be as good as gone."

"They're tracking us right now. I promise."

"Not this ship, sweetheart."

"My TV back home could track this ship," I said. "I'm sure Baumdon's friends are at least that advanced and won't be fooled by your special maneuver."

Right on cue, a crackling bolt of blue energy shot past our nose. Jack swore, but before he could issue another order, our ship rolled to the side and quickly lost altitude. The sea rushed up to meet us, and for a flickering second, I was sure I was about to meet my maker. Thankfully, we pulled out of our dive, skimmed across the water, and then started to gain altitude once more. Sadly, I could tell our speed was a fraction of what it was before. We were no longer shooting through the atmosphere. We were barely limping along.

"Damage report!" cried Jack.

"Damage reports are unavailable at this time," Daphne answered. "Sensors have yet to be repaired."

Jack stumbled. "Okay... Then..."

But that's all he got out. He just stared ahead as Daphne tried to take evasive action as best she could. For the most part, she managed to dodge the incoming fire, but we got hit once again, and as before we lost considerable speed.

As if the crippling damage wasn't enough, something else dawned on me, something that might make all of this futile since we no longer had our EVA suits. "Daphne, what's atmo like out there? Is it breathable?"

"Sensors indicate oxygen and nitrogen levels comparable to Earth," she said. "Oh, that's funny."

"Whatever that is, it does not sound funny at all."

"It has occurred to me that the only working spectrometer is in your cabin. Ha ha. Silly me. Oh well, but since there's ample vegetation on the planet, you should be fine."

"Should be is not comforting, Daphne!" I glanced at the onscreen map. We were still a good distance from the facility. "Can the engines take another micro-jump?"

"Only if you want every molecule inside them to spontaneously head off in separate directions a moment later."

I swore and hit the console with the bottom of my fist. "Then fly us to the facility ASAP. It's our only chance."

The ship rolled as Daphne brought us around. There was a loud crack, and tiny bolts of lightning arced across the computers inside the bridge. One particularly bright bolt struck Jack in the head, knocking him to the floor. The lights flickered, and the ship lurched to the side. Suddenly, there was a sickening feeling in my stomach as it rose into my throat and our ship nosedived toward the ground.

"Engines offline," announced Daphne. "Chances of reaching alien compound are rapidly approaching zero percent."

"Do something!" I yelled.

"Affirmative. Preparing inertia dampeners for crash. Brace for impact."

I managed to snap my five-point harness together before we hit. Fortunately, so did everyone else. Our ship plowed through the jungle and took down trees like a sixty-kilogram cannonball would take down a set of plastic bowling pins. Debris along with a huge mound of dirt shot into the air, and my already aching ribs took another pounding as I slammed into the harness. How they didn't turn into dust was beyond me. Maybe Mom was onto something when she made me drink all that milk when I was younger.

Don't tell her I said that.

I stayed slumped in my seat and tried to catch my breath, all the while trying to wrap my mind around the fact that I was still alive. That was one hell of a crash. Sad to say, that wasn't the first bad one I'd survived. In fact, it wasn't the only one I'd had in the last twenty-four hours. I really needed to find a new good luck charm, because since losing my original miniature dashboard elephant, we'd been cursed with ill fortune time and again.

Tolby was at my side, fumbling for my harness release. "Dakota, get up."

I stiffly pushed myself out of the seat as everyone else gathered their wits. I ran to the storage compartment where I'd stashed the archive cube and resonance crystal. I figured there was a good chance we might not make it back to the ship, at least anytime soon, and both of those I knew I would need in the future. The foremost, obviously, because it had a wealth of knowledge that spanned time and space, and undoubtedly would be the key to surviving. The latter I needed because when we got home, I needed something to sell—and that would set me and my children's, children's, children's, children's children up for life (assuming I had any, still up in the air on that one as to whether or not I want a cooing, dribbling, diaper-soiling need machine).

"Daphne, how long do we have before they get here?" I asked.

Her voice came back stilted and full of static. "ETA is approximately two minutes and thirty-four seconds."

"Damn it," I said. "We will never outrun them."

"We'll set an ambush on the ground," Yseri said. "We still have three plasma rifles, and there's only seven of them."

"That sounds like terrible odds," I said.

"Those might be the only odds we have," Tolby said.

In that moment, he seemed utterly alien to me. His face had a warrior's determination like none I'd ever seen—not even when we fought Pizlow and the Ratters back at the museum. Before, he had looked like he was going into battle. Now, he looked like a caged animal getting ready for one last fight. "If they land, no doubt they'll want to move in on our ship before whatever indigenous creatures we were warned about eat us all. We can capitalize on their haste, and once they are dead, we can take their ship."

"How are you going to ambush them if they have scanners, which they clearly do?" I asked. I mean, I was far from a great military genius, but there were a few basic things I knew about combat.

"Then we use the humans for bait," Yseri said.

"I am not bait!" I said.

"Or we could leave you behind," she countered with deadly seriousness. "They are after you, after all. Not us."

"If I may offer an alternative," Daphne cut in. "I can direct a massive EMP burst from the warp drives, which should be sufficient to crash their ship once it is in range. However, someone will need to stay behind. There is too much damage to the ship for me to do it alone."

"If we can disable their ship, perhaps we can assault the crash site and take them out before they have a chance to recover," Tolby said.

"I should also mention that in order to accomplish this, I have to crack open the warp core. Whoever assists me will not survive the resulting explosion."

"Of course," I said, shaking my head. "Why wouldn't it have to be that way?"

"Jack's still knocked out," Yseri said. "Unless someone can rouse him in the next ten seconds, that means Dakota stays."

"She's not staying," Tolby growled, fur bristling.

"That's right, I'm not!"

"Then who, Dakota?" Yseri shot back. "The Empire must survive."

"We come up with something else, that's what we do," I said. I raised my right arm to show off the intricate latticework of Progenitor tech across its skin. "Pretty sure you're going to need me to operate the webway since I'm the one carrying this around."

"ETA two minutes, twenty seconds," said Daphne. "Whatever you're planning, it will need to be put in motion immediately."

Empress coughed and grabbed everyone's attention. She was hunched over with one arm across her midsection. Dark, purple blood saturated her arm and ran down her leg. "I'll stay."

"No, Your Highness. You must think of the Empire," Yseri said.

Empress glared with the full authority of her position behind it. "I do think of the Empire. Even if Baumdon is stopped, I'm afraid I'll be too much of a liability."

"I...I can't leave you," Yseri said, sounding as weak as a newborn kitten.

Empress smiled and stroked the side of her face. "You and Jainon will bear the children of our Empire and see that it spreads through every galaxy in the universe. The light of my rule wanes, but the light of yours is yet to come."

Yseri stiffened and bowed, as did Jainon, but before we left Empress to her fate, I said something that surprised everyone, myself included. "No. I'll stay. Get Empress to the facility."

"My closest advisers and guards cannot challenge my will, what makes you think you can?" Empress asked, anger flashing in her eyes.

"Because I might be able to portal out of here before I'm basted in plasma, that's why," I said.

"Might?" asked Tolby.

"Well, should, but I guess all that depends on how well this goes." At that point, I grabbed one of two communicators stored at my bridge station and shoved it into his paws. "I'll call once I'm out. Now go."

The Kibnali hesitated as they waited for Empress's permission. Thankfully, she gave it with a short, quick nod. As Tolby headed for the door, he looked back and said, "I hope you know what you're doing."

"Me too," I said. Then with a half-grin, I added, "Remember, if I die—"

"Yeah, yeah. You want a Viking funeral."

"Damn skippy."

With that, he darted out of the bridge to catch up to Empress and the handmaidens, who had already left. I took a deep breath to center myself and then focused on the task at hand. "All right, Daphne, what did you do with the artifact and what do I need to do to bring down that ship?"

"The artifact has been safely stored in the engine room with DR-22," she replied. "And that's precisely where you need to be in the next thirty seconds."

I snatched the pouch that held my resonance crystal and archive cube, bolted out of the bridge and slid down the ladder. Once my feet hit the floor, I raced down the corridor to the engine room, all the while, trying not to listen to Daphne's countdown. I really didn't need the added pressure. When I got in, I still had a dozen seconds to spare.

A mustard-colored, light smoke filled the room. It stung my eyes, making them water, and put a salty taste in my mouth. My eyes watered as they took in the scattered debris. Everything that wasn't bolted to the floor or secured to the wall had been thrown violently around the room.

To my everlasting thanks, the portal device wasn't lost or buried under a ton of debris. I quickly snatched it from its place next to DR-22 and then turned my attention to the task at hand. "Okay, Daphne. I've got the artifact. What do I need to do to make this happen?"

"Only two things. I can do the rest. First, you'll need to find a hydro-spanner and rotate the horizontal boosters of the displacement drive ninety degrees. After that, you've got to reverse the polarity on the neighboring alluvial dampers."

"Are you sure?" I said, eyes getting wide. "That seems dangerous."

"I did say there would be a resulting explosion."

"That you did," I said. "How long do I have once the polarity is reversed before everything blows?"

"About ten seconds," she replied. She was quiet for a few moments as I went searching for a hydro-spanner amongst the debris. When I found one—and thank my lucky stars yet again that didn't take long—she asked me a question. "Do you think you can portal out of here in time?"

"I sure as hell am going to try," I said as I knelt by the displacement drive and used the hydro-spanner to loosen the mounting bolts on the horizontal boosters.

"Do you think that portal will be big enough for the two of us?"

"Aren't you in the ship?" I said, pausing for a moment and not following what she was asking.

"I am, but I can download into DR-22's artificial cortex and take over. He's a vegetable anyway. It's not like I'd be murdering him like I would my ex and his bitch of a blender."

I glanced at DR-22. He was about the size of a large beach ball with stubby, tripod legs on tracks. "Yeah, you can fit easily," I said.

"Oh good, because I'd rather not die, and if I can program a timer to set off the EMP burst and escape, I would much rather do that. I still have so much to see and do. Like kill my ex and then maybe enjoy a cold double latte."

Before I had the chance to inquire how she would enjoy such a thing, Jack burst into the engine room. He went into a coughing fit and stumbled a few times before straightening. He shook his head like a dog shaking water free after a bath, at which point he stretched his arms wide and showed off his naked glory.

"Behold! I am reborn!" he shouted. "Verily I say unto you, I am the god of stars and storm! Together, we shall smite those who oppose us!"

My mouth dropped, partly because I'd completely forgotten about him, but mostly because I couldn't believe how he was acting. "What the hell are you on about?" I said as I managed to rotate the horizontal booster ninety degrees in its mount.

Jack hurried over to me and took my hands. "Oh, my sweet goddess! How glad I am to see thee."

I jerked away. "Stop, damn it. I can't work with you pulling on me like that. And in case you forgotten, we've got company coming in sixty seconds!"

"Arrival of hostile entities is approximately forty-two seconds and counting," Daphne announced though I wish she hadn't.

Jack looked at me, pity in his eyes. "My love, has the crash made you lose the memories of who you are?"

"No, but I'm pretty sure it gave you memories of who you aren't."

"Who I'm not?" he said, laughing. "I've lived for five billion years. I've swum time and wrestled beasts of nightmares. I've plummeted from the skies and slammed into a planet's crust with the vengeance of a comet from Armageddon and lived to tell the tale. What more proof of my divinity does one need?"

"If you're so divine, help me reverse the polarity of the alluvial dampers," I snapped, returning to my work. "Because stopping the power to a coupling on the negative axis to get that done is a bit of a pain in the ass when you're only armed with a hydro-spanner and working on a deadline."

Jack picked up a metal rod lying nearby and boldly strode over to me. He took one look at my handiwork and then drove the rod through the coupling. Sparks flew with loud pops in every direction, and Jack nodded with approval. "There. Done."

I fell back in my haunches, unsure if I should be overjoyed or mortified. "Uh, Daphne. Is this about to blow?"

"Affirmative," she said. "For future reference, it would be a good idea to warn me before doing such a thing again. I'm barely going to have time to download."

The air around us sizzled, and the hairs stood on the back of my neck. I scrambled for the portal device, which I'd set on the floor moments ago. The temperature inside the room rose at frightening speed, and it took all I had to focus on setting up a portal. I know at most only a few seconds ticked by, but it felt like decades had passed before I dropped the portal in front of my feet.

Before it had fully formed, I jumped through with Jack and Daphne/DR-22 right behind.

CHAPTER TEN: DAPHNE GETS THE BEEPS

Note to self: for a portal to be accurate, it needs to have a little better direction than "anywhere but here."

Well, I wasn't quite as vague as that, which is probably why we didn't end up two kilometers straight down and inside the planet's mantle or in a geostationary orbit where we spent the last few moments of our lives freezing to death as our blood boiled. But it did mean that when we came flying out and crashed on top of some berry-producing shrubbery, I had no idea where we were.

Though I was thankful neither Jack nor Daphne had landed on top of me, as I pushed myself off the ground and felt the gooeyness of dozens of crushed berries stuck to my thighs and backside, all I could do was throw a quick check to my rear and mutter. "For the love of all," I said, plucking one of the berries off my body and noticing the neon-blue mark underneath. "I hope this juice doesn't stain skin. I'd rather not have the world thinking my ass is made of blueberries."

"Beep! Beep! Beeeeeeeeeeeeeeeeeeeeeeeep!"

The first couple beeps were low and soft, but the last was shrill and caused me to grimace. I twisted in place, searching for the source, and quickly saw that it was coming from Daphne. Her new robotic body was flopped over in one of the bushes, and her legs swung back and forth as her tracks spun furiously. Though she rocked a little, she didn't come close to righting herself. In fact, she was doing such a poor job, I feared she might damage herself further if I didn't intervene.

"Hang on a moment," I said as I squatted to help lift her top end. "Don't go blowing a gasket on me when you get your bits all in a bunch. I don't think there's a maintenance station nearby."

I dug my hands underneath Daphne's body as much as I could to try and lift her without giving myself a hernia. As I did, Jack appeared at my side, covered in dirt, berry juice, and a few leaves stuck to various parts of the body. "I love a goddess who doesn't mind going back to the basics," he said. "Here, let me help. It'll be fun to reconnect with our mortal roots by using these primitive bodies."

"Oh geez," I said as I rolled my eyes. Though I had a feeling his schizo nature would become annoying later—possibly dangerous— I did welcome the immediate help. "All right. On three, yes?"

"On three."

I gave the count and then with a great heave the two of us lifted Daphne up and onto her tracks where she settled with an unnerving rattling of parts.

"Beeeeeeeeeep! Beep! Beep!" she screeched.

I tilted my head. "What?"

"Beep! Beep! Beeeeeeeeeeeeeeeeeeeeeeeeeeeep!"

"I don't understand 'beep, beep, beep.'"

"Beeeeeeeeeeeeeep! Beep! Beep! Beeeeeeeeeeeeeeeeeeep!"

I groaned. Given all the hardships and hiccups we've had thus far, I didn't need this added to my plate. "Why don't you just talk?" I said, bopping her on the top of her dome head. "All the other robots can talk."

She spouted a flurry of beeps, whistles, and a few boops tossed in for good measure, all the while rocking back and forth.

Jack laughed and crossed his arms over his chest. The corners of his mouth drew back into a bright grin, and he gave Daphne a nod. "I understand. I'd be pretty mad if I needed a reboot as well and no one was helping me."

I shot him an incredulous look. "What are you on about? There's no way you understand that."

"I most certainly do."

"I didn't realize you were fluent in beep-o-nese."

Jack took on a smug look. "Since I'm a god, I'm fluent in many primitive forms of communication, as are you."

"I'm not God, and neither are you."

"Well, I'm certainly not the God, I don't think. But I am a god, and so are you, my dear wife. Why do you think so little of yourself? You're the same age as I am."

"Wife?" I said, eyes wide and mouth refusing to shut. "Where do you get off calling me that?"

"Your confusion does not anger me," he said. "And I forgive you for your doubts. After all, to err is human, and to forgive is—"

"Don't you dare say it!"

"...divine."

"Gah!" I almost clocked him right there. Looking back, a kind of wish I had for my own sanity's sake. Still, it's probably bad karma to punch someone for the sole reason of being nutty. So, to keep from totally losing my cool, I dug the communicator out of my pouch and flipped it open. "Tolby, bud, can you hear me?"

It only took a second or two for him to reply, and to my elation, the signal that came through was strong and clear. "Thank the furriest. I was about to call and see if you had made it out."

"Yeah, I did. Jack and Daphne are with me."

"Daphne? How?"

"She downloaded herself into that repair droid. I think she made it, but all she can do is beep at me constantly."

"Beep? Like how?"

"You know, like beep, beep, beep," I said with a shrug.

"I know that. I mean exactly how did those beeps go."

"Why?"

"Because it matters."

I rubbed my temples with one hand before running my fingers through my hair as I tried to remember exactly how it went. After a few seconds, I gave the best Daphne-beeping impersonation that I could.

"Oh, that's easy," Tolby said, sounding relieved. "She simply needs a reboot."

"See, I told you."

"There's no way you could have known that," I said to Jack. "She's way more advanced than any robot that was around when you were running about."

"Divinity aside, times may have changed, but beeps do not."

"What are you two going on about?" Tolby said, cutting into our conversation.

"Jack thinks he's a god."

"Knows," he corrected. "And so are you."

"Did the axionic deflector shell leak in the engine room?" Tolby asked.

My brow furrowed. "The what what?"

"It's an old tech thing," Tolby replied. "There would have been a lot of yellow gas in there if it had."

"Oh, yeah. That. I guess it did crack, why?"

"From what I remember, some people can get hexaisonungluoide ion poisoning from the gas," he said. "Symptoms may include delusions of grandeur and/or god complexes."

"Lovely."

"Shouldn't last too long now that you're in the fresh air," he said.

"How long are we talking about?" I asked, watching Jack stare at the ground while waving his hands at it like a conductor. I was pretty sure he was trying to orchestrate some sort of creation from the ground, but I wasn't about to press for details.

"A few hours, hopefully," Tolby said. "A day or two, tops."

"Ugh," I groaned. "I really hope it's the former. I don't think I can take him acting like this for days. How's Empress?"

"Weak," he replied gravely. "We're taking turns carrying her. You need to catch up, so we can find that webway and get out of here."

"I don't even know where you are," I replied. "Hell, I don't even know where we are."

That last thought did not sit well with me. Everywhere I looked were the same tall, thick trees with bright, spotted leaves. Alien jungle noises filled the air, and there wasn't even a single indication as to which direction our crash site was.

"That's easy enough," Tolby said. "We'll stop for ten minutes and rest. In that time, if you use the track party function on the communicator and move around, you should be able to triangulate our position. Can you see the sun?"

I looked up, and there was enough space in the canopy that I could. "Yeah. Pretty well, actually."

"Great. We're headed almost due north. Once you know where we are, you'll know which way to go to meet up."

I smiled at the simple genius of his plan. "You're too damn clever."

The call ended, and Jack tapped Daphne on the head. "You ready to give her a reboot?"

"If I knew how to, I'd say give it a whirl," I replied.

"When I was a mortal, we had control panels in the back where you could initiate a reboot."

"Yeah, we still have those, but what I meant was I'm not sure how you're getting this panel off without tools," I said as I pointed to the six screws that held Daphne's access panel in place.

"Beeeeeeeeeeeeeep! Beep! Beep! Beeeeeeeeeeeeeeeeeep!"

"Maybe Tolby still has his PEN," I said, mourning my distinct lack of pockets and wishing my PEN hadn't been stolen from me along with the rest of my usual gear back at the spaceport. "We can work on her later. We need to get a move on anyway."

Daphne beeped a few more times, and Jack didn't argue. Since he didn't comment and I couldn't understand her, I began the track signal routine on Tolby's comm using mine, picked a random direction, and started walking. It didn't take long for me to be acutely aware of how uncomfortable—and downright painful at times—it was to walk barefoot through this forest. There were several roots that jutted out from the ground as well as plenty of sharp rocks barely hiding underneath the topsoil.

"I'd give up root beer for a year if somebody would bless me with a good pair of socks and comfy hiking boots," I said after we'd gone a few hundred yards. I sat on a fallen tree and inspected the damage to the soles of my feet. They were covered in dirt and had picked up a few abrasions here and there, not to mention the tops had a few bug bites as well. "I should've grabbed an EVA suit on our way out."

"Would you like me to carry you, my dear wife?" Jack said. "Some might say it is unbecoming of the goddess to be covered in such filth."

I laughed because he was so serious about it. "And what about you? I thought you were my counterpart and you're head to toe with dirt and berry juice."

"Are you saying you want to carry me?"

"No." I was going to say more, and I think he was as well, but my comm played a little three-note tune, indicating that it had finally triangulated Tolby's position. That was exciting news until I read the display.

"What is it?" Jack asked.

"We're a hair over a hundred and thirty-six point two kilometers away."

"That's not too bad," Jack said. "A mere fun run for a couple of deities like us."

I groaned. "That's your plan, huh? Run all the way there and lose the soles of our feet in the process?"

"You're so adorable when you play mortal," Jack said. "I didn't mean run across the ground. I meant run through spacetime."

"Yeah...we could do that," I said, feeling silly that I hadn't come up with the idea myself. "Okay, give me a second to see what I can do."

Using the communicator, I pointed myself in the direction where I thought Tolby would be and checked the range one last time. I couldn't imagine a full kilometer, but I've always known how high a meter was on account that the freckle near my belly button was precisely one meter from the ground.

Using that as a reference point, I told my brain to picture a door that was a hundred and thirty-six thousand, two hundred meters away. At that point, a beautiful wormhole opened in front of us that showed a bright blue sky.

"Whoa!" Jack said, catching me by the elbow as I stepped toward the portal. "That's one hell of a view. You might want to stick your head through first."

My mouth twisted to the side, and I bit my lower lip. I didn't understand what he was talking about at first, but he seemed serious and excited enough that I should approach the wormhole with caution. So I did, and borrowing a phrase from my best bud, thank the furriest I had, for when I took a peek, the wormhole hadn't opened where I had expected, but it did open where it was supposed to, a hundred and thirty-six kilometers away in a straight line, which meant due to the curvature of the planet, it was really, really high up in the air. "Oh snap," I said, feeling my stomach drop and realizing I almost went skydiving without a parachute, which I hear you can really only do once. I backed away, and only when the portal closed a second later, I did feel a little less woozy. "How high up do you think that was?"

"Ballpark or exactly?"

"Without a rangefinder, I think we'll have to skip the latter, but I'd wager we were at least a kilometer up."

"More like one thousand, three hundred and thirty-nine point five two meters up," Jack corrected. "Well, give or take a few centimeters."

"How did you figure that out?" I asked. Though I was incredibly skeptical at the precision of his claim, I was still a little shy at challenging him directly after he'd pulled that beep diagnostic out of his rear involving Daphne.

He looked at me as if I were setting him up for a question that involved a healthy dose of embarrassment at the end. "Simple," he said. "The curvature of the Earth is eight centimeters per kilometer, and when I first arrived at the station, my ship's scanners said the planet was ninety-two percent the size of Earth. So, I did the numbers in my head."

"Just like that?"

"I'm good with numbers, what can I say?" he replied with a bright smile. "Give it another go if you don't believe me."

And so, I did, and I'll be damned if the next portal I opened wasn't but a half meter off the ground. "That's impressive," I said as I finished checking it out. "Come on, let's go before it closes up."

The three of us popped through. My feet had barely hit the ground when I heard Tolby's energetic voice from behind. "Dakota!"

I spun around in time to brace myself for the hit. Tolby launched himself into the air and nearly smashed me into the ground when he landed. His arms wrapped around my body and squeezed. I sank into that fuzzy embrace and returned the hug. "Glad to see you, too."

"I'm getting tired of one or both of us having to dodge reactor meltdowns and certain death," he said. "Can we stop that now?"

"Soon as we get out of this place, sure," I replied. "Are we ready to move?"

"I think so," he replied, throwing a glance behind him. Yseri and Jainon both flanked the elder Kibnali, who was slumped against one of the trees. "We need to get her to that facility. Even if it's abandoned, she needs the shelter, and maybe we'll get lucky and be able to scavenge medical supplies. Can you open up a portal there? I believe it's ten kilometers that way."

"No problem," I replied, looking in the direction he was pointing. "One portal, coming up."

My mind sank into the Progenitor interface, and though initially everything went as it should, for the portal opened, there was a sharp stab in the side of my head that caused me to wince and curse. At the smell of smoke and a faint popping sound coming from the portal device, I looked down and tilted the artifact. To my horror, there was a hairline crack that ran across its side, and from it came tiny wisps of smoke. "Oh damn, that can't be good."

"You broke it?" Tolby said, eyes widening.

"I didn't break it! It must've been damaged in the crash. Or maybe I did something wrong." I tried again, and for my efforts, I was rewarded with another sharp stab to my right temple and an even louder pop and show of sparks from the side of the artifact. My stomach felt queasy, and my knees buckled. Had I just destroyed one of the most important finds in all of history? I tried not to think about it, but with the scorch marks on the device's side and the smell of burnt rubber permeating my nose, it was hard not to.

"Any other time, I would've said good riddance on account of how much trouble that thing's gotten us into, but right now, what I wouldn't give for one last jump."

"Me too," I said with a heavy sigh. "I guess we're going to have to walk."

Yseri grunted. "The sun will set soon. We must hurry."

She was right, and so we did. All three Kibnali took turns carrying Empress on their backs. Even with the extra weight they had to carry, they barely slowed as we moved through the jungle—

at least, not until we stumbled upon the remains of an old spaceship and we all came to a stop.

Well, I thought it was a ship, or a shuttle of some sort since it was about thirty meters long. The dilapidated structure was metallic and had several things jutting out of the ground that looked like ribs and spars to an old fuselage, but given its deteriorated state, it could've just as easily been a root beer manufacturing plant. God, what I wouldn't have given to stumble onto one of those out here.

Turns out, however, it wasn't a ship. It certainly wasn't a root beer manufacturing plant, but if it had been, it would have been far less odd (and disconcerting) had that been the case.

"Is that what I think it is?" Jainon said, cautiously approaching the structure.

"Depends. What do you think it is?" Tolby asked as he eased Empress down and against a tall tree with rough, orange bark and leaves like pine needles.

"It looks like a Pattone, or what's left of one."

"Then no, it's not what you think," Tolby replied without giving it a second glance.

"I think it is."

"I know it's not."

At this point, I jumped into the conversation. "Would someone mind telling me what we're arguing over? What's a Pattone?"

"A Kibnali battle tank," Yseri said. "It was our main tank, if memory serves, right before the Nodari invasion."

"At which point, it didn't take long to for us to realize its armor and firepower were inadequate," Jainon said. At this point, she was next to the vehicle and started looking it over. She ran her paw across its worn surface until it found a small hatch in its side. With a grunt, she used her claws to pry it open. Carefully, like she was delivering a newborn kit, she reached inside and pulled out a sealed package, which she then turned around and showed to the rest of us with a vindicated look upon her feline face. "Now what do you have to say? Or do you want to pretend these are standard rations?"

"By the gods," Tolby said with an audible gasp. "How did one of ours get here?"

"Your guess is as good as mine," Jainon said. She tore the package open and from it, pulled out a tube of paste. Said tube was then opened, and she squirted some of its thick, green contents in her mouth. "It still has the same disgusting taste," she said with a chuckle. "You'd think time might change that."

"If there's a tank here, maybe there are other Kibnali," I offered.

"Doubtful," Yseri replied. "You'd think Baumdon would know about them."

"Maybe he did, but didn't want to say?"

"If he did know about us, he'd never have kept us together."

Jainon hurried over to Empress and tried to give her some of the paste, but the matriarch, half-awake, pushed it away. "Save it for yourself," she said. "I only need a rest."

Jainon tried again. "I must insist."

"No, you must listen."

"Your will," she said begrudgingly as she put the tube next to her. "It's there if you want it. I'm going to poke around the tank some more. Maybe we can scavenge something else, or at least, get answers."

I glanced at the sky. Though the jungle canopy obscured a lot of what was happening above, the sunlight had only the slightest tinge of yellow to it. "We should still have plenty of time to make it to the facility before dark, yes?"

Tolby nodded. "Only another two kilometers, I believe. Three at the most."

Jack, who had been quiet for a while now, beamed. "I agree, and for the record, I told you I'd get us out of this mess."

Yseri's lips pressed together, and her eyes narrowed. "If you hadn't gotten us shot down, we wouldn't be in this mess."

"As if you could've done better, kitty cat," he said, crossing his arms and staring her down.

"A blind cripple from the stone age could've done better."

"How about we not go for each other's throats?" I suggested, jumping in.

Yseri snorted. "If I were going for your throat, tailless, you'd know."

"The gods still smile on us, sister," Jainon said as she checked her plasma rifle. "Come with me, and let's see what we can dig up."

"I suppose Empress could use the rest," Yseri replied, glancing over to the matriarch. "But we shouldn't stay long."

With that, the two Kibnali disappeared inside the wreck, and for a few moments, we waited in silence. Empress muttered something I didn't catch, and neither did the others. Tolby had taken it upon himself to start walking the perimeter, and Jack looked lost in thought. Serious thought at that.

Empress muttered again, and this time, I hurried to her side. "Say again?"

Her eyes were closed, and I could tell she was in the land of the semiconscious. "I don't think I can," she said weakly.

I took her paw in my hand and gently placed my other on top. "You'll make it," I said. "We'll be safe soon."

Empress shook her head. "They...need...Empress...not me."

I grabbed her by both shoulders. "Hey, listen to me." When she startled awake and I held her gaze, I continued. "They need don't need another Empress. They need you."

Her ears flattened, and her eyes widened with fear unlike I'd ever seen. "What did I say?"

"Nothing any other wounded warrior wouldn't say who was looking after the welfare of others," I said, hoping to reassure the matriarch that she hadn't brought shame upon herself for doubting her importance.

"Good," Empress said, easing back.

Despite her front, I could see the tension in her body and hear the doubt in her voice. Due to earlier conversations with Tolby, I knew pressing Empress about possible secrets could end badly (for me), but I figured I might get a little leeway given our circumstances and the fact the other Kibnali weren't around. "If you're worried about something, maybe I can help."

Empress's eyes flickered to mine and told me I was treading into dangerous territory. "If I worry, it's because I'm responsible for their lives," she said, "and since you're asking, it's clear you don't understand the weight of such responsibility or the threat of a lifetime's regret should you fail."

"I—" Thankfully, I caught myself before I said another word. I didn't understand, even if I thought I could imagine.

"Good," she said, shutting her eyes and leaning back against the tree. Her voice carried respect and approval, and given her previous cutting tone, I was grateful for both of those traits.

"Can't say I blame her for worrying," Jack said from behind.

I turned to find him a couple of paces away, looking somber. "You know what she's talking about," I said. "You understand."

He nodded. He'd never admit it, but I could see hints of redness in his eyes and a slight sheen to them. "I was three when Kevyn was born," he said. "The day Mom and Dad brought him back from the hospital, Dad sat me on his lap and talked about how great it was going to be being an older brother—and how much responsibility it was, too. I never once took that lightly, no matter how much we fought growing up."

I let out a half-grin. "I don't think I ever took being an older sister all that seriously."

"You should," Jack said. "Brothers and sisters are the only ones you get to know for your entire life—or theirs."

I chewed on his words for a few moments. I hadn't ever thought of it that way before, and my heart grew heavy as I realized how much I'd taken my brother Logan's presence for granted. I'm not saying we had a god-awful relationship that would require a few years' worth of family therapy to straighten out, but I never had truly appreciated the place he had—or could have—in my life. All that serious thought, however, was a little too much for me delve into, and so when a funny thought came to mind, I jumped on it. "Not feeling like the divine anymore, I take it?"

The corners of Jack's mouth drew back. "Sadly, no. My head's been clear for a half hour or so now."

"Well, for the record, if you'd managed to whip off a miracle, I wouldn't have objected."

"I wouldn't have either," he said. "But I'll tell you one thing: I'll be damned if I'm going to let that stop me from getting Kevyn back."

For the first time since he'd brought up the idea, I believed his sheer will might just be strong enough to do it. "I don't doubt you will."

"Break is over," Yseri shouted, coming out of the derelict and looking even less pleasant than when she went in.

"Find anything?" I asked.

"Scrap," she said.

"And more scrap," Jainon tacked on as she came out as well.

Yseri shook her head in disgust. "I can't believe the Kibnali have been reduced to scavenging a trash heap."

"Where's Tolby?" Jainon asked, looking around.

"Over there, patrolling the perimeter," I said, motioning toward him.

I was going to ask if he happened to stumble on anything when he suddenly dropped into a low crouch and made few gestures with his left paw and tail. Yseri dashed to Empress's side while Jainon shouldered her plasma rifle and pointed it in the general direction Tolby was looking.

"What is it?" I whispered.

Jack shook his head. "No idea. But if it can spook your friends, it can spook me."

We had our answer a moment later. A deep growl came from the bushes ahead. They rustled a few times before a grotesque, skeletal creature about the size of a fifty-kilo dog with an elongated tail padded toward us. Its skin shined like copper, and its skull tapered into a long snout filled with teeth designed for tearing apart prey in the most gruesome way possible. Four sickly green eyes sat in asymmetrical sockets in its head, and all four were focused on Tolby.

The creature launched itself at Tolby with a snarl. He bolted to the side, narrowly avoiding the monster's three-inch talons. Before it had a chance to attack a second time, Jainon popped off a trio of shots.

The plasma bolts slammed into the creature's torso with deadly accuracy. Sparks flew with each hit, and chunks of molten metal sprayed in all directions. The creature staggered, and Jainon followed up with a fourth shot that struck it midskull, right beneath one of its eyes.

The monster fell to the ground with a heavy thud. There it stayed, convulsing a few times before ceasing movement altogether.

"Please tell me that thing wasn't a baby because I don't want to meet the momma otherwise," I said once I realized I was holding my breath.

Jainon and Yseri approached cautiously, but Tolby kept his distance and his attention elsewhere.

"Tolby? What's up?"

A second creature came flying out of the brush a few meters in front of Tolby, jaws open. I've no doubt that any human would've been torn in two, as my brain barely registered what took place, let alone would have had time to react. Tolby snapped off a shot with his plasma rifle, catching the thing right in the head. Its skull exploded, and before the thing hit the ground, a third monster attacked.

Tolby swung his rifle around right as the thing got to him. His weapon connected with the creature's face, which was enough to send it flying off to the side. The impact, however, was enough to cause him to lose his grip on the weapon.

But did that stop Tolby from beating the ever-living crap out of said nasty? Not even close. My best bud pounced the off-balanced monster and grabbed it by the back of the neck and hoisted it in the air. The creature thrashed from side to side in a futile attempt to rake its claws across his body.

"What a stupid creature," Tolby said with a grunt. "I should bat it around to teach the rest a lesson."

"This isn't the time to play with your kill," Jainon said with a wry grin. "Put an end to its miserable life."

"Gladly," Tolby replied before smashing the creature headfirst into the nearest tree. The damn thing was resilient because even with Tolby's incredible bulk driving it forward, it took no less than five solid rams for it to die.

"Might be stupid, but damn that thing's tough," I said as Tolby dropped its limp body to the ground.

Jainon knelt by the monster she had shot and inspected her kill. At first, she examined the torso, specifically the wounds she made, before lifting the creature's skull and looking into its mouth. The look on her face changed from intrigue to anxiety in a matter of seconds.

"What is it?" asked Yseri.

"They remind me..."

Jainon's voice trailed, and I could see the hairs on all the Kibnali stiffen. Silence lingered for a moment before Yseri broke it. "Of?"

"The Nodari."

"Do not speak of them so lightly," Yseri hissed.

"I'm not."

"Then what makes you say such a thing?"

Jainon pointed to the fallen creature. "Look at it. It's a skeletal, metallic construct and as hideous as they were, albeit a different form and color, not to mention much smaller."

"And it's not sporting bioweapons, fangs, and claws aside."

"I know."

"And it's not ripping through the stars in gigantic hive fleets."

"I know."

"And it's not coming back to life." Yseri hesitated at that those final words before tacking on, "Right?"

Jainon put one more headshot into the creature before shooting the other two again and slinging her rifle. "No. It's not, and neither are the rest."

"Then let's not needlessly worry ourselves with demons of the past," Yseri said.

"I'm not needlessly worrying about the past," Jainon said. "All I said was that these things remind me of them. No more. No less."

Empress coughed, stopping the conversation and drawing everyone's attention to her. "I think it would be best to move on, especially if these aren't the creatures Baumdon warned us about."

My eyes drifted back to the bodies of the fallen creatures. When Empress's point sank in, a shiver ran down my spine. These things could be deadly if caught off guard, no doubt, and certainly would be a thousandfold more lethal if they came at us in swarms, or herds, or whatever their groups were called. But if these weren't the apex predators of the planet, I shuttered to think what was.

CHAPTER ELEVEN: ARRIVAL

To my utmost delight, we reached the complex no worse for wear, though I'm sure the backs and shoulders of the Kibnali were on fire from carrying Empress. Actually, strike that first statement. Our bodies were no worse for wear. Our psyches, however, were not.

Over the course of the final three kilometers we traveled, we encountered no less than four other skeletal wrecks. One might've been a tank like the one we'd found before, but it was hard to tell. The others might have been spaceships, but given their horrid condition and the fact that there aren't exactly universal standards when it comes to designing these crafts throughout the galaxy, we couldn't be sure of anything. Speaking of varied starship designs, did you know what would easily be recognized by early space-faring Earthlings as a Saturn V rocket would also be easily recognized by the Portapixies of Reman XI as something that housed a mid-sized water park (their spaceships looked like spiders with party hats, to me at least)?

When we got to the facility, our bodies were tired and dirty, but our psyches needed some TLC, too. There was something incredibly unsettling about seeing so many ruins, so many ghost ships, along our journey. And if those were merely the ones we found by chance, how many more were in the area, and what caused their demise? Moreover, why the hell was there at least one Kibnali battle tank on this planet? How did they get here and what happened once they had arrived? I tried not to think about that last question but was unsuccessful.

On the more pleasant side of things, the complex was in remarkably good shape. About two dozen buildings filled the place, each standing a couple of dozen meters in height, except for the main building which stretched ten stories high. It looked like a giant snail shell turned on its side with a winding steeple coming out the top. Across many parts of these buildings ran intricate webs of circuitry, much like the ones found on my arm and the portal device. They were, no doubt, the very things Baumdon had told us about.

"This has to be a Progenitor treasure trove," Tolby said, looking around with as much awe as I was. "You'd think everyone and their mother would have looted it by now."

"Unless they didn't know what it was," I said.

"Or it's too dangerous to do so," Yseri added. She then looked over at Empress with concern, who was completely out of it. "We need somewhere to tend her wounds."

"I say we go to the main building," I said. "It's as good as any."

Everyone agreed, and we all started toward it until Tolby crouched and brought up his weapon. "I smell someone."

"You do?" I asked.

Tolby motioned to our left, toward a small, C-shaped building. "Over there."

Jainon raised her nose and sniffed twice. "Smells like Jack. Only worse, if that's possible."

"Sorry, my jail cell didn't come with a shower," Jack replied.

"Hints of the space station, too," Yseri said, adding her nose to it all. Her ears flattened, and she growled. "Must be Baumdon or one of his cohorts."

"We should kill him while we have the chance," Tolby said.

"We should get Empress somewhere safe," Yseri countered. "We can fight later."

"He could have something we could use," Tolby replied. "Or worse, he could follow and ambush us."

Tolby took one step forward, and then a figure in black composite armor bolted from behind the building. He shot out into the open like a rocket, which was good for him since Tolby's shots lagged by a few meters. As quick as the figure appeared, he was gone, ducking behind another building farther off.

I put a hand on Tolby's shoulder and gently tugged him back. "He left," I said. "No need to chase."

"I can't believe I missed that shot," he said. "He was right there."

"You'll get him next time, big guy," Jack said.

"I plan on it."

Since Tolby insisted on bringing up the rear from there on out, I took the lead with Jack and we headed for the main structure. The entrance was easy to find. Set into the west side were three pairs of double doors that were tangerine in color and slightly translucent. Beyond them we could see a few halls as well as a large inner room, but the details were hard to make out. As we approached, I wondered how we would open the doors as I didn't see any controls, but when we were within a few paces, my right arm tingled. I gave it a stretch, inadvertently pointing it at one of the doors. I then felt a tap on the back of my neck, and the doors swung open.

"Oh, that's handy," I said, checking out my arm. "Wonder if everything around here works like that."

"If it does, don't wander off," Tolby replied, still keeping vigil on our rear. "You're the only one with an interface installed."

"Maybe there's another Curator around here and he'll put one in you, too. Then we'll match," I said with a smile.

Tolby grunted. "No, thank you. I like my brain exactly how it is."

We said no more and hurried inside. The interior floor was lined with red marble tiles, each a meter square. Lights that looked like Chinese paper lanterns lined with thin wires of gold hung from a vaulted ceiling. All along the floor space sat S-shaped, black leather benches. Given the shine on each one, there was no doubt that someone, or something, was taking care of the place.

"Maybe we should let her rest here until we know where we're going," Jack said, helping the Kibnali set Empress down on a bench.

Jainon cringed along with Tolby and Yseri as their matriarch whimpered before settling. "Agreed," Jainon said. "We can split up and scour the facility while one stays guard. It shouldn't take long to get a good survey of the building."

A high-pitched shriek, like a bird of prey claiming its territory, preceded the swooping down of a grapefruit-sized, metallic sphere. Aside from having garnet-red and lemon-yellow circuitry across its skin, and a steel-blue eye in the center instead of one that was emerald green, the sphere was a carbon copy of Tour Guide, the flying drone we met back in the Progenitor Museum of Natural Time.

It swung around us, screeching a couple more times before speaking in a much more intelligible—and thankfully, less ear-shattering—manner. "Overwhelming joy! I always knew one day you...brrrrrrrrrrrpt...you brrrrrrrrrrrrrrrpt...friendly guests would arrive."

"You've had unfriendly ones?"

"Annoyance. Yes. They come in their brrrrrrrrrrrrrrpt...their brrrrrpt...their vacuum-shielding interplanetary traveling devices."

"I think you mean spaceships," I said.

"Gratefulness! Spaceships! That's the word. They come in their spaceships and try and take over."

"That doesn't sound good," I said.

"Resignation. A fact of existence. But it's not hard to deal with them," he said. "Locking the doors is more than enough since they're all eaten by the next brrrpt...the next brrrrrrrrrrpt...What's the word for a full planetary rotation?"

"Day," Tolby said.

"Embarrassment. That's it. Such a simple word."

I couldn't help but grin through all of it. "I take it your translation matrix is a bit gummy?"

"Excitement! Yes! How did you know?"

"We've been through this before," I said. "Are you a tour guide as well?"

"I am. Clarification. More like head of the visitor relations department here at Research Station Adrestia." Its eye darkened and he began to sway side to side in the air. "Admission. More like the entire department."

"The entire department?"

"Mhm."

"Would you also happen to be the last of the staff, too?"

"Impressed. Your deductive skills are exceptional."

I chuckled. "As I said, we've done this before."

"Curious. You did? Where?"

"Museum of Natural Time."

TG2—aka Tour Guide 2.0, for that's what I dubbed him in that moment—spun in place, circuits and eye lighting up. "Recognition. Exhilaration. Should've known it was you, Dakota! You're the last visitor to the museum, and you've definitively got that time-traveling aura about."

"You know about me?" I said, impressed and a bit flattered at the same time. After all, we were talking five billion years ago, give or take.

"Of course. Our records are very thorough and detailed, especially when it comes to those who buy omega-level family memberships. Guess that means now I won't be required to ask for your brrrrrrrrpppppppppppt...Your brrrrrrrrrrrrrrrpt..."

"Tiny paper devices that serve as a representation of a valid transaction?" Tolby offered.

TG2 chortled. "Tickets! Yes, tickets was the word I was after, but that is an amusing descriptive string of words as well. Would you like a tour of the facilities? It's been so long since I've had anyone to talk to—foolish looters aside—I'd be more than glad to give you a proper tour of the place."

Empress groaned and wobbled as she sat on the bench. Jack was quick to steady her, and she was quick to grab his arm to keep from falling.

"Where's your med bay?" Yseri said, hurrying next to Empress. "You must have one."

TG2 zipped over to the wounded Kibnali. A pale, blue light emanated from its eye and swept over her three separate times. "Scanning. Saddened. Hopeful optimism. I have limited knowledge of Kibnali anatomy, but we do have facilities which might be able to help."

"Might?" I repeated.

"Unless my imaging routines need defragging and rebuilding—always a possibility—she has...brrrrrrppppppppt...she has brrrrrrrrrppptttt."

"Skip the diagnosis. What's the prognosis?" Yseri asked with irritation.

"Two hours at best," he said. "Though I can extend that to twelve, most likely. At that point, she will require...brrrrrrrrrrrpt..."

"Two hours? Feels more like two minutes," Empress said weakly, looking up. She wobbled for a half second before slipping out of Jack's grasp and crashing to the floor.

Jainon was on her in a flash. "Empress!"

Yseri, a split second behind, lifted the matriarch's left arm and pressed her paw into the inside of Empress's elbow. "I can't get a pulse," she said. Her lips pressed together, and a small growl escaped as she shifted her grip. A half beat later, she relaxed, but only a hair. "No, it's there. Weak. But there."

Tolby scooped her up. "Well?" he barked at TG2. "What are you waiting for?"

"Only for you to follow," he replied before spinning around and zipping away. We ran after him, Tolby somehow being able to stay in the lead with poor Daphne bumbling along the way in the back.

We raced down the hall and passed dozens of rooms that had full-length windows and were filled with countless pieces of strange equipment. The hall curved twice before leading to a spiral ramp which then led us up and through a green, circular door and into another hall. This one had more of the same, though the temperature in there was a good thirty degrees colder than where we first arrived.

Another hundred meters or so passed beneath our feet before TG2 darted into a side room. Following right behind, we then found ourselves in a rectangular room where a table, three meters long, sat in the middle. Suspended from the ceiling directly above was a large mount which held a dozen thin, multi-jointed arms that sported everything from needles to clamps to a few things that looked like ancient depictions of ray guns from the cheesy sci-fi films of 560 PHS. Along three of the four walls were banks of computers, similar to the ones we'd seen back in the museum in Curator's office, and above those were a dozen displays, all currently off.

The moment Tolby gently placed Empress on the table per TG2's instructions, our robotic host repeatedly nudged us toward the door. "Out! Out! Out!" he said. "You can't be here for surgery!"

"Did you stick a finger in an antimatter socket?" Yseri said, brow dropping. "I'll die before I leave her side."

"Frustration. Understanding. Sterilization and relational precautions will prevent the automated system from proceeding. You must leave." Though Jack, Tolby and I started for the door, the two handmaidens did not. TG2 went to bump Jainon toward the exit but ended up flying back when she shoved him off her. "Pleading," he said. "Time is precious. You can wait right outside, and I'll keep everyone abreast of the work."

"Jainon," I said, putting a tentative hand on the Kibnali's shoulder. When she didn't rip it off, I gave it a gentle tug. "There's nothing we can do here."

The handmaiden nodded, but there was a deep growl that preceded it. Her shoulders fell, and she sighed. "Sister, she's right," Jainon said. "All we can do now is trust the gods they will hear our prayers and bless Empress with a longer life."

Yseri rushed over to Empress and brushed her forehead before leaning close and whispering something in the matriarch's ear. Empress's eyes flickered open, and she reached up weakly and took Yseri by the back of the head and brought her face close to hers. At that point, Empress spoke, but it was far too soft for anyone to hear, save Yseri. When it was over. Empress shut her eyes, and her arm fell back to the table.

Yseri slumped and shook her head before marching out of the room without a word.

The rest of us followed, and the door slid shut behind us with a hiss and a click. I plopped down next to Tolby on one of the leather benches and ran my finger over the material. It had a scaly feel to it, although I couldn't see any actual scales. Though odd, I didn't dwell on it long because TG2's voice piped into our waiting area from an unseen source.

"Diagnostic scans started," he said. "We'll have her patched up in no time...unless...oh, that doesn't look good."

Jainon put a paw on Yseri's shoulder as the handmaiden started for the door. "What doesn't look good?" she asked.

"Surprise. Tongue tied. Nothing. I mean, not nothing, just...yikes! Sorry. Forgot how big those needles were is all. Yes, that's it, just a big needle and no brrrrrrrrrrptttt..."

I muttered a curse under my breath and ran my fingers through my hair. "Do I want to ask?"

"Only if you have a better substitute for brrrrrpppt...brrrrrpt... large fountain-like squirts of liquid suspensions needed for life."

"Blood?" I offered with a cringe.

"Perfect! Blood!"

At this point, I was certain Yseri was a split second away from grabbing Jainon's rifle and breaking down the door, so I tried my best to change the subject. "Can we talk about something else while we wait? What is this place anyway? It's obviously not another museum."

"Boasting. Research Station Adrestia is an award-winning facility and devoted solely to the study of the Nekrael."

"The who?"

"The Nekrael," he repeated. "Gruesome little guys made of a living metal. They usually swarm from beneath the group and chew up anyone and anything that lands here in a matter of days. I shudder to think what they'd be capable of if they ever moved beyond their modest station on the evolutionary ladder."

"That must've been what we fought on the way over here," Jainon said.

"Probably," TG2 replied. "Oh, that reminds me, if you haven't already, you ought to put your ship into orbit. Anything parked on the surface doesn't last long."

The corners of my mouth drew back as I gave a half chuckle. "Not a problem. Ours already blew up."

"Oh, I...hang on a second. Having a little trouble with keeping a heart rhythm...Okay, that looks right. I think...Hmmm. I wonder if we have enough nano-sutures to get her stitched up."

"Hey! You're not helping!" I barked.

"Embarrassment. Where were we again?"

"You were telling us about the Nekrael and how they eat everything."

"Well, not everything, everything," he explained. "Take this installation for example. We've got repression fields that are online so most of them stay...brrrrrpppppppppppt... stay...brrrrppppptt..."

"Away?"

"No. They stay...brrrrrrrrrpt. Asleep! That's close enough," he answered. "Also, the Progenitors were a clever lot, you know? Comes with the whole ability to travel spacetime and whatnot. They coated every square centimeter of this facility in a decodapner clear coat, which pretty much makes the Nekrael gag if they get even a nibble—essentially acting as a natural repellent."

My eyebrows arched, and I nodded approvingly. "That is clever."

"Too bad they disappeared. They'd know what to do with your friend here since they used to operate on them from time to time." There was a loud crash and a thump, and then silence for a couple of beats. "Whoops. Sorry about that."

"Sorry about what?" I asked. "Is everything okay?"

"Yes. Should be. Will be. Definitely going to be one hundred percent fantastic. Well, eighty-twenty. Or sixty-forty..."

"Sixty-forty?"

"Close enough. Could I see you at the door?"

I eased off the couch and approached. I was shocked Yseri didn't follow until I realized both Jainon and Tolby had her tightly by each paw. The door slid open a half meter, and TG2 appeared in the crack.

"Come on in," he said, floating back. "Got a slight hiccup you can help with."

I squeezed through the gap and then asked my question, which looking back was fortunate because if I'd asked first, I never would have gone in. "Help with what?"

"Surgery, of course," he said as the door slid shut again with another hiss and click.

My eyebrows jumped up as my jaw dropped. "Me? What makes you think I'm capable of that?"

"Upbeat. You have hands and an interface device, which is exactly what I lack at this point. Don't worry. You're going to be a great doctor. You're not squeamish, are you?"

"Squeamish?" My gaze drifted beyond to where Empress lay. From where I stood, I could see her midsection was open via a metal spreader. Bright, purple blood stained the floor in more than one area, as well as the array of surgical devices hanging from the ceiling. In proper response to all of that, my stomach turned queasy. I leaned against the wall as my head went light. "You've got the wrong girl. This isn't the kind of doctor I ever wanted to be."

"Encouragement. Sounds like an excellent opportunity for personal growth," TG2 said. "There's no other alternative. You are currently the only one with an interface device. Now let's not brrrrrpppppppt...dawdle...yes, that will do. Need to be fast or we'll be doing an autopsy."

I took a deep breath and told myself to suck it up before hurrying over to Empress's side. I was proud I didn't throw up, though it was close for a moment there, but when I got to her side, the gravity of the situation smacked me hard. I felt as helpless as I had when I was eight and as a practical joke, some older kids convinced me I had to solve a quantum-calc problem in the next five minutes or the world was going to end. Only this wasn't a practical joke, and there was a lot more at stake here than a face full of tears. "I don't even know what to do."

"First, stick out your hands."

The moment I did, one of the devices from the ceiling swooped in and coated my hands and arms in some sort of latex-like material. "What are these supposed to be? Gloves?"

"Yes," TG2 replied. "We don't have any masks, so try not to sneeze in her guts."

Bile rose in my throat. "That's going to be the least of our worries."

"Agreement. Now then, do you see that arm on the floor? It fell off mid-procedure—shoddy maintenance and all—so you're going to have to perform its role," TG2 said.

I'm so glad my brain was quick enough to realize he meant a robotic arm, and not Empress's, because I would've fainted right there otherwise. I know I've been through some heart-stopping adventures the last week or so, but I'm really not the kind of girl who likes to see bodies mangled. "Yeah, I see it," I said. "What do I do?"

"Take the nano-suture device off it—it's the cylindrical object with all the needles coming out one end—and then do exactly what I tell you so we can close her up."

"I can do this. I can do this," I said as I bent over and freed the tool from the broken robotic arm. "It'll be like sewing up a beanbag."

"Amusement. No, it will be...actually, yes. Let's go with that. You're going to be fine, and if you don't succeed, well, we all lose a patient once or twice throughout our careers. How's your insurance?"

CHAPTER TWELVE: POST OP

I don't know how long things took. I flew on autopilot the entire time. One second I was nervously leaning over Empress's body, shaking like a newborn kitten, and the next, I was a surgical goddess, masterfully fusing cuts and tears to all of her tissue under TG2's command. At least, that's what I told myself. When we came out of surgery sometime later, I hadn't killed her. So that was good. The relief at that little fact must have shown on my face when I went out to meet the others because although I had purple Empress blood spattered all over my arms and chest, they all looked at me with hopeful smiles on their faces.

"How is she?" Tolby asked.

"Alive," I said.

"And stable," TG2 chimed in as he came from behind. "For now, that is. Her...brrrrrrrrpppppppptt...is completely shattered and can't...brrrrpppppt at all. Without further brrrrrrrrrrpt...further brrrrrrrrrrpt...specialized treatment, yes, that will do, her recovery is not guaranteed."

"But she's better than before," I added. "That's what you said in the OR."

"Yes, assuming she gets all the rest she can," TG2 answered. "I'd say she has at least three brrrrrrrrrrrrrrrrrpt...brrrrpt...day-night cycles should her body fail."

"The gods will deliver us before then," Jainon said.

"And if they don't, you'll have plenty of time to say your goodbyes," TG2 tacked on.

Yseri flattened her ears and growled. "Goodbyes are not being said. We take her back in time to when our Empire still flourished, and our own doctors will tend to her."

TG2 tilted to the side. "Back in time? Oh! Of course! Excitement! Shame at missing the obvious. You want to use our webway, don't you, to go home? Oh, I haven't seen that fired up in so long, I forgot we had one. I've always liked the way its hum fills the air."

I clenched my fists and bit my lip as I dared to hope. "You have one?"

"Of course we have one. There's one...or was one at least...on every planet we've gone to."

"And it still works?"

"In theory."

The wellspring of hope that fountained in my soul started to dry. "What do you mean in theory?"

"It works on pulpy trees. No wait, that's not right. It works on paper. Is that the phrase? You naked apes have such funny euphemisms. As I was saying, the webway works in theory. The last few times it was used, the subjects ended up inside out."

"Inside out? Literally, inside out?"

"Dark humor. And then they exploded," he added with a disturbing, electronic chuckle. "Worry not, vintage Earthling, those incidents were only due to sub-optimal power levels, which we can fix...I think."

"This doesn't sound promising," I said. "How can you not know?"

"Annoyance. Because everyone vanished and before they did, they never bothered teaching me how to fill in," TG2 said. "But I did watch a lot. I think I can brrrrrrrrrrrrrpt...can brrrrrrrpt...can mimic well enough."

I sank onto the bench between Jack and Tolby. "Is it too much to ask for one thing to go right?" I said, burying my face in my hands. "I mean, just one little thing? You'd think after nearly being blown up, kidnapped, shot down, and nearly mauled by Nek-whatevers—"

"Nekrael," TG2 filled in.

"—you'd think we were due for some good luck."

"Sympathetic reframing," TG2 said as he floated over to me. "Sounds like things could have gone a lot worse. Besides, the webway might still work. It will only have enough of a charge to produce a localized wormhole as opposed to one big enough for a fleet to move through, but it should suffice. Let's go see, shall we?"

"Right," I said with a heavy sigh. I glanced over to the others, specifically Jack, who was still sporting his birthday suit, albeit with a lot of dirt and grime. "Any chance you've got some clothes we can throw on him?"

"I do have a fabricator that should do the trick."

"Wonderful," I said, standing up. It wasn't much, I know, but at least it was something that was going right I could latch on to. I smiled, enjoyed the renewed sense of vigor surging through me, right until I realized we were minus one. "Hey," I said, looking left and right. "Where'd Daphne go?"

"Who?"

"Our little robot that was with us."

"Oh, the cute one dressed in retro?" TG2 asked, eye lighting up. "She seemed nice, but she beeps a lot. Maybe she needs a reboot."

Jack elbowed me in the side. "Told you."

"Whatever," I replied with annoyance. "Where is she?"

"No idea," TG2 answered. "I'm sure she'll turn up sooner or later."

I could only hope he was right. Though I wanted to go look for Daphne, the webway was far more important to get going, especially if repairs were going to be required. And she was slow, so it wasn't like she could wander far. She'd probably taken a left when we took a right and ended up in one of the labs. "I'd like that to be sooner since we're not sticking around."

"As would I," TG2 replied. "In the meantime, shall we get you new clothes and check the webway?"

"Yeah," I said. I looked at Tolby and the others, unsure what the Kibnali wanted to do. "Do any of you want to come with?"

Predictably, Tolby shook his head, and his answer clearly spoke for Jainon and Yseri. "We will stay with Empress. Let us know the moment you find anything."

"Copy that."

I started to leave, but Jainon spoke. "Dakota, may Inaja bless you with good fortune."

"Thanks," I said. Tolby leaned over and whispered in my ear at which point I repeated his words, which apparently were the proper response. "May her luck be your luck."

Jainon touched the top of her head lightly and bowed. "We shall see each other soon."

At that point, TG2, Jack, and I then headed for the fabricator, which wasn't far. The device waited for us down one floor and inside a nearby lab. The thing looked like an old lobster pot with three pipes coming out of the top and an array of controls at the bottom.

TG2 spent a few moments at them before the device sprang to life.

It whined like a turbine that was spooling up and it filled the air with an electric scent. After about ten seconds, it stopped, and the top opened up. TG2 bobbed toward it. "Pride. Not bad work if I may be so bold," he said. "Go on. Try them on. There's even a towel in there for you to clean up with. You humans like towels, don't you? Pretty sure I remember that's standard space equipment for you lot."

"Don't mind if I do," Jack said as he reached in and pulled out the towel. It was large, white with stripes of orange, thick, and positively comfy looking. With it, Jack gave himself a good wipe down before taking the set of clothes that were inside the replicator. What he got were fitted black trousers, a long sleeve black-and-burgundy shirt that complemented his muscular physique quite well, dress socks and a pair of dress shoes that were polished to such a shine that they could easily serve as an emergency signal for anyone marooned on an island.

"Better hope we don't have to slog through any more jungles," I said with a half-grin. "Those shoes won't do you a bit of good."

"Boasting," TG2 replied while bouncing lightly in the air. "Those aren't any dress shoes. Those are Yuenglax active dress wear. Created for the intrepid explorer who demands the ability to meet the most important client in any clime or place. They come with a six-lifetime warranty against defects and blisters."

"Never heard of them, but I'll tell you this: they are fan-freaking-tastic when it comes to comfort," Jack said, hopping up and down on the balls of his feet. "I daresay they are so good that this entire cluster of a failed expedition is totally worth getting my hands on a pair of these."

"There is no way they are that good," I scoffed.

"Would you like a pair?" TG2 offered. "We're low on material, so it can't make much other than simple weaves anymore, but I can do shoes aplenty."

I looked down at my bare feet. As much as I wanted to say no, just out of spite because I didn't want to play into the exaggerated claims Jack was making, I did need something when it came to footwear. It was a tiny miracle that they were only covered in dirt and minorly scratched up having trekked through the jungle like that. I guess that's a testament to my insistence on developing tough, calloused feet over my few years of exploration. "Okay," I said with reluctance. "Give me a pair. Socks, too."

TG2 went to work and quick as a quark, I had a pair of my very own waiting for me. "There you go."

I reached in the fabricator and pulled out my socks and shoes. I used Jack's towel to brush off my feet as best I could before putting them all on. I took a few steps around, hopped a few times, and then took a few more steps. "Damn," I said with a disbelieving laugh and smile. "These are the comfiest things I've ever put on. I swear if heaven was ever a pair of shoes, these would be them."

Jack didn't say anything, but I could see he had a bit of gloat in his face.

"Query. Shall I make you a new wardrobe ensemble as well?" TG2 asked.

"Yeah, actually, that'd be great," I replied, realizing I looked a little silly in nice shoes and underwear.

TG2 whipped up another set of clothes, similar to Jack's but tailored to me. My shirt was black, which looked much better if I do say so myself. Once I'd tossed on my new outfit, TG2 lead us to the webway. The route he took brought us back to the entrance of the building where we first met him and out the doors. We then walked around the building and between a few others that were considerably smaller before reaching what looked almost like a landing pad for a mid-sized ship.

The area was circular, raised about a half meter from the ground. Seven tall spires lined the perimeter, spaced evenly about. At the far end, twenty meters outside of the perimeter was something that looked like the claw of a giant crab jutting out of the ground and reaching for the heavens, while a few paces away from us was a small building with several antennas sticking out the top.

"Happiness. We're here," TG2 said, spinning around to face us. "I can't wait to see this start up. Shy request. Would you mind if I came with you? I've always wanted to tour the universe."

"Sure," I said, only half paying attention since for the most part, I was marveling at this technological wonder. Now that I had access to the webway, there was no stopping me on where I could go...when I could go. Don't get me wrong, the portal device was fantastic—when it worked—for zipping around spacetime on a local level, but even that had its limitations. For starters, I had to be very precise in knowing exactly where and when my intended destination was. With this, although I hadn't asked yet how things worked, I could let it do all the work.

"Why are we still gawking at this? Turn it on, babe."

I threw Jack a glare. "Babe?"

He threw me a grand response. "Only seeing if you're paying attention. In all seriousness, I'm ready to drop your furry friends off wherever and get back home."

"Sounds good." I turned to TG2. "How do we do that?"

"It is as simple as interfacing with everything else around here, though we'll need to be inside when you do—safety precautions and all," he said as he opened the door that led into the control room. "From what I understand, it's a very intuitive design if you've already mastered telling Jakpep what to do."

"Yeah, mastered," I said with a nervous chuckle.

Much like other areas of Adrestia and even the museum we were at before, the control room here was filled with...well, controls. I hadn't a clue what any did or said, or what would be displayed on the screen, but when I treated the entire thing as a giant portal device and tried to link to it, everything lit up like a party barge. Holographic menus suddenly appeared in front of us. At first, they were in an alien language, but the symbols quickly rearranged themselves into words I could read. At that point, I didn't have to look hard until I saw a blue, rounded rectangle that had the words "power on" in bright white.

"Here goes nothing," I said as I gave that rectangle a mental push.

The button changed from blue to green and then to a solid yellow. A status window appeared in the air next to it. The words displayed put a rock-hard pit in my stomach.

Reserve Power insufficient. Reroute at reactor needed for webway operation.

I groaned. "Is this what you were worried about earlier? Or is this an entirely new problem?"

"Run a type 342.2a diagnostic, if you would," TG2 said.

I was going to ask him where that was, but apparently, merely thinking about such a thing was all the interface needed to perform the task. The hologram flickered before rapidly displaying countless schematics with a wall of text running next to each one. I've no idea what any of them said, but TG2 kept his focus on all of it until it finished. At that point, he bobbed once and spun around to face me. "Frustration. The reactor is beyond repair. Optimism. We can manually reconfigure a power node near the reactor heart that will divert power away from the repression field."

"The repression field keeps the Nekrael asleep?" I asked.

"Yes."

"That seems like a bad idea to get rid of it then," I said. I then held up the portal device. "What about this? It's broken, but can we fix it and use that to leave?"

TG2 zipped over and gave the portal device a close look. "Oh! It's the actual prime mover! Here I thought it was a toy you purchased at the gift shop. What did you do to it?"

"Damaged in the crash," I said.

"Too bad," he said. "The flux capacitor is cracked, and the hexa-string-induced quantum blowback filter is ruined."

"I have no idea what that means."

"It means I can't fix that, well, safely at least," TG2 said. "Lambda Labs at the north end of Adrestia has a couple of spare flux capacitors. We use them in all sorts of projects. Our FUM, the fixer-upper machine, could pop a new one in to get it to work, but you'd be safer dancing on a neutron star than trusting anything but the most basic wormholes since we don't have any hexa-string-induced quantum blowback filters."

"How basic?"

"Spatially or temporally?"

"Both."

"Anything more than five hundred meters or five hours will do you in," he replied. "Not sure what good that will do you."

"Better than nothing, I suppose."

TG2 gave the portal device another look and chuckled. "Oh. The molanyr lattice is weak, too. Even with a new flux capacitor, you're looking at a one-shot deal. Half the circuits will liquify if you try twice, at which point it will make an excellent paperweight."

"Don't suppose you have any of those lying around?"

"Querying," TG2 said. His eye cycled through a rainbow of colors for a few moments before he spoke again. "Perplexed. I thought we did. Inventory shows that is no longer the case."

"Doesn't that freaking figure," I said with a heavy sigh.

"If we can't get it fixed here, where do we need to take it?" asked Jack with a distinct edge in his voice. "I've got to get to my brother, and this baby is the only way to go back in time."

"Polite correction, it's one way there," TG2 said. "We have multiple methods for traversing spacetime. The prime mover is merely one."

"What's another?"

"Minor information dump. The webway for starters," TG2 replied. "Some starcraft were equipped with them as well."

"Any chance there's one of those ships around?"

"Disappointment. No," TG2 answered.

"Where could we find one?" Jack asked. "A time-hopping spaceship would solve all our problems."

"Difficult to say," TG2 said. "With the Progenitor vanishing, much has been lost throughout the Universe at all points in time.

But with a few weeks at a master webway node, I could come up with a list of viable locations to explore. If those do not prove fruitful, we should...brrrrrrrrrrrpt...should brrrrrrrrrrrpt...locate a repair bench for the prime mover."

"Perfect," Jack said. "Because as soon as we're out of here, that's exactly what we're going to do: either find a ship or fix this portal device of yours so we can get Kevyn back."

"After we solve the paradox problem," I added. Maybe I shouldn't have said anything, but I felt like he needed to be realistic in all of this. Then again, maybe I was the one not being realistic by insisting he let Kevyn go, so to speak.

"I've been thinking about that, actually," he said. "And I think I've got a solution."

"You do?"

"Yeah. From what I understand, we can't save him and have the old me know he's saved, because then old me won't do everything that leads me to go back in time to save him, right?"

"I think that's right," I said, replaying his words and trying to make sure they at least sounded correct.

"Then all we have to do is save Kevyn while making it look like he's still dead to the old me," he said with a self-congratulatory smile. "Because then old me will still be dead set on going back in time to save him. Piece of cake."

"And how do we do that? I was under the impression you saw him die," I asked.

"Haven't gotten that far yet, but that seems like a trivial detail at the moment."

"It won't be trivial if we screw it up and create a black hole at our feet," I said.

Jack's brow dropped. "Are you trying to weasel out of your promise?"

"No," I said, shaking my head, though that was only partly true. "I don't think you appreciate how dangerous surfing time is.

We honestly could crack open the galaxy if we don't do this perfectly."

"If you're lucky," TG2 said with another disturbing, electronic chuckle. "You could wipe out life, the universe, and everything."

"Well, let's not do that," I said. Before Jack escalated the situation further, I threw him a sincere bone. "We'll try with everything we have," I said. "I promise. All I'm saying at this point is, we need to be damn sure what we're doing, okay? Details aren't trivial."

"Okay," he said. "Details aren't trivial."

"Now then, since we're going to play reactor engineer, I don't suppose you have an armored personnel carrier that can get us in and out?" I asked, turning to TG2. "Maybe even one sporting some phased plasma cannons or a couple of Gatling guns?"

"No, the only vehicle we have that's not in a mothball is a single-seater. There is, however, a security station we could stop at and pick up some weapons. That will keep you from being completely helpless during a Nekrael swarm and ought to serve you much better than that wimpy plasma pistol you're carrying," TG2 said.

"I guess that's something," I said.

"Only kidding. There's far too many to shoot in a swarm, but you can at least feel good about taking a few of them with you," he said. "But, the weapons ought to come in handy if we run into a stray, nonetheless."

"Can we cut the attempts at standup until we get off the planet?" I asked.

"Apologetic tone. Of course," TG2 replied. "Assurances. We ought to be long gone before they all wake up. Caution. It's still a good idea to tell your friends they should be ready to leave in the near future if they value keeping their bodies intact."

CHAPTER THIRTEEN: INTO THE REACTOR

Tolby? I'm afraid I've got bad news, bud," I said.

"You say that like we've had anything but."

I took a few quick steps to catch up to TG2 and Jack, who were already making their way to whatever armory this place had. Once I was in step with them, I gave Tolby a brief rundown of our current situation. When I finished, there was an uneasy silence on the line, so I filled the void and asked him a question. "I don't suppose you have any better ideas than turning off the repression field?"

"Somehow I think any idea that didn't result in the unleashing of a subterranean horde would be better than what you've got cooked up right now," he said.

"Yeah, I know. And if Empress didn't need a Kibnali hospital, I'd be more than willing to spend at least a couple days brainstorming, but we don't have that kind of time. We're going to have to get that power rerouted and race back before those things know what's going on."

"Which is the only reason I'm not blasting this idea to pieces."

TG2 stopped, which made Jack stop, which made me almost run smack into him. "Revelation!" he said. "There is a way we can modify the power node that would allow us to only redirect power from the repression field when the webway creates the wormhole. That would be much better than us waking the Nekrael up while we are inside the reactor."

I perked. If that were the case, I could only imagine we would be long gone by the time those creatures came from up out of the ground. "Tolby, did you hear that?"

"I did, and however you have to get that done, I'd say do it."

"Definitely," I said. "Get ready to move Empress. I'll call you when we're on our way back. We'll meet you at the webway."

"Copy. In the meantime, I'll try and track down Daphne."

"She still hasn't turned up?"

"Negative."

"Ugh. Okay. Keep me posted."

"One more thing, ask about the tank," he said.

"The tank? Oh, the tank!" I looked over at TG2. "Hey, out in the jungle, we found a Kibnali patronus—"

"That's patrone, Dakota," Tolby interjected.

"Same thing," I said, going on. "Anyway, we found a Kibnali tank on the way over here. Know anything about that?"

"Excitement! I do. The Kibnali were once studied here in-depth."

I straightened. "They were? Why?"

"Mostly to see how tough they were, I think," TG2 replied. "I'd say more, if I could, but my memory is...brrrrppprrpppttt... is...brrrrpppppppt..."

"Not what it used to be, I know," I said with a sigh. I then returned to my chat with Tolby. "Did you get that?"

"I did, though it didn't make me happy to hear. I do not like the idea of our species being test subjects."

"Yeah, I bet. Talk to you soon."

I killed the call, and a few minutes later, we entered a gray building in the shape of a dodecahedron that had about a dozen red blisters on each of its faces. The floorplan inside of the building was cut into thirds. One-third being the entryway we were in, while the other two-thirds were a couple of rooms that flanked us on either side. The walls were white with a thin, blue grid and across them, as were the floors and ceiling.

"You guys really spared no expense when it came to decorating," I joked.

"It's part of the security system," TG2 replied. "I'll spare you the details, but that grid will ensure that any unauthorized intruder is cut into a couple of thousand tiny cubes before being vaporized an instant later."

Jack gave a nervous chuckle. "You remembered to put us on the authorized list, right?"

"Insulted reaction. I would not forget such a thing. You are authorized for one accompanied entry into this facility, namely this one."

I tried to relax, and despite TG2's reassurance everything would be fine, I had the feeling it would not be. Those thoughts, however, disappeared when we entered the next room and were presented with racks upon racks of weapons in all shapes and sizes. There were cutting weapons, stabbing weapons, shooting weapons, and weapons I didn't know what they did but since they were here with all the others, I assumed they had some sort of use to them.

TG2 faced us once more and gave us both separate, long looks. "Estimating. You should each do well with a Mark IV repeater, I think."

He then led us over to one of the weapon racks where the repeaters were. They had long barrels, collapsible stocks, and holographic displays that appeared to the side when we picked them up. Those displays showed a magnified view of whatever the weapons were pointed at and were useful, I'm sure, if you ever wanted to be a sniper, but at that moment, I was hoping we'd never have to pull the trigger.

"What do they fire?" Jack asked.

"Tiny packets of antimatter," TG2 replied. "The field they are contained in will fail at three hundred meters. As such, anything beyond that, you won't be able to hit."

"That sounds dangerous," I said.

"It's a weapon. It's supposed to be dangerous," TG2 countered.

"Touché."

At that point, he gave us both a rundown on the operation of the repeaters before we had a chance to try them out in the other room, which happened to be an indoor range. I have to say, I was impressed by the mini fireworks display each one gave when an antimatter round struck its target.

When we left the security station, we'd barely gone a few steps when I caught sight of our mysterious black armor guy making a dash from one building to the next, about fifty meters away.

"Hey!" I shouted. "Stop!"

Mystery man—or alien or whatever he was—of course, didn't. He disappeared into a building, and thus our encounter ended.

"That guy is fast," Jack said, repeater shouldered and ready to fire.

"No kidding," I said, shaking my head. "What's he up to?"

"Recognition. Fe'daku? No idea," TG2 said. "He showed up four...brrrrrrpttt...day-night cycles ago. Keeps to himself to an extraordinary degree. I've never been able to talk to him."

"That's weird. Who is he?"

"Hypothesizing. Likely a beta tester from another lab who is giving one of our armored suits a run," TG2 said.

"I thought you said you were alone," I said.

"Correction. I am the only staff," TG2 replied. "Beta testers are not staff. Nor are the Nekrael. And even just counting them, I would not be considered alone."

"Right," I said. "Anyway, shouldn't you know what he's up to? Seems weird you're guessing about beta testers."

"No. We've never talked."

"Then how do you know his name?" I asked.

"I don't. Fe'daku is what I like to call him," TG2 replied. "In Polganese, it means 'lackey of my worst, incompetent enemy who should die in a glorious bonfire.'"

My eyebrows raised. "That's specific."

"Yeah," Jack said. "What's the story there?"

"Plausible deniability," TG2 said. "There is no story."

"Pull the other one," I said, wiggling my leg for extra effect.

"Really. There is none."

"Come on. Out with it."

"Annoyance. Frustration." TG2 bobbed in place a few times before continuing. "There might be another member on staff around here."

"Might?"

"Yes. And if he exists, he should die in a glorious bonfire."

I crossed my arms over my chest. "You've got to give us more details than that. What if he can help?"

"Firm refusal. No, I don't have to give details. Besides, he cannot help, if he exists. He would be useless and annoying."

Jack chuckled. "Looks like even the most advanced species in the universe can't avoid office fights."

"Irritation. There are no fights going on because that would take someone else to be around to fight with."

"Right," I said, shaking my head. "We're not here to play HR, anyway. Let's get to the reactor and get off this rock."

"Happiness," TG2 said, his eye brightening. "Follow me."

The hike to the reactor was only two kilometers outside of the facility perimeter. Most of the structure was underground, but a sizeable portion stretched about eight stories high in the shape of a crescent. The ground between Adrestia and the reactor was rough and barren, save for a single skeletal wreck of a spaceship that had probably used the clear swath of land to come down on, only to later be chewed to pieces by the Nekrael. I wondered what happened to its pilot, then realized I probably didn't want to know.

"Dakota," Jack said. "How much do you trust Tolby?"

"With my life," I said without hesitation. I had no idea where that question had come from, but I didn't like the myriad of insinuations it led to.

"And the others?"

"Not as much, obviously, but they did save my life back in the museum."

"Or saved their own," Jack countered.

I stopped, forcing the others to do the same. "What does that mean?"

"I mean, maybe they only saved you to save themselves," he said.

"Where are you going with all of this?" I asked, crossing my arms.

"Look, I'm not trying to start trouble, but if we're going to take a portal to one of their worlds, we need to be damn sure we're all still going to be friends," he said.

"I don't see why that would change."

"Depends on whether or not the bulk of them are more like Yseri or more like Jainon," he said. "Because one of those two sure was keen on blaming us for crashing here."

"I know, but she's stressed," I said. "And can you blame her? Empress nearly died and is hardly out of the woods."

"I understand why she's stressed, but I don't think she sees us as equals is all I'm saying," he explained.

"What are you proposing?" I asked.

"Nothing, yet," he said. "Only that we need to stay alert and stick together."

"I appreciate your concern," I said as we started for the reactor again. "But as long as we're laying all our cards out, none of them were going to shoot me when we first met. I can't exactly say the same for you."

"Fair enough," he said with a short nod.

The conversation died at that point, probably because I was shocked that he didn't try to defend himself, and as such, I didn't know what to say.

Anyway, the closer we got to the reactor, the warmer the air got. When we were half the way there, it was noticeable, but nothing to write home about. About three-quarters to it, the air felt like we were walking into a small room with a lit fireplace. And once we took our first steps inside the reactor, I was sure I was going into a sauna with a stuck thermostat, and I was sure I'd need to down least three canteens if I didn't want a heat stroke before this was over.

"At least it's a dry heat," Jack said, cracking a grin while wiping the perspiration off his brow. "Still, I suggest we hurry. I don't think there are any water fountains around."

"No kidding."

"Sympathetic understanding. I shall increase our rate of travel," TG2 said, speeding up.

He led us down a broad ramp that led further inside the reactor. Light, like a setting sun's rays filtering through a dirty window, came from unseen sources above and illuminated the metallic floor. Pipes and junction boxes lined the walls and ceiling, creating a complex network that I hadn't a clue how to follow as to what did what.

As we pressed on, we came across a winding staircase that we ended up descending. The steps were large compared to the ones back home, but not so much that they had been built for titans. If these were meant for Progenitors, and surely they were, I guessed that they had been about three meters tall. That thought made me happy, as it was the first concrete thing about what they looked like I could come up with. I should've looked them up when I was at the museum, and I reminded myself to check them out on the archive cube later.

The air grew stifling, and the further we went, the more I was convinced we'd be knocking on Satan's quaint summer home in no time. My head ached, and the muscles in my legs and back cramped. Worse, I realized I wasn't entirely sure how to get back out, which greatly concerned me since I was always good with spatial direction.

TG2 stopped at a four-way intersection. He hummed for a bit, looking this way and that, before he finally said. "Embarrassment. I might have taken a wrong turn. None of this looks right."

I shook my head and swore, and instantly regretted it—the foremost that is. Pain ripped through my skull for doing such a thing. "If we don't find it soon and get out of here, I'm going to need to jump in the arctic ocean to get my body temp back to normal."

"Humorous response. Understandable," he said. "But—oh, wait. Here we go."

"Are you sure?"

"Quite," he replied, hooking a left and zipping down the passage. He didn't go very far, thirty meters at the most, before coming to a stop. At that point, he faced the wall where there was an oblong blister set into an otherwise flat spot. From the bottom of his spherical body, TG2 extended a thin wire that reached out and touched the blister in the middle. The blister rotated and disappeared into the wall, revealing what looked like a gold coin the size of a dinner plate with microprocessors embedded all along its surface. "Here it is," he said proudly. "If you'd be so kind to pull it off, I'll do the rest."

"Pull it off, how?" I asked. "Like grab and yank?"

"If memory serves, you'll need to give it a quarter turn counterclockwise first and then it should come right off."

"Right, Jack, watch my back," I said. "I don't want any of those things popping up on us."

As soon as those words left my mouth, I braced myself for the pass at me he'd invariably make. Maybe I shouldn't have been so jumpy in that regard since he'd been mostly decent since we left the gas station and "rebooted" our threadbare relationship, but still, given all that he put me through in the beginning, you can't blame me. That said, I was surprised when he didn't say anything but, "You got it."

I gripped the sides of the coin, which was tricky as it was barely five centimeters thick and twisted with all my might. The damn thing didn't budge. I tried again. And again. And again.

On my fifth go, Jack looked over his shoulder. "Maybe we should trade places."

"Maybe not."

"Why? Because you want to show the world you don't need a man to do that?" he said. Though he tried to come off as joking, there was enough in his tone that made me think otherwise.

"No, because I'm a terrible shot, and if someone needs to pull the trigger, especially when antimatter is concerned, I'd rather that someone not miss a lot. Like me."

Jack chuckled and wiped his forehead on his sleeve. "None of that's going to matter if you keep taking your sweet time. We're both probably ten minutes away from being cooked medium rare."

I sighed and realized the pressure upon my eyes was almost unbearable. "Fine," I said, stepping away and unslinging my rifle. "I'll watch. You do it."

"That a girl," he said while taking my spot. His meaty hands grabbed the coin on both sides and then with barely a grunt, he spun it to the left and popped it off its mount.

"Wonderful!" TG2 exclaimed. "Now, just switch red to blue and—"

A Nekrael slammed into TG2 from behind, its jaws clamping down on his body. The moment the two hit the ground, its jaws snapped shut, crushing TG2 into pieces.

CHAPTER FOURTEEN: USING THE WEBWAY

W hat the—"

Thank whatever gods and goddesses might be out there that Jack decided to shoot rather than question current events because that was about as far as I got in my shock before the Nekrael leaped at my face, jaws open. The only thing that stopped him was a well-placed shot to the head.

The creature's skull exploded in a brilliant display of fireworks, sending fragments of metallic bone in all directions. Its body bounced off my chest and hit the ground while I stumbled backward.

"This is bad," I said, unable to look at anything but TG2's shattered body and the monster's corpse at my feet. "This is really bad."

"No kidding! Help me figure this out."

Jack's command snapped me back in the moment. I darted over to the power node, and beneath the disc we'd removed were a number of handles that we could rotate. There were strange symbols alongside each one, and I had no idea what any of them

147

did. That said, there were two that were in alignment with red bars that could be turned ninety degrees and line up with blue bars.

"Do you think that's it?" I asked.

"I was hoping you knew since you're the one with Progenitor tech installed."

"Sorry, this upgrade didn't come with a degree in Progenitor engineering." I thought for few seconds then came up with a grand idea. We might not know exactly what to do, but if someone was in the control room at the webway, that someone could probably tell us when the power flipped on. Thus, I whipped out my communicator and called Tolby. "Tolby! I need you at the webway, pronto."

"Say...again...way?"

I slammed the bottom of my fist into the side of the wall. His reply was so garbled I was lucky to get three intelligible words out of his transmission. "Get to the webway. Now!"

"Empress...ready...time or..."

"Tolby, I hope you can understand me, because I can barely understand you. Yes or no, can you get to the webway? Empress can wait, but I need you there now."

"Yes."

"Call me when you're there. Got it?"

"...affirma..."

I gave Jack a sheepish, nervous look and shrugged before shouldering my repeater. "It might take a few minutes for him to get there," I said. "I'd rather not get jumped again."

"Agreed," Jack said, raising his weapon and pointing it in the other direction.

Seconds seemed to drag for hours. Sweat continued to pour from my forehead and ran into my eyes. My mouth felt like sandpaper and my throat a desert. "Hey," I said, voice hoarse. "If I die down here, I want a Viking funeral."

"Then you better not die, because I'm not dragging your body out," he said. "You're not that cute."

"Gee, thanks."

"—kota? I'm…"

I instantly perked at Tolby's voice. "Repeat? You're there?"

"Yes."

"Oh, thank god," I said. "Is there still a holographic display up?"

"Yes…but…says…power…out…"

"Yeah, I know. I'm trying to fix that now. Let me know if it changes," I said. I then turned briefly to Jack. "Keep me covered?"

"You got it."

I went back to the handles and turned the first one from red to blue. "Anything?"

"—gative."

I grunted. I guess it was too much to ask that my first try produced results. I gave the next one a turn so they were both on blue. "How about now?"

"Nothing…are you…"

At this point, I counted the handles as well as the switches nearby and realized the total possible combinations were far more than we had time to test. "Any ideas?"

Jack glanced over his shoulder. "Try putting the disc back. Maybe that is all that's left."

I nodded and grabbed it before putting in place and giving it a quarter turn. As soon as I did, there was a low, steady vibration in the ground as well as a steady, pulsing sound that carried through the air. "Now?"

"That did it!" Tolby shouted, his voice crystal clear over the commlink. "Whatever you did, you just got our ticket home. The power readouts are full and the webway has all sorts of lights along its edge."

I smiled, but that faded when Jack looked graver than an entire set of pallbearers. "Did he say the power readouts are full?"

It took me a half second to put everything together. My jaw dropped, and my pulse quickened. We hadn't set it up to draw power later. We'd already rerouted the power, which was why we had such a good transmission, and that meant the repression field TG2 had talked about before was gone.

"Maybe we can fix it," I said, darting back to the disc.

Before I put my hands on it, Jack grabbed me by the shoulder and yanked me back. "There is no time. Look."

I glanced down the hall, and beyond the shattered remains of the Nekrael, six more came toward us. They stumbled as they went, as if in a drunken stupor or waking up after an exceptionally long nap.

"I've got a feeling there are a lot more on the way," Jack said, drilling them all with well-placed shots to the head.

When the last one hit the ground, screeches echoed from far away, screeches that were answered by dozens more. Within the span of a few seconds, those calls drew nearer and seemingly came from all around.

"I've got the feeling I don't want to find out how right you are," I said.

"Me either."

We pivoted on our heels and took off running. Down the hall we went, racing through the maze of passages. Too often they looked the same, and since I was bordering on a heat stroke, the extra exertion on my body turned my headache into an extreme migraine with a side of dizziness. I stumbled off the walls and nearly fell down a set of stairs. When we finally reached the stairs that led up and out, we were at least graced with a slight cooling of the temperature.

I'd barely gone up half the flight when I caught movement out of the corner of my eye. I spun around in time to see two Nekrael leaping upon us from up high. Reflexively, I held up my hand to block the attack. Instead of it getting neatly chomped off, the two creatures flew back like they'd been knocked in the head with a giant baseball bat.

"Did you see that?" I said, laughing and stumbling. "Did you? Holy snort I did it again!"

"Lovely, sweetheart, but that's not going to stop the rest from making us lunch," Jack said. He paused long enough to put a few shots into each as they struggled to regain their footing. "Now move!"

I did, but not before I tried to use my new-found superpower again. I shot my palm forward again and tried to knock one of their bodies back, but nothing happened. I wanted to try a few more times to figure it out, but Jack tugged on my shoulder, and I knew we had to go.

When we got back to surface level and had the exit in sight, I called Tolby on the commlink once again. "Tolby! We are leaving!"

"What the hell is going on? What's all that shooting about?"

"The Nekrael are attacking us out of the woodwork," I said. "We've got to get out of here before we're their breakfast."

"What are you—"

There was a loud crunch from Tolby's end followed by him groaning.

"Tolby? Tolby!" I shouted. "Answer me!"

He didn't, and so my mind raced with a thousand variations on worst-case scenarios as I ran full tilt for the facility. The muscles in my legs burned and my sides cried in agony under the immense strain I put under them as we sprinted the entire way back. My vision dimmed along the way, and I was forced to stop for far longer than I would've liked in order to cool down and keep from passing out.

In the momentary lull, Tolby came back, which eased my panicked heart. "Be careful, Dakota," he said, sounding like he was coming off a weekend binge with a hangover the size of Jupiter. "That guy got the drop on me."

"What guy? The one in black?"

"Yeah. Shocked the hell out of me with his suit when I grabbed him."

"And?"

"I don't know. He left before my head cleared and I got to my feet."

Jack snorted. "Why do I get the feeling this is only the tip of the iceberg when it comes to weird around here?"

"Probably because I'm feeling it, too," I said. I wiped the sweat off my brow and took a few tentative steps. My muscles ached, but at least I wasn't light-headed anymore.

"Can you run, or do I need to carry you?" Jack asked.

"No, I'm good," I said. "Let's go."

We raced over the barren terrain in a mad dash to get to the portal. When we were about a hundred meters from Adrestia's perimeter, the ground ahead of us burst open and out flew a Nekrael. It landed about fifteen meters away, and it barely had time to pivot before Jack cut it down with some well-placed repeater fire.

Another flew out of the hole a moment later, heading right for my face. Instinct, again, saved me. My hand shot up, and I telekinetically punched it so hard half its face caved in. The creature flopped to the ground and spasmed before Jack finished it off with a few antimatter rounds.

"You pack one hell of a punch," Jack said. "Maybe I shouldn't have antagonized you before. My dashing good looks might have been a thing of the past."

"Yeah, you're probably lucky I didn't shatter your skull," I said as we started to run again.

When we got to the webway, Tolby was waiting for us at the control building. Empress lay on a makeshift stretcher that was being carried by the handmaidens.

"Planck's end, Dakota," he said. "You're as red as a boiled lobster."

"I might as well be," I said as I hurried over to the control room. "That reactor was hotter than a supernova."

Everyone followed me inside, and once the door shut behind us, I linked into the webway interface. To my surprise, I didn't have to start anything up. In fact, there was a nice holographic display already up that showed several options on what I could do.

"What on earth is this all about?" I muttered, reading what was up. "Someone's already used it."

"The webway?" Tolby asked.

I nodded. "Your black-armored visitor, I'd wager. Went back in time a few days ago."

"To where?"

"Here. The planet."

"Why would he do that?" Tolby asked.

It was a good question, and one I felt had serious implications about what was going on. Sadly, I hadn't a clue as to what the answer was. All I could offer was a shrug. "No idea."

"If that doesn't affect us leaving, who cares?" Yseri said, tone sharp.

"As far as I can tell, it doesn't," I said, double-checking the system. The entire thing had an incredibly intuitive design, so finding information about all things time-wimey regarding its abilities was simple.

A dozen seconds later, I found the targeting system and began scrolling through a myriad of planets I'd never heard of before.

"Odd," Tolby said.

"What is?"

"All those are Kibnali worlds."

"Isn't that a good thing?" I asked.

"Yes, but still odd."

"Well, where do we want to go?" I asked. "Looks like we have quite a selection."

Tolby studied the display for a few moments. The planetary list had thousands of places to go, if not tens of thousands. "Find Kibnai, our homeworld, and make sure you set the year to well before 7822, or you'll send us right into the Nodari War."

"Will do," I said, scrolling through our options. Changing the date was easy enough. I gave us a hundred years' worth of padding, figuring I wanted the Kibnali Empire to be as advanced as possible, technologically speaking, without running into any issues with the Nodari. Sadly, however, Kibnai was nowhere to be found. "What do you suppose that means?"

"I don't know," he said. "That's a question we'll have to find the answer to later. Look for Paetalia. It would be our next best bet as it was one of our earliest colonies and at the heart of our empire. You'd like it there. Warm beaches. Plenty of hunting to do, and the best Jungor rum you've ever had—tastes exactly like a root beer float, only with an incredibly strong kick of alcohol."

"I do like the sound of that," I said. "Though I'll pass on the hunting part."

"Your loss."

I soon found the planet's listing, and with Tolby's approval, I made the selection. The moment I did, I felt something enter my mind. It was like a snake burrowing into my very being. I suddenly found myself looking down at my body as if my soul had a bird's eye view, but that lasted only for a split second. My view pulled away at a mind-boggling speed. I saw the planet we were on for a heartbeat before it shrank to nothingness. Stars zipped by at a rapid pace, and before I knew it, I saw the entire galaxy, which then shrank away before I could fully take it in. I saw galactic clusters and superclusters, and then I found myself racing toward an unknown place in the universe—a place I soon realized was the home of a modest, oceanic planet with a couple of mountainous continents.

My normal vision returned, and I was back in the control room with everyone else. A deep, throbbing hum filled the air. I looked up to see spacetime distort at the webway before it bubbled and gave a gorgeous view of a seaside beach with snowcapped mountains in the distance. I wasn't sure of their significance, or why they had suddenly appeared, but I did fall face-first into the cold floor and wondered why my ears were filled with panicked voices.

The blood oozing from my nose was a little unsettling, too.

CHAPTER FIFTEEN: A GIANT MEETING

You know what's weird? When your memories turn to goo, you don't realize it. It's like being super drunk. You have no idea how far from sober you are, but all your friends do. All you can do is hope you don't make a complete ass out of yourself, which isn't likely when your inhibitions are lower than my ability to pay my rent on time.

As I sat up, my hair flipped in front of my face, and I grabbed a lock with excitement. "Brilliant!" I shouted. "I always wanted to be a redhead!"

"No, you haven't, and no, you're not."

I turned to face Tolby and wrapped some of my hair around my index finger while pulling it taught so he could see. "Oh yeah? What do you call that? That's fiery red right there, and I'm pretty sure I know my childhood dreams better than you."

"That lock is brown, not red, Dakota."

"I don't know what games you are trying to pull, but this," I said, tugging the hair a couple of times, "would be the envy of any phoenix."

Tolby shook his head. "You probably don't even remember what brown is, Miss Mush for Brains. Do you know who I am or where we are?"

"Yes, I do, Tolby, thank you very much," I said, taking to my feet. I then proceeded to give him a quick rundown of recent events before folding my hands across my chest and smiling. "Looks like forgotten memories are thing of the past, huh? Tell me I missed something."

"Well, I wouldn't say 'forgot' is the right word," Tolby replied with a grimace.

"Then what would you say?"

"Well for starters, the ship we stole wasn't crewed by dinosaurs," Tolby replied. "And there was no ice cream fight back on the station. And you don't own a multitrillion-credit corporation that sells plush toys."

"I think my controlling interest says otherwise."

"Reality would beg to disagree."

I balked. "Are you sure?"

"Very."

I rubbed my temples and tried to concentrate on my memories. But as much as Tolby said they weren't true, I could clearly remember everything from how I started up Cuddle Monsters Inc. to the launch of the IPO to our total domination of all the plush-toy social media channels. Our first massive success was a plush Euryale doll—you know, the gorgon who was Medusa's sister? We dressed her up in a beautiful bridal dress because that's flipping hysterical. Can you imagine a gorgon getting married? The groom would have to be blind or he'd be turned to stone. I suppose at least her hair would be one-of-a-kind thanks to her snakes. But as real as all that seemed, I couldn't deny the fact that Tolby still looked dead serious with a hefty dose of concern as well. "I'm not the CEO of Cuddle Monsters Inc.?"

"Afraid not."

My shoulders fell. "Damn. That would have been so awesome. Hey! I know. When we get back, we can use some of the money from the resonance crystal to start it up. Won't that be grand?"

"Spacetime warp complete," a deep, electronic voice said from the nearby console. "Webway will be safe to approach in thirty seconds. Twenty-nine...twenty-eight...twenty-seven..."

As the voice continued, Yseri jumped in. "Okay, she's not dead. Either get her on her feet or on your back so we can get home!"

"I can't make the medevac come any faster!" I said. "If we move now, how will they find us?"

"There is no medevac! Only that wormhole you opened up!"

When I gave the handmaiden a stupefied look, Tolby hoisted me up and spun me around so I could see the outside. "*That* is our ticket out of here."

"I thought we just came out of that."

Tolby groaned. "Great. I think instead of erasing your memories, this time it's adding to them. I'm not sure which is worse."

Our announcer at this point reached the end of his countdown. "Spacetime fabric stabilized. Webway is now safe to use."

Jainon hammered the button next to her, and the door opened. "And that's our cue to leave."

The handmaidens were the first out, with Jack right behind. Tolby practically had to drag me out as I still didn't understand why everyone was in such a panic. Did we have a movie to catch? That would explain it, although there are always three hours of flipping previews, so I was certain we still had time.

We were barely out the door when the ground rumbled, and the thing I thought looked like a ginormous claw from before...well, it really was a ginormous claw, but it was attached to an even more ginormous creature that pushed out of the ground and sent rocks and debris flying. It came rushing at us on a dozen pairs of legs that supported an elongated, segmented body. Its head reminded me of a lobster, only with ten eyestalks and a pair of jaws that opened like scissors, and at the end of its back was a brightly colored tail with numerous barbed hooks arranged in a wide fan.

I hesitated, as did everyone else.

Jack raised his repeater and started firing into the monstrosity and screamed, "Get through the portal!"

That was enough for us all to get moving again. I ran for all I was worth toward the wormhole. Tolby was right behind, while the handmaidens followed, carrying Empress on her stretcher. Jack brought up the rear, but since he was shooting the hell out of the Goliath (a name I came up with on the spot), he trotted more than ran at full tilt.

The Goliath roared as multiple antimatter rounds stuck its body. Though it reared back in pain, Jack's attack didn't come close to killing it. Worse, Fate, the Universe, or karma (which sure as hell wasn't mine) decided we needed more of a challenge. Before we could close the distance and jump through the wormhole, Goliath smashed through one of the webway spires.

Bolts of electricity jumped in all directions and gouged huge chunks out of everything they hit. Everyone scattered to keep from being fried. Goliath, on the other hand, continued his rampage. He grabbed a boulder-sized chunk of rubble and chucked it through another spire.

The portal distorted into a dozen different shapes, from Mobius strips to hyperboloids to Apollion gaskets, before plowing through the ground like a runaway comet. The planet surface buckled and stretched as the webway platform was pulled under. A huge crack split the ground in two, raced outward, and ran under one of the nearby buildings, causing it to collapse.

Goliath started toward us, but it was forced back when a huge fountain of lava erupted from where the wormhole had torn through the ground.

"Dakota, look out!" Jainon screamed as molten rock rained down.

Operating on pure instinct, I leaped to the side, and not a moment too soon. A boulder the size of my bed smashed into the ground where I'd been only moments ago.

Through all the chaos, Jack kept firing at Goliath. When I noticed he was still trying to bring the monster down, I remembered I still had my repeater slung over my shoulder and decided to put it to good use. Even though I was a terrible shot, Goliath was as big as a barn, so even I would have had to work at missing him.

The antimatter rounds from the two of us tore into the Goliath's head and body. His legs failed him, and he came crashing down. For a dozen seconds we dumped shot after shot into his bulk, and only when our barrels were glowing red did he finally die.

Goliath had barely ceased moving when a half dozen Nekrael bounded over his body, charging right at us. Reflexively, I squeezed the trigger on my repeater, but all that came forth was a series of beeps and a bright warning on the holodisplay that read: OVERHEAT.

I suspect Jack's weapon needed cooling as well, as he didn't shoot either.

Jainon and Tolby, however, brought their rifles to bear and snapped off a dozen shots. Four of the monsters fell to their lethal fire while a fifth had its head shattered when Yseri joined in. The sixth barreled toward me, only to be greeted by a telekinetic punch by yours truly.

I knocked that stupid thing back a dozen meters, caving in half its skull in the process. Tolby followed up my hit with a couple of shots, finishing it off.

As the bodies of the Nekrael smoked around us, we all stood holding our collective breath and taking in the smoldering ruins of the webway.

"No. No. No," Yseri said, her voice climbing in both pitch and panic. "This can't be happening."

"Keep it together," Jainon said, her weapon still at the ready.

"Keep it together? We're dead!"

"Stop it!"

"We're finished!"

Jainon swiped her claws across Yseri's shoulder and roared. "You are a handmaiden of the Empress! Now act like it!"

Yseri snarled, but before she could offer any sort of retort, her gaze went over Jainon's shoulder, and she gasped. "More are coming."

Everyone spun around. Beyond Goliath's body, more Nekrael approached with methodic caution, like a pack of wolves realizing their prey had horns. Only our horns wouldn't last forever, and given the amount of screeching in the distance, the Nekrael numbered in the hundreds, if not thousands.

"Run," I whispered.

No one argued.

We retreated the way we'd come, more or less, in an effort to get back to the main building. I say more or less because we had to take a scenic route thanks to dozens of Nekrael that had climbed out of the ground and gave chase. For every one we shot, another quickly took its place. We eventually ditched the entire horde by going through a smaller building and locking a bunch of doors behind us. The Nekrael had numbers on their side, but thankfully their smarts were severely lacking.

Once inside the main building, we closed everything between us and the outside until we were back in the med bay. After a brief break to gather our wits, we split up to scavenge anything of value. I hadn't come up with much, and ten minutes after the start of the search, I was slumped on a bench with my elbows resting on my knees, staring pitifully at the total of our newly found, meager resources.

"Is that all you could find?" I asked.

"That's what I could find that I could figure out how to use," Jainon said. "There's a lot of tech scattered throughout the rooms, but the previous owners didn't leave us with any instruction manuals."

"So what did you get?"

"Welders and a few portable cameras that are linked to the monitoring station."

"That's something," I said, waving my hand in front of one of the cameras and watching the live feed play on the screen near Jainon. "At least that will give us a better shot at knowing if and when they come."

"Exactly."

"Don't suppose you've seen any Nekrael on any of the feeds from downstairs," I said, really, really hoping the answer would be no.

"Only on occasion, thanks be to Nashir," she said. "But our field of view is limited. There aren't a lot of cameras in place. I did spot Fe'daku about ten minutes ago."

"You did?" I asked, leaning in to check out the displays better. "I thought he left."

"As did I."

"Under more normal circumstances, I'd say we try and figure out what he's up to," I said. "But since he got the drop on Tolby, I doubt he's the chatty type, and I think we need to concentrate on shoring up our defenses here."

"Agreed," Jainon replied. "We could handle a sizeable attack if we funneled them through a chokepoint, but I'm worried that there might be more of those giant ones. If there are, concealment and making this floor as inaccessible as possible is our best defense."

"Yeah," I said. The handmaiden was right, but I didn't want to think how right she was because that only made me realize how I might never see my family again. They must have been going out of their minds with worry by now, or rather, had gone out of their minds. I mean, at this point, they were all long dead and forgotten, all the while never knowing what happened to me. Or did that not happen because I'd get back in the future? Thinking about all of that made my heart ache, and thankfully, Jainon cut into my thoughts.

"How did you fare?" she asked.

I hiked a thumb over my shoulder to my contribution on the table. "Found a spool of cable. Figured we could use it for rope at the very least, which is always handy."

"Simple things can often be the best things," she said.

"I also found this," I said, pulling out the archive cube and bringing up a holographic map of the entire complex. "It's not an engineering blueprint, but it's a hell of a lot better than nothing."

"Are you Taiso in disguise?" Jainon asked with a hearty laugh.

"Who?"

"Taiso, the messenger," she repeated. "Granter of knowledge to explorers and champions of the gods when they need it most."

"Oh, yes. Taiso," I said. "Naturally, that's who I thought you meant. I thought you said Play-Doh."

"Your knowledge of the gods is abysmal," she said. "Though since you're hardly a favored race, I can't blame you that much."

"Aren't you the kind one?"

Jainon rubbed my head with her paw. "I tease," she said. "You can't be that lowly, after all, if you were blessed with finding this map."

I couldn't help but smile. "You seem genuinely optimistic about such a small development. It's not like we didn't know where we were."

"True, but this is huge, nevertheless," she said. Her words carried so much energy in them, I couldn't help but feel like I'd discovered the cure for the Oriddean plague.

"Thanks."

"I mean it. No general can win a war without intel, and before this, we had practically none. We didn't even know what the battlefield we were fighting on looked like, save a harried run through it.”

Yseri, who was standing guard over Empress, grunted with disapproval. “Don’t delude yourself. We’re not winning any wars.”

That was the first time Yseri had said anything to anyone since we’d made our retreat. All she’d done was stand vigil over Empress, who had slipped from consciousness once again. Given the disgust in Yseri’s voice and the building rage in her eyes, I wished she would’ve stayed silent. She looked part maniac, part demon, with only a thread of rationality keeping her from going into a suicidal-homicidal meltdown.

“With Nashir’s guidance and our faithfulness, we shall get out of here, sister,” Jainon said, her voice soft but firm. “If for no other reason because the gods have not snuffed out our life, though they could have a thousand times by now if they so wished.”

Yseri cackled. “The gods have seen us through this? What gods? If they are there, they toy with us for their sick pleasure. No, my dear. The Universe has merely caught up with what’s left of the Kibnali, and it is finally going to make us extinct.”

A rumble shook the building. The vibration was strong enough to rattle the archive cube right off the table. We all tensed until the quake stopped.

“Can I worry about that one?” I asked. “It was stronger than the other three.”

“I would,” Yseri said. “Who knows what damage that wormhole did underground? But there’s no need to listen to me, I’m sure. I’m not the one connected to the gods. See what the almighty battle priestess has to say on the matter.”

“Your continued lashings are not helping,” Jainon said.

“Neither are these supposed gods,” Yseri replied.

Jainon’s fur bristled, and she growled. “Others have been shaved and exiled for less.”

“I’d like to see you try,” Yseri said, squaring off with her sister. “It’s convenient, isn’t it, that only a select few can ever speak to them and the rest of us have to go by your word as to what is and is not true?"

"You know any can commune if need be," Jainon said.

"I know any can drink your poison for a hallucination and risk death in the process," Yseri countered.

The door leading out slid open with a hiss, and Tolby came through carrying an armload of jars and a half dozen bracelets. "Found some food—tastes like peanut butter and chocolate—and some hands-free commlinks cleverly disguised as fashion wear," he said. Though his arrival momentarily doused the heated exchange, he was quick to pick up on everyone's body language. "What's wrong?"

"*She* is what's wrong," Yseri said, pointing a claw at me. "She and that other one."

"Dakota is not the enemy," Tolby said as he set his loot to the ground, all the while maintaining eye contact with the handmaiden. "Stress and the Nekrael are."

"And incompetence," Yseri said, "which is something these outsiders have heaped upon us from the beginning."

"She's not an outsider," Tolby replied. "She's bound to us by ritual and combat, as we are bound to her."

"You would side with her over us?"

"I'm not siding with anyone!"

"If Empress dies, you best not stand in my way," she said, eyes narrowing.

Tolby went to speak, presumably to rise to my defense, but I didn't need him to do that for me, or want him to feel like he had to for that matter, especially since I was the one who bent spacetime to my will...well, sort of. Brain mush and all. "News flash for you," I said. "If it weren't for me, you'd have blown up with the museum."

"If it weren't for you, it wouldn't have been destroyed in the first place."

"It was going to explode anyway!"

"Only according to some," she said. Yseri crouched, and her claws flicked open.

"Don't," Jainon said, putting herself between Yseri and me.

Yseri snarled and shooed a paw at me. *"Ko adaki de toko sayshooni keshnai."*

My face scrunched. "What?"

Jainon gave the translation. "A second war is never an answer to the first."

My muscles tightened, and a tingle ran through my right arm. Though my repeater was propped against the wall, and I wouldn't ever use it on Yseri, I was primed to knock her back a few meters with a good telekinetic punch. Though I hadn't mastered the ability by any stretch of the imagination, I felt confident I could use it now if need be.

"If you want to blame me for some of this, fine, I get it," I said, trying to defuse the situation as best I could. "But right now, we need to work together if any of us are going to survive."

Yseri didn't say a word, but Jainon did. "Agreed."

"Good, because the first thing we need to do is seal ourselves off," I said, using the archive cube to show the basic floor plan of the building we were in. "There are two stairwells and three halls with pressure doors that we can close, and weld shut. If we do that, that ought to keep them from wandering up here. As long as we don't throw a party and form our own mosh pit, we should be safe for at least a day. The Nekrael don't seem very smart, and they're not the greatest trackers in the world, either."

"Again, agreed," Jainon said.

"If Baumdon was telling the truth before about the Nekrael being nocturnal, we should hunker down until morning," Tolby said.

"Good point," I said. "If they go away at daybreak, we could probably slip into some of the other buildings to find food and supplies."

"That would be great if we could, but our priority has to be coming up with a way off this planet," Jainon said. "Even if Empress wasn't wounded, we can't stay here for long."

"Baumdon said this was a tourist attraction," I said. "Maybe we could send out a distress signal."

"Like the kind that got us in trouble in the first place?" Yseri said.

"Do you have a better idea?"

"If this new signal of yours ends up like your first one, sticking your face in a Nekrael mouth would be infinitely better."

"Infighting will kill us all," Tolby cut in. As true as his words were, they fell on deaf ears when it came to Yseri.

"Defending failure, are you?" she said. "Even a kit knows how troublesome she's been."

"Stop," Jainon said with an uncharacteristic fierceness. "Arguing over a distress signal is pointless if it's not possible. Before we rip into each other any further, we need to know if we can even do such a thing."

"We can," I said, adjusting the map from the archive cube so that everyone could see. "There is a communication array that's east of here, but there's a lot of open ground between us and it. With night almost on us, we're going to have to wait before calling for help."

"Or putting out an ad," said Yseri.

"Say again?"

She grinned at me in the most devilish of ways. "Seems you and Jack are worth a lot of money. I bet we could get a few ships for you. Or even a fleet to help us get started on rebuilding our Empire."

Tolby was in her face with flattened ears before I had time to fully suck in a breath. "She's not for sale."

"Yet," Yseri replied evenly, her eyes still focused on me.

"Ever," he countered.

"You would save her over Empress?"

"I refuse to lose either."

"To the death?"

"If I must," he said, to my everlasting thanks.

Yseri held his stare for a moment before she smiled. "Neither of us believe that."

Feeling as if my fate was going to be decided for me in the next few moments if I didn't do something, I cut into their standoff. "We don't need to send out a distress signal," I said. "Jack's lifeboat is still docked at the station. Maybe we can remote pilot it to pick us up."

Jainon, who'd been neutral in our exchange up until now, perked. "Can we?"

I bit my lower lip as I wasn't sure. The idea was born more from desperation than certainty. Jack's lifeboat was an old, mid-first-century AHS piece of crap, but if memory served, almost every ship in that era still came with remote-piloting capabilities. That said, we had two enormous hurdles to overcome. First, I didn't know if we could communicate with the lifeboat even if we had Progenitor tech at our disposal. Second, I had no idea who was going to pilot it. Without a remote cockpit control system, there would be no direct video to watch, and thus, even if we could talk to the lifeboat, whoever piloted it would have to send and receive massive amounts of binary data—something none of us were capable of.

The door slid open, and Jack strode through, repeater slung across the back of his shoulders, with Daphne in tow. "Look who I found. You can thank me now and kiss me later. Or thank me now and kiss me now. Or kiss me and kiss me again. I'm not picky."

I darted over and gave our little robot a massive hug. "Daphne! You couldn't have picked a better time to show up!"

"Says the girl who abandoned me," she said with despondency in her voice. "Not that I should blame you, I suppose. You probably saw a gorgeous blender, didn't you? I bet she had twelve speeds, a shatter-proof jar, and a four-horsepower motor."

"And you can talk again!" I said, laughing. "Oh, this is perfect. We might actually survive."

"I don't see how me talking does that, but it's nice of you to try and make me feel better."

"How did you fix her?" I said, looking at Jack.

"All it took was a hard reboot, as I said," he said with a touch of gloat in his voice. "Cut my thumb getting her maintenance panel open, but other than that, it was a snap. She's still pretty banged up though."

"Jack, please tell me that lifeboat of yours has a remote autopilot."

"Damn skippy it does. Do you think we skimped on basic software before we left port? But unless you've got some deep, hidden pockets with an RCCS, Daphne here can't do it without a comm station."

"There's one here in the facility, but whether or not we can use it is still up in the air," Jainon said, pointing to its location on the map.

"Works for me. I'm assuming we're waiting till the nasties leave us alone," Jack replied. "I've seen several wandering outside."

I nodded. "In the morning we'll go. Till then, we can bolster our defenses."

"I should point out that I am too damaged in my current state to adequately communicate with and pilot the lifeboat," Daphne said. Thankfully, before my heart sank too much, she added, "I believe if certain nonessential internal components are cannibalized, that is something that can be corrected, provided someone here is skilled enough in that sort of thing—or at least, can follow my instructions. We might even be able to use the fabricator to make new parts."

"How long will repairs take?" I asked.

"Seven hours. Maybe less."

I looked over to Tolby, my god of tech repair. "What do you say, bud?"

Tolby whipped out his pen and gave it a twirl. "I'll have her ready in half that."

"How much loot should we try and grab?" Jack asked.

"What loot?" I said.

"The loot here," he said, with a sweeping gesture. "It's not going to take that long to barricade a few doors. What are we going to do with the rest of the time if not find some treasure? Watch a furry leader barely breathe?"

The room filled with growls as the three Kibnali glared at him. I was the first to comment. "Really?"

"No offense," he said, taking a step back, "but I'm not the going to sit around here and pretend to be somber when I could be doing something productive."

I tossed a purposeful look at Empress. "Given how she's doing, I think that's the least you could do."

"You've got that all backward," he said without a hint of self-censure. "If you want to go about thinking this is where it ends, fine by me. I, however, am sticking with my winner's mindset, and that mindset says that before my next birthday, I'll be lounging in my yacht back home, surrounded by the most beautiful specimens of female beauty and arguing with Kevyn on where we want to go for our next dig. And you know how that's all going to happen? With a nice haul of Progenitor tech and your handy artifact. *Capisce?*"

It honestly took me a good five seconds to wrap my head around his words and try to formulate a reply. I mean, how the hell was he thinking about money and women when we were trapped on an alien world with Empress clinging to life?

"A crude and selfish mindset, but a proper one," Yseri said. "I would do well to follow his lead. We all would."

If my jaw hadn't hit the floor with Jack's comment, it certain did with Yseri's. "Did I miss something?"

"She means no matter what, we need to see ourselves in the future," Tolby explained. "The heart that doubts is the heart that dies."

"Exactly," Jack said. "So, let's finish battening down the hatches so we can find our sweet, sweet treasure."

CHAPTER SIXTEEN:
R & D

I don't know if there's such a thing as reincarnation, though many cultures are quite fond of it. My favorite take on the idea comes from the Gerganagaphaxians (try saying that three times fast). They're convinced that all souls exist in a realm that's like a huge travel terminal for those waiting to go on holiday. It's full of light and chairs and that's about it. From that room, there are an infinite number of gates where you can tour whatever universe you want to via whatever corporeal form life takes. Your body is, in essence, a cruise ship, and once it's over, back you go to the terminal. Sometimes you get to take little memories back with you like mementos, but since each universe is so different, and thus your memories are pretty useless from one to the next, no one does. Also, they believe that the duty tax for those souls bringing them back is so ridiculously high, nobody can afford to pay.

Anyway, as I mentioned, I don't know if that's right, but one thing I am certain of is that I was never, ever a professional welder in a previous life.

Now don't get me wrong, I'm not about to blame the equipment Tolby found. The Progenitor welders he had gotten his paws on were incredibly intuitive to use. They looked like old-fashioned revolvers that had a fan of spikes coming out each side. Those spikes created a near-opaque force field that shielded the user from not only the intense light when using the welder but the sparks and little flecks of molten metal that jumped around as well. It even had automatic temperature adjustment so that the plasma jet it created was at the optimum temperature for whatever material was being used. Nifty, huh?

So, one might think with such advanced technology at my fingertips, I would've been able to seal off the door I was assigned in no time. I don't want to get into the details of my spectacularly poor performance, but let's just say that by the time I got three-quarters of the way finished, I'd nearly set myself on fire three times, almost burned off my thumb and forefinger at the first knuckle twice and ended up giving my inside wrist a nasty second-degree burn.

"If you make little circles instead of going back and forth with the welder, it'll come out better," Jack said. "You'll work faster, too."

I let go of the trigger so that the welder turned off and glanced at him over my shoulder. "I'm almost done. You're not that far ahead of me."

The corner of his mouth drew back. "I finished two doors, and you haven't finished one. Tolby and Jainon have long since finished theirs, too, babe."

"I thought you were going to stop that," I said, returning to the weld.

"Old habits," he said. He waited patiently for me to finish, which didn't take long when I decided to take his advice and use the technique he'd suggested. "Not too shabby. You could get good with a little more practice."

At first, I eyed him skeptically, but when I realized he was sincere, I relaxed and stood up. "Thanks."

"Now that we're dug in like a New Georgia tick, we need to talk."

"About what?"

"Us being sold like cattle," he replied.

"That's not happening."

"Yet."

"I know Yseri is taking things hard, but even if she was going to trade us for a ship, Tolby would stop her."

Jack snorted and shook his head. "Would he? I know he's your best friend and all, but who's he going to side with if it comes down to saving his entire species or some girl he's known for a few years?"

I sighed and leaned against the wall. Any other day, I'd have cold-cocked him for suggesting such a thing. In the time that I'd known Tolby, he was the most fiercely loyal partner one could have traveling the galaxy. That said, even I couldn't shake Yseri's final words to him when they butted heads. She didn't think he'd side with me over them. Enough of me feared the same. "Empress isn't flat out dying. We have time."

"Look where we're at, Dakota," he said with a sweeping gesture and a deep laugh. "One thing we do not have any amount of is time. Even if we did, even if we got off this rock, do you want to hang around a group that's looking for an excuse to cash you in?"

I raised an eyebrow. "What are you suggesting?"

"We get Daphne to the comm station, have her pilot the ship down, and take off as a party minus four."

I balled a fist at my side and used all my restraint not to swing or telekinetically punch him through a wall. "I'm going to forget you said that," I said with a deep breath. "If you say it again, all bets are off."

Jack held my gaze without backing off in the least. "Leaving all of them here might be harsher than I should've been. Let me amend that to 'once we're off this rock, we part ways ASAP,' but don't blind yourself to reality. One of those Kibnali wants nothing to do with you, and two others are lukewarm to your presence at best. That's not the kind of odds you want, five billion years from home, especially if things get worse."

"I'm not ditching Tolby," I said. "Ever. *Capisce*?"

"You're loyal to a fault," he said, shaking his head and crossing his arms. "Why are you insisting on destroying yourself?"

"There's no other way to be," I said. "I'm sticking with him until he gets sick of my company and shoots me out an airlock himself."

"This isn't only about you anymore," he said as he dropped his brow and stepped toward me.

I retreated two steps out of caution and prudence. "Stay back."

"Why are you acting like this? I'm not the one who's threatened you."

"You're not? You sure as hell aren't wooing me." My words, thankfully, smacked some sense into him. When he straightened and eased his posture—slightly—I capitalized on it as much as I could. "We're all scared," I said. "So, I'm cutting you and Yseri some slack, but that's only going to go so far. If you want me to help you save Kevyn, you've got to keep a level head."

To Jack's credit, he took everything I said in stride. "All right," he said with a short nod. "I'm cool as a void bath, and I'll trust you at your word. But at the same time, if you want me to stay sane, you've got to promise me there's a line in the sand when it comes to how you'll let them treat us."

"There is, and believe me, she's gotten far closer to it than I'd have liked."

Jack nodded again. The harshness to his face and voice faded away, and his usual larger-than-life attitude returned. "Something else, if you've got the time."

"What?"

Jack smiled from ear to ear. "I want to show you something."

"If it has anything to do with your pants, I'm turning this welder back on," I said, only half joking.

"You've already seen that," he said with a chuckle. Jack then pulled the archive cube out from his pocket. It was displaying a holographic map of the area as it had always been, but now it was showing a building other than the one we were in. "We need to go here."

"Why?"

"It's Adrestia's data center and holds all of the Progenitor research files," he said. "If we can bring those home, not only will we be set for life, but we will be the most technologically advanced couple in the galaxy—perhaps even the universe."

I arched an eyebrow. "Couple?"

"Relax, sweetheart," he said. "I only meant couple as in a group of two people. Besides, I don't think finding a couple of hotties to hook up with afterward is going to be hard. Fame and fortune tend to make that easy. So, what do you say? When morning comes, let's swing in and see what's there."

I scrolled through what limited information the archive cube had on the building. There wasn't a lot, basically what Jack had already said. As such, my mind had to fill in the gaps, which it did gleefully. I wasn't so interested in getting more to add to my fortune, especially since I still had that resonance crystal, but I couldn't deny bringing back more Progenitor technology, or at least their research and possibly even schematics, was irresistible. Who knew what that lab held? What if the portal device paled in comparison to what they were developing here? They probably had inventions I couldn't even dream of.

A thought dawned on me that ended all of that speculation. "They'll never go for it," I said. "At least not until we've secured a way out of here. Not that I can blame them, especially since the last time I took a detour for knowledge, we nearly got eaten by Mister Cyber Squid."

"We don't all need to make a run to the communication building," he said. "Besides, how long would it take to give one building a quick sweep?"

I shrugged. I couldn't argue that it wouldn't take long, but it's not like we were on a relaxing dig. I sighed. "Our priority has to be getting off this planet," I said. "Unless…"

"Unless what?"

I dug through the records in the archive cube some more, hoping to find more detail as to what might be in there—something that would prove to be mission critical. All I came up with were vague generalities until I hit a small portion of text that dealt with the top floor. "Now that's something," I said, pointing to what I found. "There's another lab in there, one that has stasis tubes for specimens."

"Stasis tubes like the ones we could put Empress into?" he asked, practically reading my mind.

"That's my idea," I said. "TG2 said she could still go from serious to critical condition at the drop of a hat, so even if we do get aboard your lifeboat, she's hardly out of the woods. If we stick her in stasis, that would give us all the time in the world to find her proper medical attention."

Jack's smile was so bright and infectious that it could have lifted the spirits of a prisoner who had more tally marks on his dungeon wall than he had hairs on his head. "Then let's tell the others," he said. "Cause we're going to be rich."

"And save Empress's life."

"Of course. But admit it, the tech is going to be a nice touch."

Rumblings, deep from inside the planet, shook the building. Everything around rattled, and my knees weakened.

"And here I was hoping we'd seen the last of them," I said with a forced smile.

"Me, too," Jack said. "What say we kick this plan into gear before the ground splits open and we get a first-class tour of this planet's mantle?"

"I say that's a fine idea."

I double-checked my weld job before we headed back to the med bay. Not that I knew what I was looking for in terms of quality, but the bead I'd created that fused door to door frame seemed as if it would do the trick. I mean, surely it would hold for a while, right? Even if the Nekrael did come and battered down the door, we'd have enough time to get out another way. Unless, of course, these earthquakes did us in. But surely, *surely*, the Progenitors made structures that could resist the hell out of a little ground movement.

We'd barely gone a dozen paces when Jack gently touched my elbow and brought us to a stop. "Sorry about before," he said, looking everywhere but at me. "About imposing on you back there, I mean."

"It's okay."

"No, it's not," he said. "Every time my mind quiets for even a second...it goes right back to...to that bridge...and..."

Jack stopped, and after I gave him a few moments to continue, which he didn't take, I decided to spare him the silence. "We're getting him back."

"Right," he said with a short sniff and straightening of the spine.

"And apology accepted," I tacked on.

"Thanks. Can we get moving? Because if this conversation continues, I'm going to need a few drinks."

"Probably best, seeing how there's no bar around," I said. "Though if you see one, I wouldn't mind an Interstellar Irrigator."

"Girl after my own heart," he said.

With that, we returned to the group. When we got there, not much had changed. Yseri still kept to Empress's side, and the matriarch lay on the table, unconscious. Her paws were folded over her chest, which gave me the willies because she reminded me of a body during a viewing at a funeral. Jainon sat at a row of monitors and looked at us briefly before returning to watching the camera feeds on screen. They didn't show much, thankfully, only the occasional Nekrael on the first floor and maybe a dozen wandering around outside.

Tolby hadn't moved since I saw him last. He had Daphne's midsection split open and was tinkering with her insides while a small pile of robo-guts, circuit boards, actuators, and couplings lay at his feet. Since he didn't have a sour look upon his face, I assumed progress in getting Daphne capable of interacting with the lifeboat was going well.

"Get ready to celebrate, my furball friends," Jack said, bright and cheerful as ever. I think the only thing that kept Yseri from ripping him a new one, literally or figuratively, was the fact that his gusto was so out of place, none of the Kibnali could wrap their head around his demeanor.

"Say again?" Tolby said.

"We've found a little something to solve all our problems," he said. He then nodded toward me. "Dakota, front and center. Show them what we've got."

I rolled my eyes as I approached the group as I hated how little tact he had and how he roped me into it. I couldn't think about that, though, I knew. We had real concerns. "One building over is the data center," I said, showing them the holographic map from the archive cube. "Top floor has a specimen lab with stasis tubes."

Jainon spun around and popped off her seat. "Stasis tubes like those back at the museum?"

I shrugged. "I would assume."

"That's wonderful!" she said, laughing and releasing no small amount of worry. "Yseri, we can put Empress in one until we can ensure her complete recovery."

To my surprise and delight, the other handmaiden wasn't sour on the news. "Yes...that's good news."

"Good? That's fantastic. The gods smile upon us, sister! I knew they would!"

Yseri went back to her recent charismatic self and snarled. "More like it's up to us, again, to save the Empire."

"Either way, I'm thinking we need to get over there sooner rather than later," I said. "There's no telling how long it will take to prep one for transport. And now that I think about it, I'm not sure how we're going to power it either."

"That's easy," Jainon said. "They have self-contained power supplies that are good for ten years before needing a recharge, so you can transport whatever you've got more easily."

"How do you know that?"

"I used to tinker with the ones back at the museum in my spare time, which was a lot. There are a few simple things to do to disconnect it from the main power, but that shouldn't take long."

"Okay, then Jack and I will hop on over and get it done before we come back for Daphne and make a run to the comm station," I said. "Once we call in the lifeboat, we can pick up the stasis tube off the roof, fly over here, pick everyone else up and be gone."

Jainon shook her head. "No, I'll go. It's a simple procedure if you know what you're doing, but I don't want to risk one of you screwing it up and putting us in the middle of a mushroom cloud."

"Then Jack stays here," Yseri said.

"No, I'm going with," he countered.

"No, you're staying here. If those things find us, Empress will need all the help she can get to get out. And with Tolby still working on fixing Daphne, someone has to patrol the halls."

Jack went to argue but quickly shut his mouth. Apparently, he didn't miss the finality in her voice that dared anyone to challenge her. "Okay, I can stay," he said. He then turned to me. "You got this, right?"

"Yeah," I replied.

Jainon and I were about to leave when Tolby took a second look at the building. "What did you say this place was?"

"A specimen lab."

"No, the building."

"Data storage."

"That's what I thought you said," he replied. "Don't turn this into a run for another archive cube."

My body straightened, and I felt the shock hit my face. I shouldn't have been all that surprised, seeing how he was my best friend and knew me pretty well, but still, he practically accused me of having ulterior motives. And they weren't ulterior. They were supplemental. "My main concern is Empress. I promise."

"Is that all?" he said.

I hesitated, not because I wanted to lie to him, but because I didn't want to get into it, especially with Yseri around. She still looked like she could go for blood at any moment. "If I see something in arm's reach, I might take it," I said, "but I'm not planning on running around blindly looking for technological treasures."

"Promise?"

"I promise."

"Good," he said. Then, with a seriousness that dwarfed any judge's sentencing, he added, "Because if you do, the Nekrael will be the least of your worries."

CHAPTER SEVENTEEN: AN UNEXPECTED CHAT

You'd think we would've left right away, what with Nekrael getting more numerous as the minutes passed and the planetary surface continuing to destabilize. I mean, at least I was under the impression we were on a timer.

Jainon had other ideas—ideas that revolved around me practicing my telekinetic punches while she, Yseri, and Tolby engaged in some sort of ritualistic sex. Now, I'll admit the former idea had been a good one. The latter, however, I'm certain had been a convenient excuse to get their freak on with my bud, despite Jainon's claims that the day and hour were ripe for a blessing from the gods—and thus, the assurance that not only would our mission to get a stasis pod be a total success, but the Kibnali Empire would be rebuilt to an even greater glory than before. Yseri didn't care much for the religious bend, but she did have a near insatiable appetite for pregnancy. I guess those hormones finally overcame her need to stand sentry by Empress's side.

At least they were being quiet.

As I waited for their romp to finish, I stayed in the room with Empress and practiced punching a large, spongy ball Tolby had found. It didn't weigh a lot, and I have no idea what it was supposed to be for. Neither of those things mattered though, and the fact that it was exceptionally quiet when I smacked it around was awesome. After all, I couldn't exactly go pounding the walls or making a ruckus with the equipment and not expect our chompy alien friends to pay us a visit.

After about twenty minutes, ten of which I'd gotten good enough to knock the ball around anywhere I wanted, I realized my arm cramped and my breathing felt labored. I needed a rest, so I dropped in the chair next to Empress.

She kept her eyes closed, even when I said a few words to her, though she did stir a bit and waved a paw at me to stay quiet. Realizing she needed rest more than entertainment, I grabbed the archive cube. At first, I was going do a little fun reading on random museum exhibits I'd missed out on, but then Jack's warnings about the Kibnali, their attitude, and their history started to haunt me. Did he know something about them that I didn't? Were they all bent on total domination of anyone and everyone they encountered? Or was that simply how they were before they were nearly wiped out. Perhaps near extinction had changed their minds.

Still, I had to know.

I paged through the cube's records and brought up the mountain of information the Progenitors had on the Kibnali. True to Jack's word, their history was rife was conflict, long drawn-out campaigns that saw the toppling of other civilizations en masse and the subjugation of thousands of species. As the most technologically superior race ever, save maybe the Progenitors, there was nothing anyone could do to stop them, and I had no doubt that had the Kibnali ever met humanity, we would've become their pets—at least, those of us who were known to be kind to the domesticated cat.

Correction, they were the most advanced race until they stumbled upon the Nodari. Though the Kibnali won their first few encounters with them—skirmishes on some insignificant recently colonized planet named Oorda—the Nodari quickly adapted and waged a long, bloody campaign that ended at the Kibnali homeworld. Yet despite their continued loses, the Kibnali, apparently, still saw themselves as the favored race of the gods, ones destined to rule over everyone and everything, right up until the end.

But what about after the end, I wondered. Did defeat bring some humility to Empress and the others? I cycled through a few pages to find her entry. It wasn't hard to locate, even if I didn't know her name—assuming she had one other than her ruling title. After all, she was the last matriarch, the one that ruled the Kibnali right up to the Last Act of Defiance, where the Kibnali turned their own star into an interstellar bomb.

It was near the end of that entry I paused. A single line, tucked near the end of the section, shorted my brain to such a great degree I was certain I was staring at the wrong text. When that turned out not to be true, my next thought was that the Progenitors had errored or were fantastic intergalactic pranksters and this was their latest gotcha to be played. The line in question? It was nothing more than:

Empress Suiko died in an attempt to contact the gods, leaving her Empire without a matriarch a mere four days before the Last Act of Defiance.

I leaned back in the chair and stared blankly at the wall. Empress Suiko died? How could that be? Did someone else die and the entry was made in error? Did the Kibnali clone her? Did the Progenitors? Did they have some sort of resurrection technology unknown to all? Maybe. Hell, probably, right? I mean, look at all that they could do. Bringing back the dead would probably be a parlor trick to them.

If Empress had died, did she know? Or was it like a blank spot in her memory? Moreover, did Yseri and Jainon know? Surely they did given their high status. But what about Tolby? Maybe. Maybe not.

Then a new thought dawned on me. What if she was an imposter? Could that be? A thousand more questions flooded my mind ranging from how they would all react to me approaching the subject to what they might do if it turned out my imposter theory was true and that came to light.

"Stop it, Dakota," I said, reining in my overactive imagination. "This is silly."

"What is?"

I jumped out of my seat to find Empress sitting up. Her legs dangled over the edge of the table, and her eyes focused on me. "Nothing," I said, nonchalantly turning off the holodisplay of the article I was reading.

"What you were looking at says otherwise," she replied.

"That silly thing? Oh, I—" I stopped myself from going any farther. The game was over before it began. At that point, I figured I should tackle this head-on. "Are you the real Empress Suiko?"

The matriarch glanced at the door before sighing heavily. "No," she said. "The charade won't last much longer, truth be told, so you might as well know now."

Her admission was so blunt, I hadn't a clue how to react. I had been right, yet I couldn't take pride in that for some reason. The only thing I could think to say was to ask the obvious. "Then who are you?"

"A *pegami*," she replied. "You might roughly translate it as a doppelganger. Each ruling matriarch has seven scattered around. We are the most trusted and closest Kibnali, surgically reconstructed to look, sound, and act like her highness, in order to thwart assassins and keep the Empire together should the beloved matriarch fall until a successor can be named."

"What happened? I'm so confused how any of this came about."

"Empress Suiko consulted High Priestess Samatu on what to do when the Nodari were but a system away from our homeworld, but Samatu did not live through the ritual."

"A ritual like the one Jainon did back at the museum?"

Empress nodded. Her eyes glazed over as she recalled the memory as if she were shielding herself from untold emotional pain in order to recount things from a distance. "A similar ritual, but more intense, more dangerous. High Priestess Samatu traveled to the Other World to get advice from Nashir, the creator god and maker of spacetime. But as I said, she did not survive, and so Empress Suiko made the journey as well, desperate for an answer."

"And she never made it back, either," I guessed.

Empress's tail swished a few times, and her ears fell. "No, she came back," she replied. "When she returned, however, she was struck with madness, and in a moment of clarity before she ripped out her own throat, she told us two things. One, that we must perform the Last Act of Defiance in four days' time, and two, that I would take her place in order to ensure her will be done."

"Were Jainon and Yseri there, too?"

"No. No one is left alive who was there," she replied.

"Why didn't you tell them?"

Empress laughed and then winced, grabbing her right side in pain. "Why would I? We never expected to live. Who could have foreseen the intervention of the Progenitors in taking four of us the very second before we died?"

Had I been the religious type, my answer certainly would've been something along the lines of Nashir had been looking out for them. Since I wasn't, I certainly didn't want to go down that path, but I also didn't want to trample on their beliefs, as I knew such things were important to their species. "Why haven't you told them now?"

Empress's stature shrank even more, so much so I half believed I would tower over her if we stood side by side. "Because I didn't want to," she admitted. "Though I've ruled for a short time, I've ruled well, and fair, and wisely—even if that rule was only for a few days back home and then again when it was only myself with Jainon and Yseri back at the museum. And honestly, I don't want to die. When a new Empress is named by the council of eleven—the council that has been long eradicated—old *pegami* are given a choice: exile or an honorable death."

"What?" I said, shocked beyond belief. "That hardly seems fair."

"Fairness and duty do not often go hand in hand," she said. "The tradition is there to ensure the line of succession is never challenged by the old guard, so to speak."

"Well, screw that," I said. "You're not bound by that anymore. As you said, the council isn't around. Yseri and Jainon love you. They'll never send you off like that."

Empress put a paw on my shoulder and squeezed. "It's kind of you to say such things, but their loyalty should never be to me, even keeping my deception out of it. Their loyalties are and must always be with the Empire, first and foremost."

"There is no Empire without you, though," I argued. "Who would rule?"

"That's precisely it," she replied. "Who would? Both Jainon and Yseri could make a valid claim to be matriarch as they each hold equal offices in the high court. While I would like to think they would work things out peacefully, that might not end up being the case if my...abdication of the throne is not handled well."

"I still don't see why they even need to know," I said.

"Because we're going home," she replied. "They're going to have our surgeons look me over, offer the best medical care that the Kibnali have to ensure my life is preserved, and when the doctors examine me, they'll learn who and what I am. *Pegami* have markers in both blood and genes so that they can always be identified."

"Then how—" I stopped when the door whisked open and in strode Yseri, whose eyes lit up at the sight of Empress awake and sitting up.

"Empress!" she said, hurrying over. "You're up!"

"Not a word," Empress whispered to me before the handmaiden got within earshot. She then eased herself back on the table and turned to Yseri. "I've only been awake for a moment, enough to stretch my limbs. I feel I should rest more, save my strength."

"Of course," Yseri said. She stroked Empress's forehead as the matriarch shut her eyes. After a few quiet beats, Yseri looked at me. "Did you wake her?"

"No," I said. I then figured I'd tack on a white lie to head off any questions about what we talked about. I didn't know how to handle the recent revelation, but I did know I needed more time. "She opened an eye and watched me bat things around, and then decided to sit up for the show."

"Did she now?" Yseri said, skepticism lingering in her tone.

"Check it out," I said, putting as much of an upbeat voice as I could into my words. I took aim at the practice ball off in the corner and using my telekinetic powers, I popped it into the air. The ball sailed toward us, and with a second strike, I drilled it to the far corner before hitting it once more before it struck the wall. "Pretty good, huh?"

Yseri straightened. "Not bad, tailless. Maybe you'll earn your spot yet."

"Thanks," I said, not sure how to take her politeness or praise. Were her stress levels coming down finally and I wouldn't have to bear the brunt of her frustrations? That would've been nice, but I feared that was far too hopeful.

"Does your skin still itch?"

"Sometimes," I said, rubbing the right side of my neck. I'll be damned if it hadn't been bothering me until she'd said something. "From what I understand, that's the implant further integrating itself into my nervous system, which in turn allows me to use all of its abilities."

"Where did you learn that?"

"TG2 had mentioned it on the way to the reactor," I explained.

Yseri was silent as her tail switched to and fro. "What other powers will that grant you? Or is it limited to using the artifact and knocking things around?"

"I don't know," I said with a shrug. "He didn't say before we got to the reactor and then, well, everything went to hell."

Her gaze drifted to my arm and hung there a few beats before shifting back to Empress where she now lay sleeping. "I would like to think of you as a true warrior one day, tailless. The universe is a dangerous place."

"So I've come to learn, but I'm not looking to be a warrior," I said. "All I want is to get home."

"Of course you don't," she said with a grunt. "Such limited ambition, though not unexpected. Regardless, that thing will make you a formidable warrior, something we should learn to harness."

My gut tightened as her voice took a more sinister tone to it. "Harness for...?"

"For the Kibnali Empire," she said. "If you, a weak tailless, can fight as you do with such technology, what could we do with it? I dare say we could drive the Nodari into extinction with our warriors equipped with such devices."

I didn't like where this was going because she was probably right, and given our previous conversations, I didn't think she'd be one to opt for a peaceful meet and greet should a rebuilt Kibnali Empire come in contact with people. Then again, humans weren't always known for their polite first encounters either.

The door opened, and Jainon came through with a happy glow about her face. Upon her entry, Yseri stood. "Are you ready to take the tailless out on your mission?"

"Almost," Jainon said, practically strutting like a runway model over to me. "I'm enjoying the after moment some more."

"Funny, I don't remember that as being part of the ritual," Yseri quipped.

"The hour of Inaja has not passed," Jainon said. "The blessings of healthy kits can be yours. No one made you leave so quickly."

"I'm done with meaningless rites to win favor from pointless gods," Yseri spat. "Inaja will not see your kits born because she is a lie, like the rest of them."

Jainon's ears went back, and the battle priestess growled. That, however, was the end of it. Instead of pressing Yseri on the matter, she lifted my chin with one of her paws and with the other, flicked open a single claw. "Ignore her blaspheme and hold still. Her fears are getting the better of her."

"What are you doing?" I said, eyes wide and heart pounding.

"Honoring you for your first successful major battle," she said.

"And what battle would that be?" Yseri asked with a distinct snort.

Jainon kept her eyes focused on me. "The cutting out of the *Revenant*. She was integral to the success of our boarding party."

"Hardly a battle," Yseri replied. "A light skirmish at best. She is not deserving of such an honor."

"Lucky for her, that honor is not yours to give," Jainon said. "Now then, Dakota, your single heart. Where is it?"

I was so caught up watching the two go back and forth I practically forgot I was the one who needed to answer. It probably didn't help much either I thought the question to be an odd one. "In my chest?" I replied, tapping a hair off my sternum.

Without warning, Jainon lifted my shirt up so high I'd have easily gotten past any bouncer at a night club with ease. Thank god Jack wasn't in the room. Using her open claw, she began carving into my chest and left boob. I reflexively pulled back, but a glare from her put me back in place. I knew it was important not to flinch during such rites thanks to Tolby's instructions during my initiation, but still, she could've warned me.

"Long before Hisoshim, eldest son of the most ancient Nashir, would become god of war and peace, he took it upon himself to kill one of each kind of creature in all of creation so that he would know what it was like to fight and take the life of anything alive," she said. "While you have many battles yet to walk even a pace in his footsteps, the first battle is always the most important, for no others can come without it. Thus, as Nashir honored Hisoshim by detailing his son's first battle onto his unblemished skin, we, too, honor you by giving you new scars that tell your story for all to see. From this point on, you have earned the title *Ralakai*."

I didn't know what to say, or if I should, so I said nothing. Instead, I focused on keeping the pain burning in my chest as far from my mind as possible by counting sheep. It didn't work so well, and my eyes watered, and my toes curled the entire time.

Finally, after I was a few seconds away from excusing myself from further honors due to the pain, she stopped, dropped my shirt, and stepped back. "You can relax now, *Ralakai*," she said. "Though I have nothing to cauterize the wounds, they aren't serious enough for worry, and truthfully, will work for the better in the end."

"How's that?" I asked, grimacing as I looked down at my blood-soaked shirt.

"They will scar even more and thus, strengthen their testimony," Jainon said with pride.

"You're still a tailless," Yseri said, shooing her paw at me. "Bouncing a ball around does not change that."

Yseri's remark stung, I'll admit. I've always hated feeling like an outsider, even though with them, I was. I guess I was so used to being around Tolby that considering him as anything but my best friend, and thus family, never occurred to me, and that naturally meant assuming he—and others like him—would see me in the same light. That said, I was also done getting walked all over by her. "You can sit there and mope if you like," I said. "But this tailless is going to get your Empress a stasis tube, which is a hell of a lot more than you're doing."

Jainon, to my surprise, laughed and quickly ushered me to the door. "I suggest we get moving before things get ugly."

I nodded in agreement, but before we left, I glanced over my shoulder and blew Yseri a kiss.

CHAPTER EIGHTEEN: SIDE EXPEDITION

Originally, I'd thought we were going to use a more normal method to get back to the ground, like hopping in a turbo lift or unsealing a passage and using the stairs. But after some debate as to how noisy either of those options might be, and all the Kibnali saying they didn't want any of our defenses weakened for even a moment until we had to get Daphne out to the comm station—who still had a few hours' worth of repair by Tolby's estimation—Jainon and I decided on a less conventional method of leaving the building.

I leaned over the edge of the balcony and looked at the ground, which was twenty meters below. A lot of the area was blanketed in darkness, but with one and a half full moons in the sky, there was enough light to get a vague idea of what was down there. For me, at least.

"Looks clear," I said, keeping my voice low.

"Except for that Nekrael over there, the two others over there, and the third sniffing around directly below us," Jainon said. "But maybe their eyesight is as bad as yours. Why don't you give it a go and see what happens?"

"Ha, ha. Very funny."

Jainon grinned. "There's nothing funny about your pitiful night vision. It's a wonder your species survived beyond the stone age without being eaten."

"Being the only ones with fire helped," I said. "Do you want to wait them out or try another way down?"

"Let's wait a little. We can spare the time, and they seem oblivious," she said as she carefully watched the creatures below. She soon turned around and leaned against the wall. "Do you have any cards? Tolby says that's a fun game your kind has come up with."

"No," I said. "I guess we'll have to pass the time chatting."

"The horror."

"I can barely stand it," I replied. Speaking to her put me at ease, despite our predicament, and I knew should we come out of this alive, we would become great friends. "Question for you: when we're out of this, what do you plan on doing?"

Jainon rubbed her belly. "You mean aside from having a thousand kits?"

"Yeah," I said, wincing. "Sorry, that sounds like a lot."

"Not all at once," Jainon said with a laugh. "Over the next century would be a nice, leisurely pace."

Up until now, I thought she was being figurative, but then I realized she was being quite exact in her number. "You're going to pop out ten babies a year? Holy snort that sounds painful."

"Painful? Why would it be?"

"Oh, never mind. That's just another fantastic human trait you're not blessed with, enormous pain in childbirth," I said. "Well, assuming you don't get nerve blocks, which I don't understand why anyone wouldn't."

"It hurts for your females to give birth?" she asked, tilting her head. "I wonder if the gods created you as a cosmic joke. It's the only thing that would make sense."

"Hey!"

"I mean no offense, but you're a strange species," she said. "Next thing you're going to tell me is that you can't even hold your breath for more than a couple of minutes."

I frowned. "I can go two and a half, thank you very much."

"There are heretical Kibnali myths that speak of early scientists using gene manipulation to shape our ancestors so we could rise to greatness," she said. "Perhaps you should look into such engineering and correct these flaws of yours."

"That's a myth? What's the truth, then?"

"The truth is much simpler," she replied. "The gods created us directly so our empire could stretch from one side of the universe to the other. We are the chosen ones."

"Not according to Yseri," I said. I immediately regretted the words that popped out of my mouth, as I wasn't sure how Jainon would feel about such a challenge, even if it was inadvertently made.

"She's always been a...what's the phrase in your culture? She's a grass is still hungry sort of Kibnali."

"A grass is still hungry?" I repeated.

"Yes. Such a strange metaphor," she said. "What does it mean? Do plants on your world have stomachs? Although I suppose the hungry part is figurative as well."

I thought about it for a second, confused at first, but then it dawned on me what she probably meant. "Do you mean glass instead of grass? Like you see the glass half full or half empty?"

"No, but I do like that much better," she answered. "It makes more sense and your people would do well to use it instead of the other one."

I laughed. "Okay, we'll work on using it. So why is Yseri like that?"

Jainon's tail switched through the air, and her voice became morose. "She is one of the last of the Kibnali. The number of Kibnali she's witnessed die defies comprehension. Is it any wonder why she might not think the gods look after us? After her?"

I bit my lower lip and felt terrible for not having more empathy for her. "She shouldn't be standing. I mean, you'd think she'd be a psychotic mess."

"Which is precisely why I know the gods still favor us," Jainon replied. "If they were not bolstering us at our most desperate hour, as you said, we'd all be a psychotic mess. Relatively speaking, we've come away from the destruction of our home, our kin, unscathed."

"I hadn't thought about it like that," I said. I was far from convinced that the Kibnali held the favor of the gods, or that there were gods, but one thing I did come away from this with was a much deeper appreciation for how resilient the Kibnali were—far more than I'd ever be, that was for certain.

A rumble from below cut into my thoughts, and then the ground shook enough to make me stumble into Jainon as well as convince me the entire building was coming down. Thankfully, the handmaiden kept me up, and Progenitor engineering allowed the building to stay upright.

"I think we should get going," I said. "The Nekrael will be the least of our worries if this instability continues."

"Agreed."

"Speaking of the little monsters, did they leave yet?"

Jainon turned around and leaned over the edge. She only spent a few moments checking the area out. "Looks like it," she said. "Want to go first and see?"

Before I could answer, my commlink crackled to life, and Tolby's voice came through loud and clear. "Dakota, are you inside yet?"

"Negative," I said. "We had to wait a few minutes for some Nekrael to wander off. We're about to go in now. Why, what's up?"

"Remember that giant crab thing that took out the webway?"

"Goliath? How could I forget?"

"You named it?"

"Yeah. Seems like a good fit to me."

"Why do you get to name it?"

"You got to name Mister Cyber Squid," I said. "I think it's my turn now."

"If you start calling yourself David, I reserve the right to dump root beer on you when we get home," he said.

"Don't worry. I happen to like my name, but when we get back, feel free to buy me a root beer float."

"I think you still owe me for the last one," he said. "Beverages aside, can you get eyes on Goliath from where you're at?"

I glanced at Jainon, who was anchoring the cable I'd found to a point on the balcony railing so we could rappel down. She waved a paw at me and said, "We've got a few moments. Go see what he wants."

"I probably can," I said to Tolby. "I think this balcony wraps around the whole building. Give me a moment. Will this take long?"

"I don't think so."

"Good," I replied. "His body is probably a couple of hundred meters away though, right? Not sure I'll be able to see very much, especially in the dark."

"The area is still lit up enough," he said. "You should be able to see what I'm talking about."

I wasn't sure what he meant, even when I got to around the building and looked across the facility grounds to where the webway had once been. Sure, there were still lights from the control room and a few nearby towers that illuminated the area in whites and light blues, but there wasn't much else to see other than torn-up earth and a ruined webway. "What am I looking for?" I asked. "Doesn't look like anything's going on. There aren't even any Nekrael as far as I can tell."

"Exactly," he said. "I can't see any on these vid feeds either."

"So?"

"I mean I can't see *any*," he repeated. "That includes Goliath or any of the others we killed."

I squinted, trying to pierce the darkness. It didn't help. "Are you sure? His body has to be there. We nearly melted the barrels on our repeaters bringing him down."

"I'm sure, and despite the simple design of your eyes, you should still be able to see him, too, if he was there."

"How is that possible?" I asked, feeling my chest tighten and mouth dry. "He was missing like a third of his torso when we dropped him."

"I don't know," he said. "I'm not saying he magically got up. What I'm saying is Baumdon mentioned these guys having a voracious appetite. So if they ate Goliath that quickly without leaving a trace, there must be a ton of Nekrael out there now we haven't seen. So be careful."

"You know I am."

Tolby replied with a huff.

"Okay, I can be careful when I need to be."

"This is one of those times you need to be."

"Right." I chuckled, which to my embarrassment came out more like a snort. "We're going. Keep me posted if anything else pops up."

With that, I ran back to Jainon and filled her in. She took the news well, and judging by the look on her face, she had about as much concern for the missing Goliath as I would have if someone had told me my bicycle tire was low on air. "We'll keep an eye out," she said. "Tolby has said you're the adventurous type and love rappelling."

"Yep," I said as I put my hands on my hips and smiled. "Been loving it ever since I tried it for the first time on my eleventh birthday. Man, that was a fun birthday, right up until a flash storm ruined the cake."

"Glad to hear. I mean about the repelling, not the cake," she said. Jainon wrapped the cable around her chest and then between her legs to create the makeshift harness before checking out the ground once again. "Let's get this done."

"You don't sound too enthused."

"Never been fond of this, to be honest."

"Pretend you're sliding down a giant curtain," I said.

"A curtain? Why?"

"You know, cats...curtains..." My voice trailed as she looked at me with a blank expression. "Never mind. Let's go."

"Humans are odd. Likeable, but odd," she said. With that, she went over the railing and rappelled down into the dark.

After a few seconds, the cable flopped a few times, signaling that she was free, and it was my turn. I followed suit and made my own harness before rappelling down as well. I came down a little fast too fast and ended up chafing my back and my left hand on the cable.

I was still freeing myself from the impromptu harness when Jainon gripped my shoulder, digging her claws in just enough to freeze me in place. "What?" I whispered, eyes scanning the gloom for any signs of movement.

"That smell," she said. "Plasma bolts have been recently fired."

"You can smell that?"

"You can't?" Her tail twitched, and her lips drew back. "Don't answer that. You've probably highlighted your species' shortcomings enough."

"Thanks. You're too kind."

Jainon pulled her plasma rifle off her back, and even though I did the same with the repeater TG2 had given me, I was glad she took the lead. We hurried across the ground that separated the main building from the data center in no time, and though we had seen some Nekrael not that long ago, we saw no signs of them now whatsoever.

The data center was similar to the main building, being of a spiral design, like a snail shell turned on its side, only it was half the size both in diameter and in height. We followed the curved outer wall for about fifty meters before coming to the entrance. As we got to the door, she turned and said something completely unexpected.

"You should procreate with Jack."

I was so taken aback by the abruptness and bluntness of her statement, I nearly dropped my repeater. "I should what with Jack?"

"Procreate. Become a mother by having him multiply with you and create babies," she said.

"Yes, I know what procreate means."

"Then why the surprise?"

"Because I don't want to?"

"Is he diseased? Or frail for a human male? If so, your ideal mates must be incredibly large. He's much more muscular than you are."

"No. He's...look, why are we talking about this? Even if he was my type, I don't want to be a mother."

"Not now or ever?"

"Not now for sure. I've got so much I want to do and see."

Jainon stared at me, and I got the feeling as if she was trying to decide whether or not I was serious. "What could be greater than seeing the lives you create? Seeing the continuation of your species? Seeing who will drive you onward as battle approaches and who will inherit your mighty Empire? Besides, being a mother would be good for you."

"How's that?" I said, starting to feel insulted.

"Throughout the entire universe, parents of advanced species protect their offspring with a fury unlike no other," she said. "Being a mother would awaken the warrior in you, make you more confident and deadly in battle. Perhaps then, you'd walk by my side as we advance on danger instead of behind. Not to mention, if you had children and you were to ever fall in battle, your death would fuel a burning revenge your children would have for your enemies. How could all that not be for the better?"

"That's a lot to unpack," I said, amazed at how different we saw parenthood. Though in retrospect, maybe I shouldn't have been that surprised, given what I knew about the Kibnali. After all, they were a prolific race whose chief aim was to span the entire universe, one way or another. "How about we talk about this later, like when we're off this planet instead of outside waiting to be a tasty snack?"

"As you wish, but in the meantime, I suggest you pretend you have offspring, or want them, and fight and act accordingly."

I shook my head in disbelief, and we slipped inside the data center. The lobby looked similar to the main building, or rather, I think it had looked similar at some point. There were the same red marble tiles, but they had splatters of thick, ochre-colored goop. Scorch marks blackened the walls where fist-sized chunks had been torn out. A single bench remained intact, although it was overturned and pressed against the wall. The others were in more pieces than I had fingers and toes. Lantern lights still hung from above, but most were torn or shattered. Only three offered light, and minimal at that.

Despite the cloak of shadows that draped everywhere, spotting two of Baumdon's lackeys who'd been eviscerated and had slumped against the far wall was easy. Spotting the four dead Nekrael nearby wasn't hard either, especially since one of them was practically at our feet. Several of their limbs bent back unnaturally or were missing altogether while numerous gaping holes allowed us to see inside their bodies.

I pointed my repeater at its head and gave it a nudge with my foot. "Think it's dead?"

Jainon kicked it once in the side before driving her heel into its neck. There was a soft crunch, and some of that ochre-colored goop oozed out of its mouth. A putrid, metallic smell soon followed. "It's dead."

"How long ago do—"

Jainon held up her paw, silencing me, before she went into a slight crouch. Her eyes scanned the lobby with her plasma rifle following. As she did, she made a dozen quick gestures with her tail while her ears twitched like unseen feathers were tickling each. After a few seconds, she turned to me and glared.

"What?" I whispered.

The Kibnali grunted. "I was telling you to cover our right flank while I checked out the bodies."

"Did you forget I'm not a kitty commando?" I said with amusement. Probably an inappropriate comment given our circumstances, but it's always cracked me up how I could crack myself up pretty much anywhere. I stifled a giggle before mustering up my best apology. "Sorry. It's how I manage stress."

"When we're out of here, you will need to train with Yseri," she said. "Now follow me and watch that right flank."

Jainon approached Baumdon's former partners like the slightest misstep would have her catch a tripwire. I stayed a few steps behind and to the side and kept my eyes to the right where a hall branched off from the lobby. Halfway to the bodies, movement caught my eye. I snapped around. The Nekrael we'd left behind twitched and raised its head. Its once lifeless eyes looked at me with a faint green glow.

"Sonuvabitch!" I shouted, bringing my repeater to bear and squeezing the trigger. Antimatter rounds hammered it and the floor a hundred times over before I stopped shooting.

"What did you see?" Jainon asked, rapidly scanning the area.

"That Nekrael was still alive!"

"Impossible. I crushed its neck."

"Look, I know what I saw."

Jainon opened her mouth to argue some more when the other three Nekrael began to move as well. Like the first, they started with twitches, but in the span of a few heartbeats, they were clawing toward us across the ground, dragging their broken bodies and leaving a smeared, yellow trail behind.

"Great, they can regenerate," she said, sounding more annoyed than alarmed. Three well-placed shots later, they each dropped with new smoking holes in their skulls. "I wonder how long it takes them to rebuild."

"You seem calm about this," I said.

"Fought worse," she replied.

"Worse than monsters coming back to life?"

"Sadly, such an ability isn't solely theirs," she said.

"The Nodari?"

She nodded. "Their blood was flooded with nanomachines that worked incredibly fast. And if you didn't incinerate the bodies or blast them with finely tuned EMP devices, those nanomachines could even bring a body scattered in a thousand pieces to life in under an hour. Sometimes within minutes."

"Cripes." I looked at the monsters we'd killed. They were frightening enough. I couldn't imagine what it would be like to fight something like them—or worse—that could come back to life after virtually any sort of wound.

"Tolby," I said, opening a comm. "There's something you need to know."

"I'm really starting to hate it when you call me like this."

"Me too," I said, still keeping a sharp eye on what was left of the corpse. "The Nekrael don't stay dead."

"What do you mean they don't stay dead?"

"Exactly what I said. You kill them, and they get back up. Jainon said it was like the Nodari, but not as bad."

Tolby growled. "Let's hope their similarities end there."

"No kidding," I said. I was about to end the call when a thought dawned on me. "Hey, I thought of something. The Progenitors had these guys under control, right? Do you think we could find something around here to combat them with?"

"Now there's the first useful idea tailless has had in a long time," Yseri chimed in.

Jainon put her paw on my shoulder and tugged. "Gods willing, we'll be blessed with something for precisely that, but we need to get back on track."

After I agreed and ended the call, we took the side hall from the lobby and followed it as it curved into another large room. This one had vaulted ceilings with large columns and intricate circuitry spread throughout. On either side were a handful of smaller rooms, perhaps the equivalent of our offices, while at the far end was the turbo lift we sought that would take us up to the lab. The air had a smoky aroma to it, and before I could figure out the source, Baumdon burst out of one of the side rooms, firing madly back the way he'd come with his pistol.

He must have dumped three dozen shots into whatever was there before he stopped shooting. With shaking arms, he ejected a spent powerpack from the weapon before slapping a new one in place. After that, he doubled over and caught himself on his knees and muttered to himself while gasping for breath. "Must find something...anything...to keep them away."

I wasn't sure if we should shoot him or not. I guess I lack that true killer instinct. Jainon, however, did not. She coolly raised her rifle, but before it came to bear, Baumdon looked up and dove sideways with reflexes that would put any Venetian mongoose to shame.

Shots flew from all three of our weapons, and Jainon and I bolted for cover. I ended up in one of the offices next to the doorway, while the Kibnali priestess was about five meters away, hiding behind a column. During a brief lull in the shooting, Baumdon darted behind a column at the far side of the room. I took the time to catch my breath, but the peace didn't last long. Plasma zipped through the air in both directions, each shot leaving wisps of sweet-smelling smoke lingering all around.

I shot back as much as I could, trying to contribute—try, of course, being the operative word. Though Jainon possessed incredible aim, I can only assume Baumdon had a few favors owed to him by the gods or Fate or whatever runs the show because he always seemed to be a hair away from actually being hit.

My contribution, as I alluded to, was paltry at best. I did succeed in making a mess of everything around him, and even took out something that looked like windpipes crossed with a toaster that was hanging in the office behind him. I didn't think it did much or was particularly close to Baumdon's location, but after it exploded in a shower of sparks, our former captor decided to try his luck at parlay.

"Shooting each other at this point seems counterproductive," he said. "Wouldn't you agree?"

I couldn't help but snort. "I think you're the one who shot first."

"Can you blame me for being jumpy? I didn't think you survived your ship exploding, let alone that there was anyone else here."

"Don't worry. There's a lot of other things I can blame you for."

"Some of that blame better be at yourself, because you are the one who marooned us all on this planet."

His words incensed me so much I couldn't help but look around my cover and stare him down. "Blame myself? Are you out of your mind? You tried to imprison us all and when we wouldn't have it, you shot us down on this forsaken, monster-infested rock."

"I only disabled your ship so you'd stop running," he said as if that made things better. "I'd fully intended on picking you up—alive I might add. We never had to be stuck down here."

I glanced at Jainon, who motioned for me to keep him talking as she slinked around the room to get to his flank. "Don't you dare try and pin this on me," I said. "This is one hundred percent all on you."

The argument went silent for a beat before it dawned on me that Jainon was nowhere to be seen. I wasn't sure what that meant. Hopefully good.

"Blaggin Fraktaurs!" he shouted. I saw plasma bolts fly from his position and into the office he'd come from.

An ear-shattering shriek that sounded like equal parts dying horse and ripping metal filled the air. Out of the room stumbled a skeletal construct that was two and a half meters tall with scythes for arms and a nightmare for a head. It had a dozen eyes set across a sweptback forehead and a jaw filled with teeth to make any great white jealous. A coppery exoskeleton encased its body, and thus it looked similar to the Nekrael, only much bigger, save Goliath. As terrifying as this creature was, I guess I should be glad Goliath hadn't managed to squeeze in here as well.

"Dakota, make for the lift!" Jainon shouted as she directed all of her fire into the creature.

I ran as she and Baumdon continued firing. It died—or at least, ceased its attack—by the time I'd run into the lift, but not before it had pounced on Baumdon with its powerful legs and driven one of its scythes through his hip.

"Top floor," Jainon said, voice shaking like the Reaper had dropped her a line to say he'd be over the next day.

I hit the button while the Kibnali handmaiden kept her weapon trained on Baumdon and the fallen monster. I didn't ask why we weren't going to help him, especially since his cries of agony were echoing in my ears. I didn't have to. As the turbo lift door slid shut, I caught sight of the creature moving once again.

CHAPTER NINETEEN: STASIS TUBES

What was that thing?" I asked.

"I don't know, but I think I've got a good idea why this planet has never been colonized," she said, lowering her rifle and leaning back against the wall.

"At least that's one mystery solved," I said, forcing a chuckle. "Would make a good story at some point, though, right?"

"Only if I were the main character. You're too boring," she said.

"Me? Boring? I'm Little Miss Time Traveler. It doesn't get any more exciting than that."

"You *were* Little Miss Time Traveler," she said. "Your only interesting characteristic is currently broken. Now you're back to being a normal naked ape with terrible vision and a horrific sense of smell," she said. Despite her words, her tone was light and playful. "Face it. Put me on the cover, and you'll be an instant intergalactic hit, author wise."

"No way. I'm not sticking a Kibnali on the cover. You kitties already have enough of a god complex as it is. I don't need to feed your ego any more."

Our conversation cut short when the turbo lift stopped and the door slid open, instantly reverting both of us to take-care-of-business-and-don't-get-killed mode. We stepped out of the lift and into a lab that was semicircular in shape. Monitors along the wall flickered to life as we entered and bathed everything in the room in dim, azure light. On a raised, hexagonal platform stood a half dozen opaque stasis tubes while a bright yellow, five-fingered claw the size of an industrial refrigerator hung from the ceiling.

I wrinkled my nose at the acrid taste in the air, and it didn't take long to find the source. A wicked crack ran along the side of one of the stasis tubes, and rust-colored liquid pooled around its base. From the hole in the tube sprouted a formation of rose-colored crystals. Well, I assumed they were rose-colored as thick, black mold clung to most of it. "My exemplary Progenitor engineering background has led me to believe we should use a different tube."

"Exemplary, huh?" Jainon said, amusement in her eye. "And where did you go to school for that?"

"You know, *the* university."

"Of course. Now let's put your degree to work so we can get out of here."

We made a quick, thorough search of the lab. Thankfully, no Nekrael were around or any other nasties waiting to get the drop on us. Equally as awesome, there weren't any other ways in other than the lift, so we didn't have to worry about watching multiple entrances.

"Looks like they have their transportation shields up," Jainon said, tapping the opaque covering on the stasis tube she stood next to. "I think you can lower it at one of those consoles."

I picked one at random and hurried over to it. I made the connection to the computer easily enough as I had with everything else my cyber arm allowed me to tap into. Once I mentally double-tapped the black-and-purple icon in the middle of the screen (which looked like an abstract unicorn dancing around a planet—

the icon that is, not the screen), an image of some nameless desert at night with six moons hanging in the sky and a handful of alien flora scattered about popped on screen. Another icon then appeared front and center that looked like a wheel turning. After a few spins, it disappeared, and finally a proper menu appeared at the bottom than I could navigate through.

"Okay, I'm in," I said as I began to explore. "What am I looking for? Something to do with the stasis tubes, I'm imagining."

"I'm not entirely sure as this setup is different than what was at the museum. All I know is that the last time I played with one of these tubes that had its shield up, I got a nasty shock and shorted out the whole unit."

"Gotcha."

Several minutes passed as I worked, and Jainon said nothing, but she did check in with Yseri over the comms to see how they were doing. I didn't pay much attention to it since I could only hear her end, but from the little bit I did gather, they were doing well enough. Although I did catch something about the Nekrael wandering the first floor more than they had previously. My gut tightened at that thought.

"Sorry this is taking so long," I said, still sifting through records and options. "This workstation is tapped into everything around. Trying not to cause a disaster by picking something random."

"I think we're okay for now, but the sooner you can get to it, the better. Empress is on enough borrowed time."

"Adrestia has a vehicle bay," I said, perking up. Though it was a bit of a proverbial squirrel, I looked into it as much as I could for a couple of minutes, hoping and praying part of what was there would be a spaceship of some kind.

"Anything we can use inside?" Jainon asked.

"Doesn't look like it," I said as my shoulders slouched. "A couple of ground transports needing repair and what looks like a fusion bike. Oh, that could be fun. I used to love racing those in my teens. Well, that would be fun assuming we weren't stuck here."

"Then let's not waste any more time on it," she said. Though her voice was calm, there was an edge to it, like a straight razor pressed to the skin.

I nodded and went back to my sleuthing. It wasn't much longer before I found what we were looking for.

"Got it," I said proudly. "This whole menu section is dedicated to this lab specifically."

"Are those the stasis tubes?" she asked, pointing to a list on the screen.

"Maybe?" I punched the selection, and to my delight, it popped up a submenu with six distinct areas. At the top of five of them were serial numbers and the words "Tube status: online" and then a bunch of data beneath. The sixth was the same, but instead of being listed as operational, it simply said "unknown."

"You are truly a gift from the gods," Jainon said, nuzzling the side of her face into mine. "The Deep One smiles on us. Drop the shield on one of them so I can take a look."

"You got it." It only took two tries. My first attempt, somehow, ended up turning on a few more lights in the room, which was nice. Truth be told, I got a little excited and misclicked. When I corrected my error, the shield surrounding one of the stasis tubes faded away, but the tube was not empty inside. Instead, it held a creature that looked like it came straight from the depths of hell.

Its body was encased in a bronze exoskeleton with flecks of amber throughout. The thing stood on a pair of sizeable legs that were probably ripped from a velociraptor on steroids. Each of the three claws it had on its feet could no doubt open up a battleship like a tin can. Five limbs came from its torso, two thick ones at the shoulders that tapered into elongated hands with four digits each, and three more sprouting from the chest that were similar, but smaller and thinner. Six compound eyes, all green, surrounded its skull. Curled horns came from the top and ended near its jaw—a jaw that sported teeth like daggers. Spines ran down the center of its back, and barbs jutted out from the elbows, knees, and heels.

Jainon stumbled back as she seated her plasma rifle against her shoulder, but she did not fire. "Dakota," she whispered. "Double-check that tube is operational."

"They are all. We just had the status window up."

"Check it again!"

I jumped at her command and quickly turned around to face the screen. When it cycled back to the summary data, it was as I said. All tubes were online and working as they should. "We're in the green."

"Good...good," she said, more to herself than me, I think.

"Nodari?" I asked, as that was the only thing I could think of that would strike such fear into her heart.

"Yes," she replied, her voice barely a whisper. She sucked in a breath and tore her gaze away from it long enough to say a few more words to me. "A scout, but don't let its looks fool you. It's one of the deadliest things in the universe. If it gets loose, there could be a hundred more of them in a week."

"A hundred in a week? Are you kidding me?"

"It would depend on how much biological and raw material its nanomachines could scavenge, but such numbers would not be unheard of."

"What the hell is it doing here?"

"Being studied, I assume," Jainon said. "Or was, at least."

My chest tightened, but before it could go into A-fib, I took a deep breath and went back to the computer and lowered the shields to other tubes. As long as that thing was staying put, we'd be okay. At least, that's what I told myself. "What are in the other ones?"

Jainon circled the group. Her face hardened more and more with each one she passed. "They're all filled with scouts, too."

"Is there a way we can dispose of one safely so we can still put Empress in a tube?" I asked. "Maybe the records can tell us something. Surely the Progenitors had some way of handling these guys, right?"

"I can only hope."

I wasn't sure where to start, but I did stumble across a set of logs for one of the subjects. I brought up one of the first ones and waved Jainon over before I read aloud. "Local date 435.2.598. Tech Primarch Valaris logging. Guided evolution of Specimen VL-624 is complete. Base proteins stable, and we seem to have solved the problem of their sudden deaths after being alive for sixty days. T-virus will be introduced into the wild Nekrael population in three months provided we replicate our success with VL-624. Repression fields along with secondary and tertiary defenses are still demonstrating they are more than enough to keep Nekrael and emerging Nodari under control during study. Fire blossom failsafe online."

"They created the Nodari?" Jainon said, shaking her head. "Why?"

"Probably the same reason they made the portal device which ultimately wiped them out, because they could," I said.

"Too bad the Nodari didn't wipe them out."

"Going by the precautions listed, I think they realized how deadly the Nodari were," I said. "I don't think they appreciated how deadly messing with time could be."

Jainon nodded. "You're probably right. See what the other entries say."

I scanned through the list and ended up picking the third log from the end because three was lucky and made me feel safe, and I really needed to feel safe right then.

"Local date 438.8.101. Tech Primarch Valaris logging," I said, reading the entry. "Nodari show remarkable strength and cunning in one-on-one combat. We decided to pit them against the Kibnali ahead of schedule to see what they're capable of at this stage and have been astounded by the results. Out of ten matchups, not a single Kibnali has survived individual combat without weapons.

I'm putting in a request for a re-evaluation of our defenses before we move on to new stages of study, which have been slated to start next week after Tulian's birthday. Note to self: Tulian is allergic to apritut oil. Find substitute so we don't have a repeat of last year."

"Damn them!" Jainon shouted, slamming her paw onto the top of the console. "They used us for their own disgusting experiments? By the gods, if they dropped the Nodari into the Kibnali Empire as a test, I'll travel to whatever dimension they vanished to and rip them apart myself."

"Why couldn't they have wanted to study something cute, like dalmatian puppies?" I said, massaging my temples. "You'd think they'd want to know where they get their adorable nature from. Is it tied to their spots? Their button noses? Hyperactive tails? Who knows? Whatever the answer is, it would've been a lot better for us, I'll tell you that much."

"Move on to the last one," Jainon said, pointing to the screen. "We need to know what they did with the Nodari. Or at least, what we can do to stay alive."

I nodded and brought up the final entry. Once again, I read aloud. It didn't take me long to wish I hadn't found any of it. "Local date 438.8.115. Tech Primarch Valaris logging. Remaining staff has disappeared. It's been eight days since we lost contact with what's left of our fleet. All the Nodari, save those in stasis, are gone as well. I can directly attribute this catastrophe to the opening of wormhole NGI-02882. I can only assume the paradox backlash predicted by Master Chronologist Nelag has not only come to fruition but is now sweeping across the universe and wiping out our entire species. If my interpretations of his calculations are correct, this will be my last entry, and I'll be gone in an hour. I am unsure if any of my work will remain as an echo, or if I, too, will be wiped from all of history as if I'd never existed. I am leaning toward the former as I can remember family, friends, and where I came from. But I fear it may be the latter. How does one know what one forgot? Either way, sadly, means I have no way of knowing how successful our endeavors here might be. I will be initiating the fire blossom shortly once I find the other override key. Sterilizing the planet is the only way to keep this galaxy safe. If I can't locate it, I'll have to trigger an emergency cascade by shutting off the repression fields and letting the Nekrael evolve into Nodari."

When I got to the end, Jainon was staring at the screen. Had fur not been covering her body, I'm sure I would have seen the color drain from her skin. "We've got to get off this planet right now."

I swallowed. Hard. "I doomed us all turning off that field, didn't I?"

"It certainly hurt a lot more than we thought," Jainon said. "Even if this fire blossom doesn't trigger, that field was keeping the Nekrael from evolving into the Nodari. We'll never survive a planet full of them."

"No," I said, trying my best to argue with reality. "There's got to be more to the defense around here than that."

"If there is, we can't risk betting on it," she said. "We've already seen the Nekrael heal from mortal wounds, and we've already seen a more advanced one take out Baumdon downstairs. If that's how fast they can evolve, who knows how long it will be till we're fighting Nodari en masse?"

My mouth dried, and the hairs on my neck stood as I turned all of this over in my head. "What about Goliath? Please tell me he's not a shadow of what's to come, too."

"I don't know what he is," she confessed, "but I don't want to stick around to find out. We need to warn the others and get Daphne to the comm station."

Agreeing wholeheartedly, I called Tolby and gave him the rundown of everything that'd transpired over the last ten minutes. When I was done, he didn't say a word. I couldn't even hear him breathe. "Hey, talk to me," I said.

"I...I can't believe this is happening," he finally said.

"Me either. But we can—"

A deep rumbling preluded the chaos that followed. The room quaked before everything tilted sideways and the floor buckled. The giant claw thing on the ceiling ripped free of its mounts and came crashing down. Only it didn't stop at the floor. Instead, it punched a hole right through it.

Jainon managed to grab on to an outcropping on the wall before she slid too far. I, on the other hand, did not possess feline reflexes or sharp claws to dig into things. As such, I slid toward a gaping hole in the floor with stasis tubes and consoles tumbling right behind.

CHAPTER TWENTY: THINGS GET WORSE

I screamed all the way down into the hole, considerably more as I approached the lip and got a nice view of the four-story drop I was about to enjoy. A half second before I went over, all I could do was wish I could fly, or at least, knock myself to the side. Then I realized I could.

Well, I realized I had a half-baked idea that might let me, but when your choices are try something that even a schizo wouldn't consider realistic or becoming a gooey pancake, I'll take the foremost any day of the week.

I twisted sideways as I went over the edge and pressed the palm of my right hand into my chest. The telekinetic blast I let loose shot the wind out of my lungs as it knocked me back in the air. I think getting kicked by a bucking warhorse would've felt better. But at least when I hit the ground and rolled, I'd only fallen three meters instead of the twelve to the ground floor and ending my life as a quaint splat.

"Oh...god..." I said between gasps of air while staring at the sunken and twisted ceiling.

"Dakota! Dakota! Are you hurt?"

Jainon's panicked voice took my mind off my immediate misery. "I'm alive," I said, though I wasn't confident enough yet to move, fearful I'd broken something and due to all the adrenaline, I wouldn't know it yet. "I guess that's something."

Her upside-down head peeked through the hole in the ceiling. Carefully, she reached out and grabbed a rebar that jutted out. With all the skill and confidence of a master gymnast, she used it to flip down and land in a three-point crouch at my feet.

"How did you land here?" she asked.

"Directed a telekinetic blast into my chest midair."

"Clever. Must have hurt."

"You've no idea."

"Can you stand?" she asked. "This building could collapse at any moment."

As if the building were listening in on the conversation and wanted to accentuate her point, it rumbled again, and its support columns groaned in response. "I think so," I said, but it was more hopeful thinking than sure diagnosis. With another set of groans from the supports echoing in my ears, I shot to my feet and immediately regretted doing so. The pain lacing my ribs and tailbone had to make childbirth feel like a relaxing massage.

Jainon grabbed me by the upper arm, keeping me from tipping over. "Easy," she said. "Don't nosedive down that hole."

"I'm okay," I said, then chuckled painfully. "Well, I'm alive. Okay is relative."

The comm bracelet on Jainon's wrist beeped, indicating an incoming call. My brain shorted out for a half second before I realized I'd lost connection with Tolby at some point, and the last thing he probably heard was me screaming my head off. It took me another second to realize why he was calling her and not me. The one I had was missing, and in its place was a nice bruise. Apparently, it tore off during my mad scramble.

"Tolby," Jainon said, answering the call. "Is everyone safe over there?"

"For the moment," he replied with a notable sigh. "Where's Dakota?"

"She fell down a hole that opened up in the floor, but she's walking," Jainon replied. "We'll call you back in a few. That earthquake tore this place apart, and I'm worried it's going to collapse."

"I understand, but the moment you two are free, let me know. I'm going to check our defenses. That rumble shook our building more than I'd like."

"Is it still safe to be in?"

"I think so."

"Make sure," Jainon said. "And be safe."

As Jainon finished the conversation, I eased over to the hole in the floor and peered down. Scattered on the ground floor were all of the stasis tubes—well, what was left of them. If the shells weren't split, their tops were mangled. If their tops weren't mangled, their bottoms had shattered. Worse yet, after a distinct popping sound and shower of sparks from one, I realized their power supplies had been destroyed as well, which meant the stasis fields inside were no longer.

Claws from a demonic hand eased out of a crack in one of the tubes and began pushing the metal aside. My eyes were glued to the spectacle with awe, as if I were watching a baby raptor fight its way out of the egg it was in. "Jainon," I said, waving her over. "This building is going to be the least of our worries."

The Kibnali hurried over and cursed up a storm when she saw what I was pointing at. "Maybe the building will collapse on top of them and buy us some time."

"Preferably without us still inside," I said, scooping up my repeater, which had miraculously not fallen to the lower floors.

Jainon and I darted over to the turbo lift doors. The control panel on the side was no longer lit. This wasn't surprising as the wall it was mounted on was cracked and the panel itself was tilted forward, exposing a portion of the back which likely wasn't meant to be exposed. The other things that tipped us off to its broken nature were the occasional popping sounds of short-circuited electronics and the accompanying burnt smell.

"Help me get the door open," Jainon said, setting her feet and pushing against the door, trying to get it to slide. "We can use the maintenance ladder to get down."

"Why are you so sure there is one?"

"Because the turbo lifts in the other building had them. I saw them when we were sealing the place up."

"I suppose that's as good a reason as any," I said as I came to help.

Together we tried, but after several seconds of us accomplishing even less than Sisyphus, I realized we needed a new strategy. It had to be a strategy that was quick and effective. And since the only things we had at our disposal, tool wise, were big guns, that's what I went with.

"Move," I said as I squared off with the door and raised my repeater. "This will only take a second."

Jainon grinned and dashed to the side. When she was clear, I held down the trigger, and the barrels spun to life. Antimatter slammed into the turbo lift door, each round taking chunks out of it half the size of my fist and issuing bright explosions of light as they hit. In a matter of seconds, I'd chewed it up so much that after I stopped firing, Jainon only had to reach over and give the remains a playful tap to send them tumbling down the elevator shaft, leaving us with a large hole to use.

"That looked like a lot of fun," Jainon said. "I think you need to let me borrow your toy one of these days."

"It was a lot of fun," I said with a playful, slightly evil chuckle.

I flung the repeater over my shoulder and looked into the elevator shaft. Spotting the ladder was easy. It was bright yellow against a flat, gray background. Like the staircase in the main building, the ladder was obviously built for creatures larger than the average human as the rungs were spaced further apart than I would've liked, but they were still manageable. Well, they would've been manageable if my sides hadn't been pulverized. With every rung I went down, fire ran through my torso and weakened my grip.

"God, this hurts," I moaned as my eyes watered.

"It will hurt more if you fall," Jainon said. "Control the pain. Don't let it control you."

Easier said than done, I thought, but we continued down with a balance of care and speed. Thankfully, we managed to descend the shaft without me falling. I feared that the door on the ground floor might not open when we reached it, or worse, the turbo lift above would come crash on our heads, but Fate continued to smile on us for the moment, and Jainon managed to slide the door open with relative ease.

We'd scarcely gotten out of the shaft when a Nodari scout pushed free of the heaping wreck of stasis tubes that had once kept it prisoner. It stood over two meters tall, and somehow looked ten times more terrifying than it had before—probably because now it was moving and looking right at me.

The damn thing roared, and with one smooth motion, it ripped a chunk of metal from a nearby tube and heaved it at my head. Sharp reflexes and a little bit of leftover divine favor from whatever deity still had pity on me were all that kept me from being impaled.

Jainon opened up on the creature with her weapon. Her plasma rifle shot it a dozen times in the chest and face. It staggered backward before stumbling over a stasis tube and landing on its back. The handmaiden rushed over, and before it could get up, she shot it three more times. Its legs twitched violently, like an insect's who'd had an extra helping of INVAS-X bug killer, before the whole thing went still and she backed away.

"It'll be up within an hour," she said. "Maybe even less, given all the material around here."

"What about the others?" I asked, picking myself up off the ground.

As soon as I said that, I wished I hadn't since Murphy's law #423 of hazardous space exploration immediately kicked in. Across the room appeared two more of the scouts. They came at us from two different angles with such speed I'm a little surprised they didn't precede a sonic boom. Jainon fired at the one closest to her. As before, her aim was deadly, and she punched seven holes in the creature's torso, neck and face in under two seconds.

To my credit, I wasn't completely useless. From pure reflex, I used a telekinetic punch and hit the thing with an excellent uppercut. Its head reeled back, and I knocked it off balance. As it tumbled and sought to regain its footing, I brought my repeater to bear and squeezed the trigger. I wasn't anywhere near as accurate as Jainon was, but since I basically had a Progenitor mini-gun, I didn't have to be. Antimatter rounds vaporized everything in a cone in front of me, including most of the scout's body.

"Hot damn," I said, ceasing fire and gawking at the devastation I'd caused. "Tell me I'm good."

"You're adequate," Jainon teased. "I'll make you good one day."

"Thanks, sensei."

Jainon's brow dropped, and her ears twitched. "What's that beeping?"

I hadn't noticed it before, but as soon she said it, I realized that the noise was coming from my repeater. To the side of the holographic display was a new status that I'd never seen before. "Warning: Low energy" blinked repeatedly in yellow, and beneath that was the line "13% remaining."

"I guess I need less spray and pray," I said. "Either that or figure out a way to swap power packs or recharge whatever's in here."

"Can you do that?"

I shrugged, hating that I had to. "TG2 I'm sure could have. Maybe if we got back to the armory we could figure it out, assuming we can even get in. Maybe it will recharge on its own like my arm."

There was a loud thud behind us, and I spun around in time to see the original scout that Jainon had shot was starting to move. Not a whole lot, mind you, only a twitch here and there of a foot or hand, but that was infinitely more movement than when it was dead moments ago. "Let's continue this conversation outside, shall we?" I said as I backed away.

"Absolutely."

With our committee reaching a unanimous decision, we darted out of the room and raced back down the hall to the lobby area. Baumdon's lackey was still there, and so were the Nekrael, but the latter were slowly moving now, too. Neither one of us said anything until we got outside and looked at the sky. Up until that point, I'd have sworn we'd seen it all, but I was wrong.

I was so, so wrong.

Hanging amongst the stars were bright red points of light arranged in a repeating, hexagonal pattern as far as the eye could see. I had no idea what they were, how they got there, or what they were going to do, but in the deepest parts of my soul, I knew I wouldn't like the answers to any of that.

"Tolby, we're out," Jainon said, putting in a call to the others. "We can't wait until the morning to get Daphne to the comm station. We've got to go now. The Nodari scouts are loose."

"Ha!" Tolby shouted, sounding like he would be perfectly at home in an eighth-century PHS asylum.

"Ha?" I repeated.

"Yes, ha," he said. "Care to take a guess why I opted for that?"

My gut twinged. I sucked in air between my clenched teeth. "We've got bigger problems?"

"If by bigger problems you mean the entire planet is going to be sterilized in under an hour, then yes, we have bigger problems."

CHAPTER TWENTY-ONE: TIME CRUNCH

Under an hour?" I shrieked. "How?"

I didn't really need to know how. At least, not truly. My brain, trying to protect what was left of my sanity, plunged itself into that sweet, sweet sea of denial. To my brain's utter sadness, my eyes went back to looking at the night sky, more specifically, to all those angry red lights floating in it.

And then, of course, my ears took in Tolby's next words and completely ruined the reality disconnect my brain was going for.

"The fire blossom launched a couple of minutes before you two called in," he said. "I'm staring at a countdown timer."

"Can't we stop it?"

"I have no idea," he said. "I'm willing to venture that if we could, it'll take a lot longer than an hour to accomplish because I'm not seeing any sort of cancellation button."

"How could there not be a cancellation button? Everything has a cancellation button! Even spam has a cancellation button, and it's been weaponized far greater than some stupid planet killer!"

"I guess the Progenitors didn't get the memo," he said. "Why are you arguing with me about this? It's not like I can help it."

"Because I don't want to die!" I shouted. "Can't you reboot the system? Isn't that what you always do? Find the control, alt, delete buttons. That'll do it."

"There are no control, alt, delete buttons!"

"How much more work is needed on Daphne?" I asked.

"Two hours, minimum," he said. "And that's counting some risky shortcuts."

"We don't have two hours, Tolby, and we need Jack's lifeboat!"

Jainon's paw found my shoulder. I turned to face her, and she shushed me with a claw. "We're going to have a lot less than an hour if you two don't quiet down," she hissed. "It's a wonder the Nekrael or the Nodari aren't on us already."

I glanced to the sides and then back the way we'd come. Everywhere I looked was clear, thankfully, but she was right. That could change, and our power packs were low. I probably couldn't use my telekinetic punch much more either as I noticed my arm once again felt icy. I guess I hadn't noticed in all the excitement. At least it, like my portal device, would recharge over time. Too bad that thing was still busted and even if we did get it fixed—

"I got it!" I said, doing a mini hop filled with excitement. "We make a run to the Lambda Complex, find that FUM thing, repair the portal device, and pop back in time."

"Assuming you can do all that, then what?" Tolby asked. "We can't go back more than a few hours, remember?"

"We run through the gate the webway opened," Jainon said, filling in the rest of my brilliant idea. "There's a small window of opportunity from when you opened it and that monster destroyed one of the spires."

There were a few moments of silence before Tolby spoke. "I can't believe I'm agreeing to this, but okay," he said. "We'll hold down the fort until you're back. Be fast, though, we don't have a lot of time."

"No kidding."

The call ended and Jainon and I headed for the Lambda Labs. According to the maps I'd seen of the area, the labs were more of an underground bunker with a single entrance point in the southwest corner of the facility than a huge network of buildings. I didn't think it would be hard to find. That, of course, said nothing about getting access to what we needed. After all, everything that was buried across the galaxy—from fusion missile silos to dog bones—tended to be well guarded. And well, if the Progenitors built this place knowing there might be Nekrael and Nodari scouts wandering around, there had to be one hell of a guard dog inside.

I didn't have the luxury to wonder for long what sort of Cerberus awaited us. After we'd successfully dodged a few wandering Nekrael, we got to the edge of an alley, and I flattened myself against the wall when I saw what lay ahead.

About fifty meters away, camping right outside the squat, sloped building that led to the Lambda Labs, was Goliath along with a dozen Nekrael. They weren't doing much other than occasionally shouldering each other or taking the random swipe that seemed mostly harmless (Goliath swipes notwithstanding as every time he whacked a Nekrael, he cut it in two). Sadly, despite their pointless action, their very presence made sure we'd never get to where we needed to be.

"Tolby, I need a time check," Jainon whispered.

"Forty-seven minutes," he said. "Are you in yet?"

"No. The gods have seen fit to test us once more," she replied. "Not sure how long it's going to take to get around this latest obstacle."

"What sort of obstacle?"

"Goliath and Nekrael. They're right outside the lab entrance."

"I see. I suggest finding a way to move them in less than forty-eight minutes."

"Tolby, check the cube," I said. "Is there another way in?"

"One moment," he said, sounding hopeful. There was some rustling on the other end of the line before he started talking to himself. "Let's see, where are we anyway? Nekrael research sites maybe? Damn it, there are a few. Maybe this? Gah, stupid ad. Do I really need shampoo for my spatula collection? Sorry...all right, here we go. This looks like our place. Let me bring up the maps...and...perfect."

"And?"

"And there's no other way in."

I balled a first and was tempted to punch the wall with the bottom of it, but I was rational enough to stop myself. We didn't need the extra noise. "Are you sure? There has to be."

"I'm sure, Dakota," he said, irritation in his tone. "According to this, the Lambda Labs are dedicated to resonance cascade scenarios, so it's a high-security place with one way in and one way out."

"Well, hell."

Jainon eased out of the alley and checked the sides before slipping back next to me. She then detached the communicator from her wrist and put it around mine. "I'll draw them away," she said. "Get in there. Get that device fixed and get Empress out of here."

"What? No," I said. "That's suicide."

"The Empress's life is more important than mine," she said. "She must survive above all else."

"No, she—" I caught myself before I spilled the secret, but not fast enough for Jainon to pick up on my error.

"She what?"

"She...wouldn't want you to throw your life away," I said.

"I'm not throwing it away," she replied. "I should be able to lose them running through another building. Once I do, I'll meet you back with the others."

My throat tightened. I needed more than her prophetic skills to rely on, even if that something was utterly childish. "Pinky promise?"

She stared at my tiny, extended digit. "What is that supposed to be?"

"Just...uh...wrap your pinky around mine and swear you'll make it back."

"How does this help? Is this something your gods command you to do?"

"No," I said. "It's an oath."

"Bound to our pinkies."

"Yeah...look, never mind."

Jainon shook her head and quickly wrapped one arm around mine. "If pinkies bind humans, then arms bind the gods. I swear I'll return safe, and together we'll look back on all of this with fond memories."

I laughed at the butchering of the ritual. "Thanks, but I don't think I'll ever look back at any of this with fond memories."

"Nonsense. With all the adversity we've faced and battles we will have won, how could we not?" With that she disengaged and slapped my shoulder. "May Inaja bless you with good fortune."

"May her luck be your luck," I replied.

Jainon touched the top of her head and gave a slight bow. "We shall see each other soon," she said. "Move the moment they're clear."

"Will do."

Jainon darted a good fifty meters to the side before coming to a halt and raising her plasma rifle. She roared with such fierceness, if I hadn't known better, I'd have bet my resonance crystal she had an entire Kibnali battalion behind her.

A few of the Nekrael took note and turned toward her. The rest, Goliath included, followed suit when she fired a quick, three-round burst into the crowd. Two of the shots dropped a couple of the monsters by turning their heads into vapor. The third shot caught Goliath in the neck and did little other than piss him off.

But that was the plan.

She pivoted and disappeared from my sight, a thunderous herd of Nekrael chasing her with Goliath in the lead. Though he wasn't the mutilated corpse we'd turned him into a while back, he still had chunks missing from his body and ran with a sizeable limp. That last bit is probably the only thing that kept Jainon from being a Goliath chew toy. She was faster, but not by much.

The instant they were gone, I bolted. Footsteps resounded in my ears, and I feared the Nekrael would be drawn back to my clomping. A glance over my shoulder alleviated those fears. All still pursued Jainon, and with every second, the distance between me and them grew.

"Thank goodness," I said with a smile and a sigh.

That smile faded when I reached the bunker door. It sat recessed in the wall by a quarter meter and looked like a giant gear. Next to it, sitting on a pedestal about a meter and a half tall, was a console, square and green. Thin, white lines ran across an otherwise black background. I hoped that meant it was on standby and not broken.

I tapped the screen a few times after trying unsuccessfully to make a connection with my Progenitor interface. For whatever reason, when I tried to mentally extend to the console, I couldn't find it. It's weird to describe, I know, but it felt like although my eyes were telling me the screen was right there, my brain—the Progenitor enhanced part at least—was screaming back, "There's nothing there!"

I huffed in frustration and glanced over my shoulder. A few Nekrael wandered the area, maybe a hundred meters away. Most, I assumed, were still chasing Jainon. *Good*, I thought, *but not good enough. They'll be back soon.*

I tried to connect again and failed. Tapped the screen a few times, and that failed, too. I even kicked the door twice and was rewarded with a sore set of piggies for my effort.

With the fire blossom burning over my head and frustrations mounting, I brought my repeater to bear. "Screw it," I said. "Let's see what a little antimatter will do."

A small porthole opened next to the door a split second before I began firing. From it, a probe, like a tennis ball on a stick, shot forth. It stared at me with a large, yellow eye for a split second before speaking. "What do you think you're doing?"

"Coming in?" I replied, fumbling over my words. "Wait, who are you?"

"Who am I? I could ask you the same thing! Think you run the place, do you? Just going to barge in here with your antimatter repeater. Ha! Like that'll work. We've got a photonic gravitational prism array augmenting our repulsion fields. You'll never tunnel your way in here."

"No? I mean, I thought no one was left."

"That's what you get for assuming. Now go away."

"Hey! I didn't assume," I said, feeling very put off. "Tour Guide said so, or whatever his name is."

"That figures," the little probe replied, sounding even more put off than I was. "Just the same. I might as well be dead to him, and him to me. Haven't bothered with his company since I caught him cheating at marbles."

"Do all of you play marbles?" I asked, thinking back to the museum where the Curator ended up loving the game. I shook my head and scolded myself for getting distracted before he replied. "I need to get in. There are Nekrael everywhere."

"Yes, I'm aware. That's why the fire blossom is up."

"Right, so I have to get off this planet," I said. "Like, now."

"No, you have to get off in forty minutes, give or take. Depends on how fast your spaceship is, you know? Which, I'm guessing, you don't have."

"Let me in!"

"Can't. No unauthorized access is allowed."

I ran my fingers through my hair and grabbed a fistful in frustration. "I've got an omega-level family membership," I said. "Doesn't that give me access to the tour or something?"

The probe perked and sounded impressed. "You do?"

"Yes! I'm Dakota Adams!"

"Oh," it said, its voice turning wary and its body easing back into the hole from which it came. "In that case, have a lovely day."

"Now what?" I shrieked.

"We've got excellent records on you," he said. "Don't think it was lost on me that you happened to be the last visitor to our museum before it went belly up."

"That wasn't my fault!"

"And you probably didn't have anything to do with the *Revenant* exploding either."

"How did you know about that?"

The probe chuckled. "I told you, we have excellent records. And since I don't want my lab, my home-sweet-home being obliterated like that art gallery you summoned a black hole inside, you can toddle off now."

"I didn't ruin any art gallery!"

"Maybe not yet from your point of view," he explained. "You know, time travel, timelines, and whatnot."

I groaned. My eyes found the portal device at my side and another brilliant, probably ultimately-stupid-and-full-of-plenty-of-consequences-later idea popped in my head. I pulled it free and showed the artifact off. "If you don't let me in, the last thing you're going to do is surf an event horizon."

The probe gasped. How, I'm not sure. It clearly didn't have lungs. Maybe it was part of its translation matrix. But there was definitely a gasp. "You wouldn't."

My eyes narrowed. "Try me."

"I might."

I pointed the device at the door. "Remember the museum?"

"I wasn't there."

"Remember the art gallery?" I growled.

The probe shot back inside. I kept the war face I had, though inside I was one sad puppy thought away from breaking down with an ugly cry to dwarf all others. I had one stupid job to do, get inside a measly little bunker, and I couldn't even do that.

A hiss, like an ancient steam engine, preceded an awful screech of metal on metal that nearly had me clawing out my eardrums. The door drew back and then rolled to the side.

I bolted in.

CHAPTER TWENTY-TWO: LAMBDA LABS

Once I cleared the threshold, the door rolled back into place and sealed with a pressurized hiss. Inside the bunker, I was greeted with frigid air that nipped my face and crystalized my breath. I rubbed my arms as best I could and cursed between shivers. I hate being cold with a passion, probably more than I hate being chased by a swarm of Nekrael with a side of Nodari scouts topped with a Goliath or two.

Okay, maybe not topped with two Goliaths, but definitely one.

The L-shaped room I was standing in held a handful of consoles to the side, all of which were iced over. A few recessed lights in the low ceiling gave the area much-needed illumination, but it wasn't enough. Especially when I saw that there was an open lift straight ahead and the lights weren't enough to illuminate the entire shaft. Stumbling down that would have put a damper on all our plans to get out in one piece. At least the shaft was slanted at a forty-five-degree angle so if I did topple over, I could enjoy the tumbling sensation before braining myself on whatever was at the bottom.

Yet another flying orb, looking very similar to Tour Guide and TG2, came flying up from the shaft and stopped in front of me. Whereas Tour Guide and TG2 always seemed upbeat and pleasant, before he even spoke, this guy had annoyance written all over him.

"How may I be of assistance in helping you with whatever disaster you're concocting?" he asked, staring me down and not doing any of the bobbing, bouncing, or playful spinning I'd grown accustomed to.

"I'm not concocting a disaster. I'm trying to escape one."

"One you made, I'm sure," AB1 replied.

I named him AB1 at that very moment because he was being an annoying bastard, and I tacked on the numeral one because I felt I'd eventually need a two and three down the road. "Your friend made the mess when he said to shut off the repression fields. All we were trying to do was get home."

AB1's eye color shifted to a dark purple. "Pegasan did this? I should have known. Probably was going to run off with you as well, right? Leave me here to get vaporized with the fire blossom while he enjoys traveling the stars."

"I didn't know anything about vaporizing you, but he did want to tag along once we got the webway working."

"Where is the little traitor now?"

"A Nekrael bit him in half," I said, cringing as the memory came back to me. It was unreal how much strength those things had in their jaws, and given what they did to a droid, I hated to think about what they'd do to someone made of flesh and blood.

"Serves him right," he replied. "What's your plan now? You are aware that this bunker won't survive the fire blossom, aren't you?"

I held up the portal device. "Need to get this working again. I understand there are extra flux capacitors here and we could use one to fix it?"

For the first time in our conversation, AB1 noticeably perked. A soft, emerald-green light swept over the portal device, and once he was finished with the scan, he went back to looking sour. "Your lattice matrix is practically goo, which means after the first time you use it, your circuits will fry. And don't even get me started on how basic of a wormhole you can safely make."

"I know all that," I said, realizing I'd spent far too much time standing around already. "All we need to do is hop back to when the webway was opened and get through before everything goes to hell. That's it."

AB1 perked again. "You had the webway open?"

"For a few moments, yes."

"Why didn't you say that to begin with!"

"You never asked!"

"Details, details," he said. "I'll fix Jakpep for you, but you're taking me along. Deal?"

"Abso-freaking-lutely," I said, blowing out a huge puff of air.

"No time to waste then. Let's go."

Feeling better about our chances at this point, I followed him to the lift with hope in my step. It was probably a delusional hope, like someone bounding up to a slot machine that "was due" to pay out big, but when you're teetering on the edge of obliteration, you'll cling to anything good, much the same way I figure prisoners who'd spent thirty years in a smelly dungeon would get excited about a cupcake on their birthday.

As the lift descended, I put in a call to Tolby to catch him up on things. "Hey, bud," I said. "I'm in Lambda Labs. Should have the portal device repaired soon. How are things on your end?"

"Still holding our own," he said. "The Nekrael are all over the place now, though. Something has them riled up."

"That would be Jainon," I said. "She gave me her comm band and then drew their attention so I could get in. You'll need to watch for her."

"She took on a planet full of Nekrael and Nodari?"

"More like gave them something to chase," I replied. "She'll be fine. She's got kits to worry about, you know?"

I threw on that last part, hoping it would help placate Tolby's angst as well as mine. It was a good point, though maybe I should've considered the notion that this might make him rush out to her defense. Then again, Tolby was the level-headed one between the two of us.

"Looks like I'll be in for another fight," he grunted. "Where did she run to?"

"Easy, bud," I said. "She'll come to you."

"Not if she gets swarmed."

"She won't."

"Damn right, she won't," he shot back. "You worry about getting that device up and running. I'm going to the balcony to see what cover fire I can provide."

The call ended as the lift shuddered and groaned to a halt. The air was a good ten degrees colder than above. Aside from feeling— or maybe I should say not feeling—my lips turning blue, I started to wonder how many fingers I'd lose to frostbite before this was over.

We traveled down a short hall, which ended in an observation room about twenty meters wide. The far end had full-length windows that overlooked a factory built on a circular floor plan. Countless machines, presses, robotic arms, conveyors, and half-built components in storage bins lay underneath a network of catwalks. Like the consoles above, ice kissed most of it.

"Why's it so cold down here, anyway?" I asked. "Hoarding ice cream?"

"Thermostat broke," AB1 replied.

"You've got to be kidding."

"Nope."

"Why not fix it?"

"The lower temp prolongs my circuits and makes me feel a hundred thousand years younger than I really am. You should try it."

"No, thanks," I said, teeth chattering. "I don't want to be a frozen mummy."

"Suit yourself," AB1 said as he hooked left and started to descend a long, curving ramp that ran the circumference of the factory. "If you're so averse to a little drop in temperature, why don't you turn on your heater?"

"What heater?"

"The one in your arm."

I looked at my cyber arm. The circuitry still glowed a light orange. "I didn't know it had one."

"Officially, it doesn't," he replied. "But you can have it continually run self-diagnostics which in turn will heat things up a tad."

"How?"

"The same way you think through anything with that thing," he said.

"Right," I replied, feeling irked. Would it kill the little guy not to be so condescending? Probably. I let his attitude go and followed his instructions.

Okay, arm, thoroughly check yourself out for the next ten minutes, I thought.

At first, a tingling sensation started in my shoulder, and soon after I could feel warmth returning to my body. Not much, mind you, but enough that I felt confident I wouldn't die of hypothermia before the planet was obliterated. "That's handy. What else can it do?"

"Didn't you read the instruction manual?"

"I didn't get an instruction manual," I replied, putting bite into my words. "The Curator from the museum installed it and didn't give a lot of tutoring. I didn't even know I could throw telekinetic punches until earlier today."

"One of the niftier features of having a Mark IX Titan interface sewn into your arm," he explained. "It essentially draws power from your micro power cells and then releases it in a localized area of spacetime."

"Is that why my arm feels cold after I've used it a few times?" I asked. "Because I've taken energy away?"

"Yes. And you'd know that if you read the manual."

"I told you I didn't get one."

"It's in your arm," he said as he unlocked and opened a fire door which we then passed through. "I suppose I shouldn't be that surprised. According to records, you humans hate reading the manual. Always want to jump right into a live tutorial. That's probably how you ended up blowing up the museum, isn't it?"

I was going to argue, but we reached the end of the ramp and stepped into the factory, so I didn't feel like carrying on. The facility looked impressive in terms of the sheer complexity that each machine had.

Some were shaped like upside-down spiders with barrels protruding from their bellies. Others were more of the machine-press kind, but with lots of needlelike devices aimed at the center for whatever reason. More still were surrounded by robotic claws, some empty-handed, others wielding items that probably doubled as ray guns. All had inlays of Progenitor circuitry across their surfaces. All looked like they were an integral part to building something incredibly powerful like a fleet of battleships that could wipe out a solar system from three galaxies away or a computer that could finally deduce why guys refused to put the toilet seat down.

"Almost there," he said, leading me on.

I picked up my pace to follow. My heart felt heavy the more I gawked. I was going to be leaving behind yet another treasure trove of Progenitor tech, unable to take any of it with me. Worse, it was all going to be destroyed in a half hour, and there wasn't anything I could do about it.

"We can fix Jakpep with that," he said, interrupting my train of thought. "Go on. Put him on."

I turned to see AB1 floating next to a contraption that had an empty stand surrounding a half dozen tiny, mechanical arms sprouting underneath and curling upward. Unsure what to do, I turned to AB1 for help. "Put him on what, the stand?"

"Do you need to consult the instruction manual first?"

I narrowed my eyes. "You're a mouthy little thing, you know that?"

"Apologies. I failed to bond with you using humor. Apparently, I need to not use such complex jokes."

"Whatever," I replied. I carefully put the portal device on the stand.

The stand sprang to life in a flash. I watched in awe as one of the claws began pricking the artifact on the side, and each time it did, bright circles of light radiated across the portal device's skin. This continued for a couple of minutes before one of the claws gripped the artifact's side and pulled sideways, neatly detaching the side from the main body. This revealed a glowing, ruby-red cylinder with a hairline fracture running from one end to the other. Another mechanical hand swept in and popped the cylinder free from its housing before a third came in and replaced it. The side was then stuck back on and the claws started pricking the artifact once more.

"Is it done?" I asked.

"It's configuring the new module," he replied. "Five minutes it'll be ready to go."

"Hot damn," I said, beaming like a little girl getting the pony she'd begged for incessantly over the past year. I opened up a comm to Tolby. "Hey! It's fixed! Five minutes tops, and I'm heading out."

"Excellent," he said. "We're ready to go."

"Jainon is there then?" I asked, ever hopeful.

"She arrived not even a minute ago," he said. "She said she found transit tunnels that connect all the subbasements and used those to give the Nekrael the slip."

I smiled, glad that the Kibnali had kept her promise. Perhaps the intertwined arms were luckier than intertwined pinkies. "Give her a scratch on the head for me, will you?" I said. "Actually, no. I take that back. I don't need you two to have any excuse for another make-out session until we're clear."

"You honestly think we have that little self-control?"

"Do I need to answer that?"

Tolby didn't reply, so I ended up looking to AB1 for some insight into whatever took place here. "Hey, do you know anything about what happened here?"

"Of course," AB1 said. "I have been instrumental in all research."

"Including the Nodari?"

"Especially the Nodari."

I sucked in a breath and wondered if perhaps I should stick to that wonderful island called Ignorance where things are full of bliss. "What were they trying to do with them before they all vanished?"

"The Nodari didn't vanish," AB1 said. "They were sent away."

"Away? Where?"

"I'll show you," he said before turning to the side and projecting an image of the planet we were on a couple of meters away. The planet sat peacefully in space, but circling the entire thing was a swarm of tiny, angry dots. The image zoomed in, and it wasn't long before two things happened. First, I could see details, and second, I really wish I'd stayed on that island. The dots were ships, large and organic looking, and they had to number in the tens of thousands.

"Tell me that's not a Nodari fleet."

"It's not a Nodari fleet," AB1 said right as a gigantic wormhole opened near it, at which point the ships began to enter. "Do you feel better now?"

"Holy snort! That's a Nodari fleet!" I said, eyes wide. "Where are they going?"

"Invading the Kibnali Empire," AB1 replied matter-of-factly.

"What? Why?"

"That was Adrestia's entire purpose when it was built: to engineer a species to destroy the Kibnali Empire."

Tolby, who was still on the open line, roared. "Dakota! He better not have said what I think he did."

A heavy thump sounded from behind, and I spun around to see what had made it. Shadows that draped the factory made it hard to see much of anything beyond a few dozen meters. Even AB1 seemed unable to locate the source of the noise as well. He floated forward a few paces before a Nodari scout landed next to him and with one, heavy blow, drilled him into the floor, splitting his casing.

I screamed a string of obscenities and fumbled with my repeater as I tried to bring it to bear. I never got a shot off before the creature was on top of me.

CHAPTER TWENTY-THREE: BUGGING OUT

Claws raked across my weapon, knocking it from my grasp. I scrambled backward, trying to avoid being shredded into ribbons. I shot my arm out and telekinetically punched that freakish bastard right in his big, stupid head. It fell to the side, and as it staggered to its feet, I did the only sensible thing I could think of: I ran.

I ran even faster when a monstrous roar echoed through the air. I didn't dare look behind me, but I could hear the pounding of its feet as it gave chase. I sprinted down a narrow aisle filled with machines on either side. About halfway down, there was a gap between the floor and a container, and I rolled underneath it and belly crawled as fast as I could to the opening that led to the other aisle. Pain raced through my tender ribs as I had to stretch and contort in less than optimal ways to make the crawl, and I feared I was aggravating my injuries in ways that might prove problematic later, or even fatal.

A loud crack filled my ears as the Nodari scout rammed into the container. It shrieked and sent a claw-bearing arm after me. Its first swipe missed, but the second sliced into my calf.

That newest wound hurt like hell, but I gritted my teeth and kept my bearing. I drew my plasma pistol and opened fire. Since we were both on the ground, the shots struck its shoulder and arm. It reeled away from the machine, but I don't think I did much else than piss it off more.

He rammed the container again, and a second container that had been stacked on top of the first toppled off. I dove out of the way. Thankfully, I was quick enough to keep from being squashed. Sadly, the move was made so haphazardly, unadulterated agony ran through my sides and chest, and I dropped my plasma pistol in the process. The weapon slipped under a nearby machine and was lost in the darkness.

"No, no, no," I said, spending a few precious seconds trying to find it, but such efforts were made in vain. The scout roared, and I clambered to my feet while opening a comm. "Tolby! A scout's trying to kill me!"

"A scout? Are you sure?"

"It sure as hell wasn't trying to kiss me!"

"Where are you?"

"I'm still in the labs!" I said, running. "One got in here, and I lost my repeater and plasma pistol!"

"Is there anything else you can use?"

"Other than harsh language? No."

"Get out of there," he said, sounding more panicked than I'd ever heard before. "No one has ever killed a Nodari before in unarmed combat. Not even a scout."

"I can't! I left the portal device, too!" I said, vaulting over a railing and hooking left.

"Cripes, Dakota. We're all dead without it!"

"I *know!* I was kind of hoping you'd have some secret ninja move I could use that would get me out of this mess."

"Unless you get your repeater back or figure out a way to knock it into a vat of molten metal, all you can do is run," he said. "That's my secret move."

So I did. I ran faster than Hermes himself through the factory and made three hairpin turns before racing up a catwalk. I slowed due to protests of both lungs and legs and glanced behind me. The sounds of pursuit no longer hounded me, and everywhere I looked showed no signs of the Nodari scout. That said, I found little comfort in any of it but tried to enjoy the brief reprieve.

"I think I lost it," I whispered.

"Only temporarily," Tolby whispered back. "Call me back when you're clear. I don't want to give your position away. But remember this: it's out there. It's looking for you. It can't be wrestled with. It can't be intimidated. It doesn't feel pain, or doubt, or fear. And it definitely will not cease hunting you, ever, until you're dead."

"Is that supposed to make me feel better?"

"No, it's supposed to make you realize what you're dealing with," he said. "But, Dakota, you need to know something else."

"What?"

"You've got this. For the past few years, I've had the honor of being at your side, and I've seen you survive hair-raising, grueling encounters that would've stopped a dozen of the Empress's elite guard. So don't give up. We'll see you soon."

The line went silent, and I cursed. I ran my hands through my hair and realized they were sticky. It took only a second to see why. Fine lines ran across my chest and seeped blood. My hands shook, and the world slowly spun around. I had to catch myself on the catwalk railing to keep from falling as it dawned on me how close I'd come to meeting Grimmy and how the Reaper must be toying with the idea of collecting his raincheck on our date sooner rather than later.

Despite Tolby's pep talk, tears welled in my eyes. What the hell was I going to do? I wasn't a fighter. I certainly wasn't a crack commando that took on alien shock troops as a daily warm-up to a hundred-kilometer fun run. I was simply a girl who got a little lucky now and again, and now she'd gotten in way over her head. Even casinos in Vegas weren't greedy enough to let people bet on my odds.

I slapped myself across the cheek and ended my pity party. Even if I had my doubts, it wasn't only my life that depended on my success. Hell, it wasn't just the lives of us stuck here either. Literally, the fate of an entire species hinged on my success. I cleared my eyes, set my jaw, and vowed to rise to the occasion in such a spectacular fashion that tales would be sung about my triumph for the next ten thousand years. Maybe I'd even get a few songs, or a new RPG game made in my honor, too. Wouldn't that be cool?

"All right, you little bastard," I whispered, easing forward. "Where are you?"

Of course, he didn't reply. That didn't keep me from finding him, though. After a couple of minutes of working my way along the catwalks, I saw the portal device sitting in its cradle below. My heart sank as the scout picked up my repeater and gave it a look. For a brief moment, I hoped the monster would inadvertently blast his head off, but instead he held it close to his body, barrel pointed down, as if he were well-familiar with the concept of firearms.

I guess that shouldn't have been surprising. After all, the damn things wiped out the Kibnali. They couldn't have possibly done that simply by running at them in a mad attempt to rip them apart close range. I don't care how strong they were or how acidic their blood might be. Superior firepower makes short work of swarms. You don't have to be Sun Tzu to know that.

With the repeater in the hands of my enemy, I didn't have a lot to work with in terms of assets. Worse, time was ticking away, and I needed to act, fast. Then it dawned on me my arm was a potential treasure trove of unknown abilities, and it had a manual, to boot! Now, if only I could access it—

Pages appeared before my eyes, neat and orderly. Clearly, they were a product of the Progenitor interface interacting with my brain, but damn if they didn't look real enough, aside from the translucent nature to those pages and the fact I didn't have to use my hands to physically turn them. I couldn't make sense of the vast majority of it as it all seemed to be technical specs that went way above any AP course I ever took.

"Can't you just show me the bit on telekinetic punching?" I moaned.

The pages rapidly flipped in response and landed on a detailed section that once again made little sense unless you held six PhDs in Progenitor engineering.

Undeterred, I continued to skim through until I hit a small section that sounded like I could vary the amount of energy being discharged in a punch. Either that, or it was detailing a yet-to-be-implemented feature list. It was hard to tell, and there was only one way to find out. I needed a test subject.

I turned my attention back to the scout. He wasn't near the portal device anymore, but a good five meters away. At first, I thought he might be wandering off and that maybe I could sneak over, grab the artifact, and ninja my way out, but then I realized he was systematically searching for me, all the while keeping an eye on the device. He knew I wanted it.

"All right, let's see if this will do something," I said. I aimed at a cylinder that was near the artifact and imagined giving it a gentle nudge as opposed to a wicked uppercut.

The cylinder wobbled, which made enough noise for the scout to whip around, repeater up and ready. I gave it another nudge, and it fell with a loud clank. The scout jumped and laid into the trigger. Antimatter rounds tore through everything as it swept left to right. My gut tightened, and I swore three times over, as the portal device was one stray round away from being annihilated, and with it, our chances of survival.

When the shooting stopped, the table lay on its side, smoldering and cut in two. The repair module threw sparks, and its arms twitched. The portal device, still cradled in its stand, thankfully, looked unscathed. The scout strode over, inspected the damage it had caused, and then disappeared into the darkness.

"Dakota," Tolby said, far louder than I'd ever have liked. "I hope you're out of there."

"I thought you weren't going to call me," I hissed.

"We're—"

A loud crash blasted through the line. Shouts of panic and orders took over from his end and then the all-too-familiar sounds of blaster fire.

"Come and get it, baby!" Jack yelled. I heard his repeater go to work with deadly efficiency. Between small explosions and his maniacal laughter, I heard Nekraels shriek in pain.

"Defenses are breached, and Nekrael are pouring in," Tolby said, getting back on the line. He yelled at Yseri to get down before I heard another deafening explosion. "Planck's end, that was close."

"You guys need to bug out!"

"I'm aware—Jainon! On your left! On your left!"

More shots followed, and inhuman screams blasted through the air.

"Tolby! Talk to me!" I shouted, gripping the rail so tight I'm surprised I didn't leave finger marks.

"We're headed for the vehicle bay," he said between labored breaths of air. "Meet us there, and for the gods' sake, deal with your own problem and don't worry about ours."

Those last words snapped my attention back to the lab. I caught sight of the Nodari scout below right as he aimed my repeater and fired. I bolted sideways as a spray of antimatter rounds hit the catwalk. The area I'd been in vaporized in a shower of sparks. Load-bearing supports were the next to go, and although I'd escaped atomization, I couldn't escape the pull of gravity as the catwalks crashed down in a heap of twisted, groaning metal.

I rolled with the fall and ended up jamming my back into the corner of one of the machines. The scout leaped over the collapsed structure and leveled the repeater at my head. Reflexively, I punched the repeater. The barrel turned upright as the scout fired, chewing apart the ceiling and showering us both with sparks. Before he could recover, I summoned every last bit of strength I had and directed a punch right at his head.

The monster's head exploded as if it had been hit by an angry fist of whatever awe-inspiring deity you have in mind. Chitinous exoskeleton and goo flew in all directions, and the scout dropped to its knees with a shudder before falling over.

"Holy snort," I said, laughing in disbelief.

My celebration ended a moment later when I realized from my right shoulder down, I felt bathed in ice, and my arm literally hung with dead weight. I couldn't move it to save my life and certainly couldn't feel a thing. It was simply a hanging, useless appendage.

"Crap," I said, using my left hand to pick up my right and watching it flop to my side once I let it go.

I scooped up the repeater and gave it a check as best I could with one arm. It registered less than three percent remaining energy. At least it hadn't read zero, I told myself. As I hurried back to the portal device and scooped it up, I opened up a comm to the others.

"Guys, I've got it," I said proudly, hooking the artifact to my belt. "We're in business."

No one replied.

"Guys...guys?"

CHAPTER TWENTY-FOUR: HELLO, SEXY

Tolby? Jainon? Anyone?" My voice strained, and my mouth dried.

I ran back up the ramp and tried to placate my imagination with a thousand different scenarios that didn't end with the grisly demise of all those involved. I got to the elevator topside without any trouble as well. Getting to the surface, however, was a separate matter.

The lift was painfully slow. As it crept upward, my mind wasn't focused on what little time was left. It kept tossing AB1's final words over and over. The Progenitors had engineered a species to destroy the Kibnali, and for all intents and purposes, they succeeded. I wanted to deny it all, pretend as if that ancient, all-powerful race wouldn't do such a thing, as I'd been enamored with them for so long. Why would they do such an abhorrent thing? Was there some mistake? That would explain the museum, certainly, as it was hard to imagine they'd save a few Kibnali if the Progenitors were looking to commit total genocide. Then again, maybe keeping them in the museum was supposed to be like collecting a few trophies at the end.

I shuddered at that thought and grew queasy when I thought about how Tolby and the others must have taken the news. I couldn't think about that much because when it popped into mind, I reached the top. There, I saw that the circular bunker door was still firmly in place, and since I didn't have AB1 around anymore to open it for me, that put a hamper in my escape plans.

I briefly considered the idea that maybe the scout had found another way in, perhaps using the transit tunnels that Tolby had referenced earlier. Then again, maybe he hadn't, and I'd end up using precious moments looking for a way out that didn't exist. But if there was only one way in and out, how did he get in at all with the door still shut? I realized I'd likely never know, so I opted to try and work my magic on the consoles nearby. It took a few moments for me to be able to link into one, but when I did, the rest of the room lit up with activity.

Lights along the ceiling as well as the running boards near the door cast a warm orange glow to everything around. Multiple screens displayed a myriad of information, except for the one I was looking at. That screen sat there with nothing more than a blinking cursor.

"Right," I said, realizing I needed to use my interface. "You're waiting for some input."

I shut my eyes and reached out mentally via my cyber arm, or rather I should say, I tried. My attempt was met with abject failure and the strangest sensation I'd had in a long time. Mentally, it felt like I was searching for something I wanted to say but had lost the words only moments ago—that strange void in the mind where thoughts disappear, and no matter how hard you scramble for them, you can't seem to get them back. Physically, my shoulder and arm felt like they'd suffered ice burns thanks to a naked romp in Antarctica.

"Stupid arm," I said, glaring at the limp thing. "Can't I just plug you in somewhere to get your juice back?"

It didn't answer, of course, and I hadn't a clue how to recharge the thing. The energy had always seemed to come back slowly on its own. How long that would take was still up in the air, but I couldn't afford to sit around. Even if there wasn't a self-healing scout down below, the planet had an upcoming date with Armageddon.

"Look, gimpy," I said to my arm. "If you don't wake up, you're going to get really warm, really fast, and even I doubt that's as much energy as you want to take in."

I chuckled at my own stupid humor, side effect of being so tired, no doubt. But when that remark gave me an idea, my eyebrows arched, and I grinned.

Using my left hand, I vigorously rubbed my right arm from shoulder to wrist. Damn thing was even icy to the touch. But after a half minute, enough feeling returned in my arm that I could feel pins and needles race up and down it.

"God, I hate that," I said with a shiver.

At that point, I tried to connect with the console again. This time, I felt more drunk than forgetful in the sense I slogged through getting it to work, but I did. Once I realized I was in the system, I jumped and shouted for joy before scouring the interface for some sort of user manual or main menu.

At first, all I was greeted with were a number of graphics and diagrams that didn't make sense. After another minute of persistent work, I got the console to display a menu of options where one selection was clearly labeled "Front Door Control."

Eagerly, I selected that and the opening sequence to the bunker initiated. As the door unlocked and rolled out to the side, I bounced more and more on my heels, unable to contain my growing excitement and faith we were all about to put an end to this nightmare.

I flew out of the bunker and relished the warm air that greeted me. I also gave silent thanks to whatever deities were watching out for me because there were no Nekrael or scouts in sight. With a little luck, I'd have a clean run back to the vehicle bay as well. Too bad I didn't have my lucky plastic elephant. A good rub on its belly would've sealed the deal and we'd have been back home in no time.

From what I could remember, the vehicle bay was a couple of hundred meters northeast of the main facility building. I wasn't sure what to expect inside as I hadn't seen any details on it. Honestly, it didn't matter. All that mattered was that we'd all reach it safely, and that's what I intended to do.

A soft, electric crackling filled the air, sounding almost like those ancient fluorescent light bulbs that occasionally get shown off in museums. I looked up and immediately wished I hadn't. The twinkling red lights of the fire blossom now had beams of light shooting from their centers down to the ground. One of those beams landed nearby, and although it didn't do anything other than place a red dot on the ground, it did look a lot like a laser sight homed in on its target—which probably wasn't too far off from its purpose.

"Please, please, please, don't fire for another ten minutes," I said, figuring I'd get to the vehicle bay in under five easily and having a few more minutes of padding wouldn't hurt.

I picked up the pace and sprinted full tilt to the rendezvous point. My wounded calf burned in protest, and with each stride—with each impact my foot made in on the gravel beneath me—pain shot up my leg while fresh blood oozed out of the wound.

After rounding the second corner in my personal race against doomsday, the ground fifty meters away heaved upward with a gigantic explosion. Horse-sized boulders mixed with metal and other debris shot into the air before raining down all across the facility grounds. A few larger chunks landed unnervingly close, and a rear quarter of a Nekrael practically took my head off as it slammed into the ground close by.

Staring at the smoldering crater, I tried to raise the others on the comm. "Please tell me you guys are okay," I said. My gut tightened at the silence, but it eased as static came back, which was followed by Yseri's unyielding voice that always seemed to thrive in battle.

"Tolby overloaded a power junction," she said. "We're in the transit tunnels and still moving."

"You've no idea how relieved I am to hear your voice," I said, laughing and catching myself on my knees as I doubled over. "Can you still reach the vehicle bay?"

"Without a doubt. Do you have the portal device?"

"Yeah. I'm almost there."

"Good. Perhaps Empress's faith in you wasn't completely misplaced," she said. "We'll be there in two minutes."

With renewed vigor, I sprinted toward the vehicle bay. I slowed only once when a Nekrael appeared from around a corner ahead. My right arm was still cold, but at least I could use it again. I brought up my repeater and right as the damn thing charged me, I let him have it with my last remaining burst of antimatter rounds.

They caught it across the neck and torso, tearing the creature apart. Its mutilated body tumbled to my feet. I tossed my now-empty repeater onto its head for a little extra injury and finished my run to the vehicle bay.

The vehicle bay was large, boxy, and had lots of neon-orange trim along the edges. What looked like smokestacks sprang from the roof, and around its perimeter were several small boxes—like power nodes—embedded in the ground. When I reached the building, I tried the first door I came across. It didn't slide, swing, or budge in the slightest. I also couldn't find a terminal or console to tap into. So I moved on to the next and went through the same thing. The third door I came across, thankfully, responded after a minimal amount of coaxing from my interface device. As it slid back and closed with a heavy click, I breathed a sigh of relief. A few more steps and I could rejoin the others, and then it would simply be one last crazy dash through the past and through the webway to be clear of all of this.

I trotted down the short hall I was in, hoping that Empress was faring well enough and that all the recent fighting and running hadn't done her in. Since Yseri hadn't completely lost it on the comm channel, I assumed the matriarch was relatively fine.

I opened and stepped through an interior door and ended up in the vehicle bay. Ginormous double doors stood tall at the far end. Six columns, evenly spaced around, helped support the curved ceiling above. The space to my right held a half dozen vehicle spaces, each one clearly outlined in white with their own identical sets of machinery nearby. I figured said machinery was everything needed to maintain, refuel, and repair whatever was there.

Three of the bays were empty. One held something that looked like a Candarian battle tank, only the body was sleeker and the cannon up top looked like it could level mountain ranges. Another had something considerably smaller and jeep-like, though it didn't have any tires. It simply sat on the ground. Signs above both of those bays lit up as I drew near, each one saying: OFFLINE.

The final bay, the one closest to me, had a cherry-red fusion bike. It looked every bit of gorgeous as any of the bikes I used to dream of racing when I was a teen. The massive front and rear tires looked capable of gripping any surface, on road and off. The engine housing that bulged and formed the back of the seat hinted at the fusion reactor underneath (or whatever the Progenitor equivalent was), while the aerodynamic front half-whispered tales of untold speed to anyone brave—or stupid—enough to fully open the throttle.

For a moment, both time and my current situation became meaningless, which is what tends to happen to us mortals when staring at something sent straight from heaven. You think Arthur didn't dribble like an idiot when he finally got a chance to touch Excalibur? Of course he did, and not a single knight of the round table would say otherwise.

I hurried over to the bike and ran a finger over its curves. "Hello, sexy," I said as a longing to take it for spin firmly gripped my heart.

The door across from me slid open, and I jumped as everyone came barreling through, Jack in the lead. Dirt and gore from Nekraels covered each one in no small amount, and each struggled to catch breaths that had long since been lost.

"Glad you made it," I said.

"You look terrible," Jack said, eyes wide. "You're wearing half your blood on your shirt."

I looked myself over and grimaced. It did look awful, and now that I was paying attention to it, it felt nothing short of torturous. "I've been better."

Jack hurried over and started to examine my chest, but when I batted away his fingers, he frowned. "I'm not trying to cop a feel," he said. "You need that looked at."

"When we get out of here," I said. At that point, I realized the group was minus one. "Where's Tolby?"

Jack tensed and glanced back to the handmaidens, who had Empress supported by the shoulders. Jainon shook her head, and Yseri answered in her typical fashion. Short. Cold. Matter of fact. "We lost him in the explosion."

My knees buckled. Jack grabbed me before I kissed the metal floor. "She means separated," he said. "Not lost, lost. We don't know where he is, is all."

"He's not answering his comm," Yseri added.

"That doesn't mean he's dead," Jack shot back.

"We will be if we wait much longer," she replied.

The last half of her response stuck in my head. "We can wait," I whispered. When everyone looked at me, I found my strength. "We can wait. Like you said. We've got time. It might not be much, but we're waiting until the last nanosecond."

"One last test by the gods," Jainon said as she eased Empress to the ground and propped her against one of the columns. "How long until the planet is covered in lava? Fifteen minutes?"

"Seventeen," Yseri replied.

The comm I'd taken from the *Revenant* sprang to life. I fumbled to grab it off my belt. I flipped it open and was shocked to hear a broken, winded voice that was one hundred percent Tolby's.

"Hello," he huffed. "Can anyone hear me?"

"Tolby!" I shouted, leaping to my feet. "Where are you?"

"I don't know," he said. "In the transit tunnels, somewhere. I had to use my other comm to distract them. This damn place is a giant maze. I'm trying to get to the vehicle bay, but I have no idea where I am."

I laughed as I cleared my eyes and wiped my nose on my arm. "Because you have the worst sense of direction. What do you see? Maybe I can find you on the map."

"I'm in a long stretch with some conduits running above me. I've got pretty much every damn Nekrael and scout behind me caught at a pressure door," he replied. "Not sure what's ahead. All I can see is tunnel, but it must end in a lava pool. The heat is getting worse with every step."

"He's headed for the reactor," Jack said. "No two ways about it."

I nodded. "Keep going, Tolby. It'll cool off once you get topside. I'll meet you there."

"Will do," he replied.

I started for the bike but stopped when Yseri called out to me.

"Dakota!" she said. Anger burned in her eyes, and her hands clutched her weapon in such a tight manner I worried she was readying herself for a fight with me. The words that followed didn't ease that worry. "Leave your artifact."

"Why?" I said, instinctively drawing the portal device to my chest.

"Because it's our only ticket out of here and we can't risk losing it."

"I'll make it back," I said. I knew she was right, in the end, but I also knew if I handed it over, that would be giving Fate the thumbs-up to rub me out in this mad dash to get to Tolby.

"You're oathbound to the Empress," she said. "She needs it more than you."

"We all need it," I said. "I'll be back, and then we'll leave together."

Yseri brought her rifle to her shoulder, and though she kept it pointed at the ground, we all knew it was a courtesy she reluctantly gave. "I'm not asking."

"You're going to shoot me?"

"If I must."

I looked to Jainon for help, figuring the irate Kibnali would listen to her sister. "Feel free to chime in."

Jainon flattened her ears. "She's right," she said. "Prime the device and leave it here." I went to object, but she cut me off. "Dakota, if you don't make it back, we all die. We can't take that chance. Empress must survive...the Empire must survive."

"What good is your empire if you abandon the ones you love?"

"What good is your love if you sacrifice everyone else?" Yseri retorted. "Now give us the device, right now. I'm done talking."

A beat passed between us, though it felt like a thousand years. In that time, I realized I couldn't even win a Pyrrhic victory. She was going to shoot me in short order if I didn't capitulate. "Fine," I said. "But I'll be damned if you're holding it."

"Give it to Jainon, then, if it makes you feel better."

I shook my head and shoved the portal device into Jack's hands. "He'll carry it," I said. I then tacked on a quick lie, hoping it was unneeded, but not wanting to take a chance otherwise. "And for the record, I'm setting the device to only respond to his command. So no getting cute while I'm gone."

Jack's eyes widened, reflecting the shock on his face. "You're trusting me with it?"

"Yeah," I said. "It's primed and ready to go. All you have to do is pull the trigger, and you'll be six hours in the past. That ought to give you plenty of time to get through the wormhole when it opens up."

Jack nodded with a grin. "Not worried I'll leave you behind? Got my little brother to think about and all."

I returned the grin, although it was full of tension. "I'd be lying if the thought hadn't crossed my mind," I said, hopping on the bike. "But I figure you'd rather not spend the rest of your life with the Kibnali, so you'll still need me to get him and get home." I then turned to Yseri. "Happy?"

The Kibnali handmaiden lowered her rifle. "I won't be happy until this horrendous experience is over, but this will suffice."

"Good."

Jack pulled the repeater off his back and handed it to me. "I think you'll want this."

"Thanks," I said, finding a place for it across my back. "See you soon, Jack."

"Don't be gone long, Dakota."

With that, I jacked into the bike with the interface on my arm and mentally pressed the ignition button to fire up the bike's reactor. A low, oscillating hum filled the air, and I could feel the raw power emanating throughout the entire frame. I then connected myself to the vehicle bay main door and ordered it to open.

As it rose, Jainon and Yseri raised their weapons and pointed them outside, each ready to obliterate anything that happened by. In the brief lull I had before it was game time, I caught Jainon's eyes. "Hey," I said. "One last thing..."

"Yes?"

"If I die..."

"You want a Viking funeral. I know."

"The biggest one you can make. I want flames that scorch the heavens."

The Kibnali smiled. "Only fitting for a warrior like yourself."

"May Inaja bless you with good fortune," I said.

Jainon's eyes lit up with approval. "May her luck be your luck."

I touched the top of my head lightly and bowed. She returned the gesture, at which point I opened the throttle and rocketed out of the bay.

CHAPTER TWENTY-FIVE: ONE LAST TRIP

The ground raced beneath me. Buildings flew by in a blur of motion. I kept my head low so it was protected by the curved windscreen and eased off the throttle as I approached my first turn.

Leaning, I whipped around the building like my bike was on rails. Despite the tension of the situation, the insane amount of danger to life and limb I faced, I couldn't help but smile and wish I could somehow take this bike with me. I wanted to ride it forever as the damn thing performed better than any of my wildest fantasies.

I spied a few Nekrael running at me from the sides, but the bike was too fast for them to have any hope of catching me.

I zipped around another corner, which put me on my final run to get outside the gray facility walls. Up ahead, I spied a Nodari scout running out of a building. Despite the speed and distance, I could see one arm ended not in its usual claws-from-hell, but rather some sort of organic cannon—an organic cannon it pointed at me.

Activate shields?

The words flashed through my mind, and I ended up repeating them aloud for them to register. "Shields? Yes! Shields!"

The bike slowed, presumably from the redirection of power, and a translucent yellow shell appeared around me, not a moment too soon. The scout fired three shots as I sped by, each one striking the bike dead center, or at least would have. Instead, the neon-blue bolts impacted the shield and exploded in a brilliant starburst.

"Well that's handy," I said, laughing.

Shield integrity failing.

"What? You're not allowed to fail!" I argued. "You're a superbike! Do super things!"

Shield generator is 83,392 years overdue for maintenance.

"Of course you are," I muttered.

A fourth hit the shield, and both it and the shot vanished with a thunderous clap.

"Seriously?" I said. "You couldn't have held for a bit longer?"

No.

I growled, hating whatever AI inhabited the bike. It was short, and off-putting, though I shouldn't have been too hard on it seeing how it did suggest—and turn on—the shields in the first place.

A fifth shot zipped by my head and would've taken it completely off if I hadn't already begun weaving. Shots six and seven went wide, and at that point, I felt far enough away that I straightened out and gunned the throttle. The scout became a speck in the distance in no time.

Minimal shielding aside, the rest of the bike performed fantastically. I don't know what sort of shock absorbers the Progenitors had developed for the suspension, but holy snort, I felt like I was skating on glass, even over the rough terrain outside of Adrestia.

"Looks like we're clear," I said. "Is there anything else you can do to help?"

No.

"Don't talk much, do you?" I said, chuckling.

No.

I shook my head and concentrated on driving. I didn't ease off the throttle until I reached the reactor. A thin red line from the fire blossom struck it in the middle while clouds loomed around the structure, giving it a sinister appearance. Lightning crackled from the clouds, and I had a feeling the brewing storm wasn't a natural creation, but the result of the fire blossom getting ready to decimate the planet.

I brought the bike to a halt and jumped off. As I ran into the gigantic structure, I raised Tolby on the comm.

"Bud, where are you? I'm topside with a sorta-talking bike."

His reply was broken and filled with static and plasma fire. "Down...where...can't find...out."

Don't get me wrong, elation pumped through me hearing his voice and knowing he was alive, but I couldn't help but hate how little sense of direction he had. Even with the half reply, it was clear he was having trouble making his way to the surface. He'd probably be lucky to find his way out of a paper bag at times.

"I'm on the way," I said as I punched in the comm's track party function. It immediately gave me a range, a hundred and eighty-seven meters. I sent the data to Tolby's comm as well. "Did you get that?"

"Get..."

"Did you get that?"

He didn't answer, so I asked again. All I got in return was an earful of static, but I did notice that the range being displayed began decreasing. Elated, I ran down the path Jack and I had used before until I reached the winding staircase that led deep inside the reactor's guts. I leaned against a junction box and wiped the sweat off my brow as I checked the range again.

A hundred and fifty meters. One forty-nine. One forty-eight. Down the staircase I went. My lungs sucked in stifling hot air that once again threatened to cook me in short order. I hated to think what Tolby must be suffering through, given all his fur. Then I worried he might not make it out at all due to heatstroke.

I checked the range. Eighty to go. Eighty-one. Eighty-two.

"Tolby!" I shouted, redoubling my efforts and breaking into another run. "You're going the wrong way!"

At the bottom of the stairs, I ran down one of the many corridors filled with pipes, conduits, and shadows aplenty. I paused at a junction long enough to figure out which way led to Tolby and took off again.

"I hope you've got your friend, Dakota," Jack said. His voice, steady and even, felt tenser than any tripwire. "We've got less than ten minutes."

"Almost," I said.

"That almost needs to be a yes, ASAP."

"I'm aware of that," I shot back. "I'll be there."

I cursed as the comm ended. He was right, of course, but I didn't need to hear it at that moment.

I continued to follow my tracker. Down the passages I went, turning and backtracking as needed. At the bottom of another staircase, I glanced at the tracker again. Sweat ran in my eyes, and I had to spend a few precious moments clearing them. Even then, the display was blurry. The massive headache crushing my skull wasn't helping either, but I managed to see Tolby was less than forty meters away.

"Tolby?" I shouted, running, searching. "Tolby, where are you?"

Thirty meters. Twenty. Ten.

I rounded a corner, expecting to find my best friend. Instead, I was greeted with a Nodari scout.

I yelled in fright. It lunged, claws outstretched, and I fell back, raising my repeater as I slammed into the ground. Instinctively, I brought up my foot and caught it in the abdomen as I pulled the trigger. The scout's body sailed overhead, torn to shreds by the impact of a dozen antimatter rounds.

I rolled and pushed myself up, only to find two more scouts racing toward me. Bright green plasma bolts sizzled by my head, striking each one in the face. The monsters howled and kept coming until four more shots dropped each one.

I spun to find Tolby standing there, plasma rifle ready to engage whatever else came at us.

I threw myself at him, wrapping my arms around his waist, and squeezed. "I'm so glad you're okay."

Tolby winced. "Glad to see you, too."

I drew back and noticed the purple blood on my hand and the wounds across his body. "You're hurt."

"Just a flesh wound," he said as coolly as any battle-hardened, river-guarding knight of old.

I gave him another hug. "Good, because I'll never carry your fat butt out of here."

Tolby pushed me to the side and fired his plasma rifle twice more. The head of a Nekrael exploded about fifteen meters away, and its body dropped to the ground with a thud. "Time to leave. Lead the way."

Tolby might have never developed a sense of direction. Thankfully for him, I hadn't been dubbed the queen of "Pin the tail on the dragon" without good reason. We raced to the exit, Tolby keeping sharp watch on the rear.

After taking two corners, we came face to face with a pair of Nekrael. I laid into the first with my repeater, vaporizing half of its body before it had a chance to leap at me. The second attacked impossibly fast. I squeezed off more rounds, but they didn't find their mark. A split second before it was upon me, the creature's head exploded, victim to a well-placed shot from Tolby.

"Thanks," I said, blowing out of puff of air.

"Any—"

Tolby stumbled forward and roared in pain as a Nekrael latched onto his back. Its claws dug into his sides and legs while its vicious teeth clamped down on the back of his neck. He reached back, trying to get a hold of the monster, but couldn't get a grip on the beast.

Without thinking, I shoved the barrel of my repeater into the Nekrael's side and fired. The antimatter rounds tore the thing apart, and its body fell.

Tolby dropped to a knee and blood poured from his wounds and stained his fur. I immediately went to his side, trying to hoist him up, but he batted me away. "A moment," he said with a deep growl. "Make sure no more come up on us."

"Okay, but a moment is all we have," I said.

"These things will not be the end of me," Tolby said. "I'm not going to let the Progenitors win."

"Me either, so get it together," I said.

A scout rounded the corner behind us. I cut him down with a hail of antimatter fire. Another Nekrael came at us from the front, and like the others, it met a grisly end when I laid into him with the repeater. Before its body collapsed on the floor, I spun around, weapon ready, to find yet another one of the monsters barreling toward me. Instead of trying to take it out with good old-fashioned spray and pray, I knocked it silly with a telekinetic punch and placed a few shots into its skull as it struggled to regain its wits.

"Tolby, bud," I said between ragged breaths and forced laughter. "I can't keep this up much longer."

Tolby grunted, and using his rifle, he pushed himself up. His face twisted and his eyes watered. The shaking in his legs struck terror in my heart as I feared his wounds were far graver than he let on.

"Lead the way," he said, voice wavering.

"You're good?"

"My desire for vengeance will see me through any wound."

"I hope you're right."

I only took a few steps before he found his lost strength, and as such, I picked up the pace. Within heartbeats, we were barreling through the reactor again, only this time, I could hear Tolby's distinct oaths ringing in my ears.

"I swear by the head of each god, I'll travel through all of spacetime and personally gut every Progenitor out there."

"That's going to be hard seeing how a backlash took them all out," I said.

"That won't stop me," he growled. "A quick, painless death is nothing they deserve. I'll make the gods bring them back to life, if I must, have their blood spilled."

At this point, we reached the first stairwell, and up we went. The temperature still kept the air oppressive, but at least I didn't feel like I was hovering over a scalding pot of boiling oil. We continued through the maze of passages as Tolby continued to promise all sorts of death and torture the Progenitors. Sadly, I had to stop a couple times and clear my eyes from sweat and get my bearings, which ate up precious time. Each time, Tolby put shots back the way we came.

At a four-way intersection, I had to pause yet again to remember which way to go before hanging a right and then taking our second left. This passage ended in a T, which I knew was near the exit.

"Almost there!" I shouted with glee.

"Good," Tolby said, firing three more times. "My power pack is low."

When we reached the final stairwell, I felt as if we'd been granted angel wings we were moving so fast and with such purpose. The last set of corridors went by in a blur fueled by adrenaline. Tolby fired more and more until we got to the ramp that led outside. At that point, we passed through a pressure door and I immediately closed and sealed it behind us using a nearby console.

We both jumped back as something heavy slammed into the door. It bulged outward a couple of centimeters, but it held nonetheless.

"Come on," I said, pulling Tolby along.

"Right behind you."

My legs pumped, and my lungs took in as much air as I could gulp. Sweet, fresh air kissed my face as we ran outside, and the bike I'd used to get here beckoned us over, promising freedom.

I jumped on, and as I fired up the reactor, Jack called in.

"Less than three minutes, Dakota," he said. "You better be knocking on our door."

"Sixty seconds, tops. Might want to meet us outside."

Tolby jumped on behind me, and I hit the throttle. The bike roared in response and nearly threw us both with its godlike burst of acceleration. Since I had to fight to keep us stable, I wasn't paying attention, and that's what got us in the end.

The rear of the bike exploded, and we slid out of control before being thrown. Tolby and I tumbled across the rocky ground. My repeater went flying in the process. Where, I had no idea. Tolby managed to keep ahold of his plasma rifle, which was the only thing that kept us alive for the next few seconds.

A Nodari scout, the one that had taken potshots at me on my way to the reactor, jumped out from behind a boulder, weapon aimed at the two of us. Tolby drilled it three times in the chest and twice in the neck. It fell to the ground in a smoldering hulk.

"Dakota, what's going on?"

I cursed before answering Jack's call. "A damn scout took out our bike."

"How far are you?"

"I don't know," I said, picking myself up and cringing as I did. The palms of my hands were chewed up, and I could see flecks of dirt and tiny rocks embedded in them. "Maybe a klick and a half."

A Nekrael shot out of the ground near our position. Tolby took its head off with his plasma rifle, and he managed to do the same to the next two that came flying out of the tunnel as well. The third, however, closed the distance before Tolby could kill it.

The creature rammed into Tolby, knocking his weapon to the side. Tolby swiped its face with his claws, leaving deep gashes across its face and knocking it to the ground. The thing found its footing right as Tolby jumped up in the air and drove both of his feet into the creature's neck, causing it to snap.

Monstrous bastards number four and five appeared. To my utter amazement, they didn't get far. Tolby pounced on the one closest, and while he had it pinned beneath his bulk, he caught the other midair and broke its back over his knee before ripping its limbs off and using them to beat the first to death in a matter of seconds.

"Remind me to stay on your good side," I said, both in fear and awe of what he was capable of.

Tolby scooped up his plasma rifle with bloody paws. "Later. We have a portal to catch."

We took off running again. As my feet pounded on the rough terrain, Jack spoke with an unnaturally calm voice. "I'm sorry, Dakota. I really am."

My run slowed. "What? Don't you dare..."

"Yseri! Jainon! Grab Empress," Jack said. "We're leaving."

My throat tightened. "No...please..."

"You had your chance," he said. "We're not sticking around to die. It's that simple."

The line cut out before I could say another word. My pace slowed, then stopped. I probably should have been cursing Jack's name from the top of my lungs, but I hadn't the energy or wit left to do anything.

Tolby came to my side and dropped a heavy paw on my shoulder. "Thanks for coming back for me," he said. "You didn't have to."

I chuckled through a sniff. "Don't you dare say that. Of course I had to."

The ground behind us rumbled. I turned in time to see Goliath break the surface a hundred meters away. As he pulled his massive body out of the hole, fine bits of debris rained down around us.

I grabbed hold of Tolby's paw. "We were so close, too."

"Do me a favor?" he said, squeezing my hand.

"Of course."

"If I die," he said, shooting me a playful grin. "I want a Viking funeral."

CHAPTER TWENTY-SIX: THE ARENA

Beams, fifty meters across and bright as a supernova, dropped from the sky. The nearest one drilled straight through the reactor and within seconds, a bright fountain of lava spewed into the air.

The ground rose and fell in waves. Tolby and I tumbled sideways, still embraced, and somehow, he kept us upright. Sadly, Goliath didn't fall either and charged. Tolby dropped me to his side and readied his rifle. I grabbed a pistol off his belt and aimed with my left hand as I prepped for one last telekinetic punch from hell with my right. If we were going to die, we'd at least go down fighting. I swear, I was prepared to tap into so much energy, I could have sworn my fist was encased in divine light.

Tolby and I fired shot after shot, but Goliath raised a claw and blocked every last one. Damn thing's armor suffered little more than scorch marks, something I was acutely aware of as it kept coming.

An explosion on the beast's flank knocked it sideways. One of its legs broke off, and its left claw fell to its side. A second explosion hit the top of its carapace, sending chitin in every direction.

"Go! Dakota! Go!" Jack screamed over the comm.

Confused, I pivoted to see Fe'daku driving a land skimmer at max speed. It had a broadhead shape and open top, and it floated on a cushion of air. Behind Fe'daku stood Jainon, manning the top-mounted canon. She fired one more shot into Goliath's side before whipping the portal device up and firing.

A beautiful, fully formed wormhole opened a couple of meters away. Screaming with joy, I grabbed Tolby, and we raced through. We came out the other side in the same location spatially but a few hours in the past.

As I panted for air, Fe'daku slid the skimmer through the portal, nearly taking Tolby and me out in the process.

Once the skimmer came to a stop, Fe'daku tapped the side of his helmet, causing the faceplate to disappear and revealing Jack's smiling face.

"You left!" I shouted, laughing and crying.

"We did," he said, waving us over. "Now get in. We're not out of this yet."

With a single leap, I cleared the side and ended up in the back with Yseri, who held Empress slumped in her arms. Tolby was right behind, smushing into the front. Jack gunned it a split second later.

We'd barely gone a dozen meters before Goliath lumbered through the open wormhole and gave chase. Even with a bum claw and a missing leg, he was fast. He wasn't gaining on us, but we weren't losing it either. At least lava wasn't falling from the sky. So there was that.

"You're Fe'daku?" I said, trying to put things together.

"Yep, but I think I'll stick with Jack. Much sexier, don't you agree?"

I gripped the side of the skimmer as Jack whipped us around a boulder. Cripes, he was driving fast. Not that I was complaining. We had a portal to catch and a Goliath to get away from. "How far back are we?"

"A minute from you opening the webway," he replied. "I think."

"You think?"

"It's a little up in the air right now, okay? This time surfing stuff sucks and makes my head hurt."

I chuckled as we bounced over a few dips he didn't bother dodging. "But how? AB1 had only one flux capacitor left."

"Correction," he said. "He only had one left for you. I used the rest before you got there to line all this up."

I shook my head, thoroughly impressed. I had a million questions, but they would have to wait until we weren't trying to jump through a wormhole that had a five-second window at best.

Jack reached back and handed me a spray can. "Take this. Figured you might want it."

I eyed what he gave me, unsure what to do with it. "What is it?"

"Good ole fashioned first aid synth-spray," he said. "Or close enough to it. Progenitor design and ought to be good on those gaping chest wounds of yours, unless you're keen on coming down with a nasty infection, assuming you don't bleed out first."

My eyebrows arched as I was thoroughly impressed with all he'd accomplished. I turned the nozzle toward my chest and sprayed myself down. A fine mist hit my skin and stung worse than a hundred yellow jackets out for revenge. "Damn, that hurts," I said, hitting the side of the skimmer.

"It'll get better. Had to use a few myself."

Thankfully, it did. A few seconds later, a cooling sensation replaced the stinging one.

"Bring anything else back?" I asked. "Dropship? Space marines? Snow globe?"

"No," he said, swerving to avoid a pit in the road. "They were all out of those."

At this point, we zipped inside the facility perimeter. Jack took a sharp corner to take us down a side street, and I nearly went over the side. I was going to chew him out when I saw his arms stiffen.

"Brace for impact!"

The words barely registered in my mind when the skimmer lurched, and I slammed into the back of one of the front seats. Half a Nekrael flew over our heads with a trail of ochre-colored goop closely following.

"Get off the damn road!" Jack yelled right before we hit another of the creatures.

This time, it was more of a graze. It was enough to rip off its hind legs, but not nearly enough to slow us down. And you better believe that was a good thing, because Goliath hadn't eased off our ass in the least. In fact, when I glanced back, I was sure that if he gained a few more strides on us, I could floss his teeth.

We zipped around a corner, and ahead I could see the webway, maybe three hundred meters away. The skimmer's engine roared as Jack opened up the throttle.

Jack then put his hand to his ear. "We're almost there. Get through the moment you can!"

"Who are you talking to?"

Jack pointed toward the webway. From a side building, I saw Daphne roll out and make a beeline for the center of the platform right as a big, beautiful portal opened. But it didn't lead to a beach, or any place sunny for that matter. What lay beyond was a stone coliseum that stretched high into gray skies.

"That's not what I had opened before," I said, leaning forward. "Why is it different?"

"Like I should know!"

"You've been running around here, so yeah, you should!"

"I might have fudged a few things that had some consequences, okay?"

"God, I hope this doesn't turn us inside out," I said.

Jainon, still on the gun, looked down at me with a grin. "Or make us explode."

"We've got no other options," Jack said. "It's our only ticket off this planet."

I didn't argue. None of us did. Right before we passed through, I realized the other side offered a three-meter drop we weren't going to avoid and sucked in a deep breath.

We shot out of the wormhole, and immediately the skimmer tipped forward. There wasn't a damn thing we could do other than pray for a soft landing, which I suppose since we all didn't die, was partially answered. The skimmer's nose crumpled as it impacted the sandy floor before the entire craft slid out of control and slammed into a stone slab.

I stumbled out of the vehicle and had a brief second to take in our new surroundings. We were definitely in a gladiator arena, complete with towering stands, rudimentary, stone slabs for obstacles (which also included another set of Progenitor spires for another webway), and one, pissed off monster to fight to the death when Goliath tumbled out of the portal.

The ginormous creature hit the ground with a deafening clap of thunder. The ground caved where his feet hit, sending shockwaves racing up my legs. The portal closed a moment later.

Jainon was the first to act. With blood oozing from her mouth, she leaped up and brought the cannon to bear. "Steel yourself. Nashir has seen fit to thrust us into one final battle."

"Scatter and take it from all sides!" I yelled, bolting left along with Jack as Tolby and Yseri grabbed Empress and ran off in the other direction.

Jainon's first shot hit Goliath in its left claw and carved out a boulder-sized chunk from its bulk. The next hit the creature square in the chest, but to my dismay and disbelief, the blast only cracked his armor. There was no follow-up shot.

"Gah! Arek's games!" she said. "It's out of ammunition."

"That's going to complicate things since Goliath's way more pissed than dead," I yelled back.

Goliath agreed and charged the lone handmaiden. Jainon held still for so long, I was sure she'd frozen up in fright, but at the last second, she dashed forward and ran under Goliath's attempt to smash her where she stood. His heavy claws pulverized the speeder with a sickening crunch.

"Bring it down while it's distracted!" Jainon called out, darting between its numerous legs.

"Easier said than done," I replied. I glanced around, hoping to see something we could use, but all I saw were obstacles in the arena and heavy portcullises that lead off into dark tunnels. Figuring I needed to do something, I pulled out my plasma pistol and started firing.

Goliath ignored each shot. Instead of even acknowledging my existence, he twisted and barreled after Jainon. I continued to fire, but my shots did little to his armor other than leave black marks.

"Coming through!" Jack yelled as he raced by.

My jaw dropped at the sheer speed he had. I didn't have a radar gun, but I'll be damned to a bedridden life if he didn't easily blow by at a hundred kilometers an hour. Then my jaw dropped even further when he pulled off his next stunt. When he reached Goliath's side, he jumped up and drove a fist through a joint on one of its lower legs. Exoskeleton exploded in all directions and trailed long strings of yellow goo.

The blow wasn't nearly enough to do the creature in, but it was more than enough to get it to stumble and make Jack the center of attention. Goliath swung his back end, whipping his tail at Jack. Although Jack managed to jump out of the way of that blow, he didn't fare so well against the next. Goliath batted him away with the back of his claw, sending him flying and tumbling across the arena floor.

"Jack!" I yelled, dashing toward him.

Jack managed to get up, but stayed hunched over, clutching his midsection. He staggered a few paces before collapsing against a nearby wall. Despite his obvious injuries, he waved me off. "I'll be okay. Get rid of that thing."

Since I didn't have any red potions, magic wands, or some other fairy-tale healing item, I skidded to a stop, knowing I couldn't do anything for him and began shooting at Goliath once more. The creature went after Jainon, and like before, he ignored all of my shots, making me feel thoroughly useless.

"Dakota!" Yseri shouted as she took up a position off to the side and began firing as well. "Aim for his wounds and shoot slow! Your skill cannot match your frenzy!"

I nodded and ran. She was right. My shots were too quick, too full of panic and adrenaline to be of any use.

With Goliath still intent on chasing down Jainon, Tolby flanked the monster and pumped a dozen plasma bolts into its weakened side. As the damage against Goliath mounted, Tolby's fervor for battle grew. "You should have stayed on that dying rock!"

Goliath replied by fanning his rainbow-colored tail and flicking a volley of harpoons at him. Each one whistled through the air. Tolby tried to dive out of the way, but he wasn't fast enough. One of the spears cut across his forearm while another caught him through the upper thigh, taking him off his feet.

Tolby, pinned to the ground, roared as he yanked the harpoon free. As he did, Goliath fanned his tail again, looking for the coup de grâce. Before it could be issued, Yseri popped out from behind a stone slab and put four shots into the gaping hole in his side.

Goliath shrieked, and faster than should have ever been possible, it burrowed underground.

For a few tense seconds, nothing happened, but then a wave of dirt came at me as Goliath tunneled toward my position right beneath the surface.

"Holy snort he's fast," I said, bolting sideways. I expected him to keep chasing, but his dirt trail ceased as he went deeper underground.

His stint this time wasn't nearly as long. The ground near Yseri billowed, sending the handmaiden dashing to the side. Her reaction, unlike mine, was filled with amusement.

"The poor kit is scared," Yseri said, grinning. "I would be too if my wounds had wounds."

Goliath burst from the ground right at Jainon's feet. It was only her countless decades' worth of training that saved her. She managed to jump back enough so that when the monster crested the surface, she was hit by his forehead and not taken in by Goliath's gaping maw.

The handmaiden was launched a dozen meters into the air as the three of us started shooting again. She hit the ground, hard, and managed to roll with the landing so that she lost very little time coming to her feet.

Goliath closed the distance in two seconds and repeatedly attacked with his claws and forelegs.

"Some assistance!" Jainon shouted as she scrambled. Though she'd remained unscathed up until this point, she panted heavily, and it was clear she couldn't keep free of the monster much longer.

Yseri moved in, and I lost sight of Tolby when he ducked behind one of the blocks. I ran up a steep ramp and on top of the platform, betting I'd have a better shot at Goliath's weak spot from that vantage point.

Jainon feinted left, and when Goliath took the bait, she darted right and under his heavy swing. It was more than enough to get her in the clear for a bit longer, and when he swung around to give chase, I was presented with a beautiful target: a gaping wound at the top of Goliath's carapace.

Instead of firing in reckless abandon, I heeded Yseri's earlier advice and spent an extra couple of seconds breathing.

In...out...in...out...

My body steadied, and my eyes focused on my target. I squeezed the trigger, smooth and slow. The first bolt of plasma missed, but it left a sizzling trail only a handbreadth above what I'd been aiming at. My follow-up shot struck soft flesh with a fantastic result.

Goliath reared back, fanning his colorful tail and roaring in the process. He spun around and launched a volley of harpoons at me.

Thankfully, I'd anticipated the attack once I saw that tail spread and managed to dive out of the way.

All of this gave Jainon enough opportunity to run to relative safety. And by relative, I mean, she managed to put forty meters between herself and Goliath as opposed to the three she previously had.

In the end, I guess the distance she created didn't matter, because Goliath decided to come at me instead, his newest tormentor. I didn't have the self-control or speed Jainon had, so when Goliath charged, I ran back off the platform and ducked behind a block of stone. My self-delusion of him not seeing me shattered when Goliath rammed the block at full force, demolishing the top half.

I ran, dodging falling rock, and ended up narrowly avoiding one of his claw strikes in the process. I twisted as I ran, and using one arm, I popped several plasma shots into his face. To my utmost delight, one of those shots found his left eye, and the thing popped like a water balloon.

Goliath recoiled, screeching in pain and shaking his head back and forth.

"Not bad, tailless," Yseri called out, with no small amount of pride in her voice. "We shall take its other eye and let it curse the day it ever decided to give chase to the Kibnali."

Goliath recovered and came at me with such vengeance, I was sure not even an unobtainium-powered shield generator would slow the thing. Time crawled, and my mind raced as it tried to decide which way to run. I could go left and hopefully take advantage of his blind and weak side, or I could try and dart underneath as Jainon had. Neither option seemed promising, and going right, where he still could see and smash things quite well, was clearly suicidal.

I darted left and managed to get around one of the webway spires before Goliath tracked my movement and followed. He hit the spire with his shoulder, cracking the structure, and wrapped his claw around to try and drive me into the ground.

I barely scurried out of the way. Thankfully, I didn't have to run anymore. Tolby came flying through the air with one of Goliath's fired harpoons in hand. He landed on Goliath's back, drove the impromptu spear deep into the creature's open wound. Despite his bloody leg and god knows how much pain racing through his body, as Goliath thrashed, Tolby kept his grip and wasn't thrown off.

I took advantage of the situation to put more distance between myself and Goliath, and I ended up next to Jack, who was still slumped against the arena wall. He looked up at me weakly and smiled, which was enough to know he was alive.

As much as I wanted to tend his wounds, I knew we had to finish Goliath off. But how? The wounds he'd suffered had stopped bleeding, even his most egregious ones, and maybe it was a trick of the lights or sheer paranoia on my end, but it looked like they'd healed a little, too.

"Damn thing isn't going to die, is it?" Jack said with a cough. "Even if we do drop it. It'll come right back."

I nodded. That was the problem, wasn't it? Even if we had bombs to drop, or I could telekinetically punch its head clean off, given it was designed to turn into a Nodari, it would eventually get back up. We needed to kick it into a volcano or drop it into the sun, and at the moment, we weren't fighting near either.

Then another thought came to me. Distance didn't matter. I smiled brightly as the most obvious and completely suicidal plan crystallized in my mind.

"What?" Jack asked.

"I got it."

"What!" he called out while I took off running. "I'm not going to like this, am I?"

"You'll have to trust me!"

The battle raged on between the Kibnali and Goliath, and neither side looked to be winning. As Jainon leaped back to get clear of a tail swipe, I shouted to her. "Jainon! Where's the portal device?"

"In the speeder!"

"Keep it busy for a few more seconds!" I yelled, running full tilt for the wrecked vehicle. My legs stretched under the demanding pace, and I prayed that in Goliath's rampage, he hadn't smashed the device.

"Dakota! It's still not fixed!" Jack yelled. "You're going to fry it!"

I ignored his words, and when I reached the speeder, I furiously searched through the wreck, but it was nowhere to be found. Not in the front. Not in the back. Not even on the ground nearby.

"Dakota!" he yelled again. "It's our only way home!"

"I know!" I yelled back. "Just tell me where it is!"

I spun around to see Goliath roar and throw Tolby off his back. My best bud rolled with the momentum and came to a stop behind a column. He rose to his feet, albeit slowly and stiffly. Yseri and Jainon fired more rapidly and aggressively, trading safety in distance to hopefully distract Goliath enough for Tolby to get away.

I turned back and scoured the wreck again, knowing I couldn't do anything without that device. I dove into what was left of the back seat before throwing myself out the other side and checking underneath. I was about to curse it all when a soft voice called my name.

"Dakota," Empress said. "Here."

I whipped around. Empress stood a couple of paces away leaning heavily on the wall with one hand and offering the device to me with the other. Her legs shook, and her breathing was shallow. I tried not to think about how much she must be pushing the limits of her body as I snatched the artifact.

I shut my eyes and tuned the world out as best I could. I reached out and connected with the portal device and felt its familiar presence in mind. At first, I saw nothing but heard everything from terrible roars to sizzling bolts of plasma. Then, tiny equations filled my mind. Familiar ones. Ones that preluded the opening of a wormhole. But with no console, I had no reference points, and as history had taught me, the less I knew about where I wanted a wormhole to open, the more disastrous it usually was.

I snapped my eyes open when I heard both Jainon and Yseri yell.

Tolby, flat on his back, rolled out of the way of one claw strike, but was not going to be able to dodge the next that was only a second away. Out of pure instinct, I raised the portal device and pulled the trigger.

My vision filled with more equations as the device tried to bring to reality what I had in mind: a wormhole that connected the center of Goliath's body with the sun that loomed overhead.

The air around the monster wobbled as spacetime had an acute identity crisis, and then he vanished only to reappear in front of me, not even twenty meters away. A second portal opened up in the center of the arena, blacker than any event horizon and swallowing up the entire webway platform.

A loud explosion came from the side of the portal device, shooting red-hot shrapnel in all directions, and I stumbled back.

My face felt wet and warm, but that sensation quickly faded as every semblance of self I ever had washed away.

I only had one thought at that point in time.

Man, that's a nice breeze.

CHAPTER TWENTY-SEVEN: FINALE

The wind swept me off my feet, and I found myself sliding toward the void I'd created. The fright was more than enough to spur me into action. As I struck a stone slab, I twisted enough to grab ahold and keep from being pulled into the void.

Goliath, likewise, was at first unable to counteract the enormous amount of suction the wormhole generated and it slid back as well, but only for a few moments. It slammed its pointed feet in the ground, firmly rooting itself where it stood.

"Sorban biscuits on a stick," I muttered. "What's it take to get rid of you?"

Goliath answered by lifting one leg and driving it back in the ground a couple of meters in front of him. At that point, he managed to pull himself forward.

In a panic, I scanned the area, trying to find something I could use to get myself out of this predicament. The only things that met my eyes were giant, space-faring felines who were desperately clinging to stone and column like I was and enough sand that I vowed to never look upwind ever again.

"Dakota!" one of the felines called out. "We can't hold much longer! Close the portal!"

Dakota? That name felt right. And could I rid us of that void that hungrily sucked everything down its gaping maw? In the back of my mind, I felt I could. Or at least, once could. But how?

Goliath moved again, driving another foot into the ground and shifting another meter in my direction. It wouldn't be long before he was on me and there was little I could do to stop him. All I had with me was my good looks and a spiffy cyber arm that probably hurt like hell to get punched by.

Power tingled through my side at that thought. Memories of me knocking Jack silly and pulverizing both the Nekrael and Nodari rushed back. I grinned with devilish delight remembering my powers. I might not be armed, but I did have one hell of an arm.

"Come on, big guy," I said, egging Goliath on. "Got a nice treat for you."

Goliath obliged. As he lifted his foot up, I drained every bit of energy I could from my arm and drove a telekinetic punch straight through his good eye.

Tissue and chitin exploded in every direction. Goliath shuddered and crashed to the ground. I had no time to gloat, sadly. The strength vanished in my right arm, and without its help, I slipped off the rock.

Racing across the ground thanks to the vacuum of the void, I hit Goliath in the face and tumbled off. I managed to kick off his body hard enough so that instead of being dragged through the wormhole, I ended up hitting one last chunk of stone near the portal's edge, which I desperately clung to.

Goliath disappeared into the inky black a moment later.

"Help!" I cried. My legs flopped through the portal. Stabs of icy pain shot through my feet and up my legs. "Someone! Anyone!"

The biggest of the felines, bloodier than a surgeon working triage at a mass casualty event, let go of the slab he was on and slid toward me. He slowed himself down by raking his claws across the ground, and he skillfully positioned himself so his feet anchored him against the boulder I was on while his back lay pressed against the ground.

"Don't let me go," I begged as his massive paw grabbed my arm.

"As if I'd ever," he said. Then, with a deep growl, he pulled me along the ground and out of the portal.

"Close it," he said. "You're clear."

Fog still clouded my mind, but I knew the answer on how to do such a thing was there. I shut my eyes and racked my brain for a way to get rid of the portal. The specifics never materialized, but the more I pushed for an answer, the more a swirl of equations flashed through my mind.

Pain mounted in my head, but I kept on. It probably didn't last for but a few more seconds, but it certainly felt like a lifetime. Without warning, everything fell into place, and the invisible knife that dug in my skull vanished, and along with the immediate sensation of relief came the immediate cessation of my mangling of spacetime.

Slowly, my savior and I rose to our feet, and once we were both upright, I fell into his embrace. His fur felt warm, comforting, and familiar, like an oversized teddy bear straight from the dryer. Probably shouldn't ever admit to him I called him a teddy bear on account I imagine that's insulting to giant felines. "I don't know who you are, but thanks for saving my life."

"No, Dakota. Thanks for saving ours."

An hour and a half later, I sat on the arena floor with my memory mostly intact while Tolby, Yseri, and Jainon continued to use the archive cube to try and figure out exactly where we were. And when. No one was sure. At the very least, Jainon had said the gods had whispered a bit of encouragement to her as a reward for destroying Goliath: we'd made it to somewhere in the Kibnali Empire prior to the Nodari invasion.

While the Kibnali tried to make sense of things, Empress sat quietly next to me, and we watched Jack play mechanic on the totaled land skimmer while Daphne played music nearby. Twenty minutes ago, Jack declared triumphantly he could fix the vehicle. Empress and I had our reservations. Okay, we all felt he didn't have a snowball's chance in hell. Still, maybe he'd get lucky. Stranger things had happened, and he being a total guy probably needed to do something to keep from going insane.

"You look better," I said, breaking the silence between myself and the matriarch.

"I still feel terrible," Empress replied solemnly. "At least our trip through time with Jack led to a little more medical attention."

"You guys are going to have to fill me in on that," I said.

"I'll let Jack," she said. "It's his story."

"He'll probably have a fit if someone steals his thunder," I said with a grin. I then sighed as the events of the past couple of days replayed in my head. In that short time, I'd discovered—and subsequently blown up—a Progenitor museum, managed to get myself stranded five billion years in the future, wiped out a research facility with untold riches in terms of technology, discovered the Progenitors had purposely orchestrated the genocide of the Kibnali for unknown reasons, and now I was stranded billions of years in the past on a planet on the other side of the Universe from where I called home.

I chuckled thinking about that last bit. For all I knew, we were so far back in the past neither Mars nor Earth had yet to form. Or if they had, maybe dinosaurs were the current kings of that pretty blue sphere. That might be fun getting back to. I always did want to see a T-Rex. A real one, not the clones they have in zoos. Although I will say, micro-rexes are so damn cute. Too bad they're so expensive. Stupid designer pricing. They look like they'd make fun pets.

Empress leaned her shoulder on mine and gently took my hand with her paw before giving it a squeeze. She had a surprising amount of strength in her grip. "Jack," she said. "He brings honor to your species."

Warmth flowed into my heart as I looked at the guy. Not because I'd renewed my schoolgirl crush I had had on him way back when. Our first encounter at the museum pretty much soured those feelings into oblivion. But what coursed through my veins was now gratitude and respect, which was a thousand times better. "Yeah, I guess he does," I said. "Though, I still think I should get to smack the hell out of him for scaring us like that."

"Perhaps," Empress said after some thought. "Afterward, he can sire you a great number of warriors that will carve you a mighty empire to rule—second to ours, of course."

I laughed and shook my head. "Let's not get ahead of ourselves. I'm not ready to waddle around like a penguin and look after a mini-me. Besides, I can barely remember to water my plant enough to keep it alive, and it's a cactus."

"What's a cactus?"

"A spiny plant back home I only have to water once a week."

"I suspect your children might want more than that," Empress replied.

"I hear they do."

"She wants to honor you again, as before," Empress said, looking at Jainon.

"Me? For what?"

Empress grinned as her tail whipped me on the side. "Had that question come from any other, I'd have laughed at such obvious false modesty. But how you think so little of what took place is astonishing."

"You mean here in the arena?"

"And at the facility," she said. "You've accomplished no small tasks in such a short time."

I blushed and shrugged. "I only did what I had to."

285

"I don't doubt you'll always see it that way," Empress replied. "Regardless, she wants to grant you a full title."

"I...I don't know what to say," I said, stumbling over my words. I wasn't sure what the title would be, or its ultimate significance in their culture, but it was obvious it was a great honor.

"Say nothing," Empress replied. She then grinned. "To Yseri, especially. She's still...how do I put this...tense, and Jainon should speak to her first."

"Got it."

"I don't suppose you guys found anything else about the facility?" I asked, the details of its purpose still gnawing at my mind.

"No," Empress said. "We barely got things together to get you."

"Well, thanks," I said. "Still...I wish we knew more."

Empress nodded solemnly. "As do all of us."

"No ideas whatsoever why the Progenitors hate you so?"

Empress shook her head. "None, though they wouldn't be the first species to curse our existence."

The conversation paused a few moments, and we watched Jack work. Predictably, he was getting nowhere. Not that I could tell being an expert Progenitor mechanic, but we could see it by the look of utter frustration that had made a home on his face.

"Poor guy," I said. "He doesn't have a prayer to get that fixed."

"I know his heart," she said. "He won't stop working until his brother his safe."

"You're probably right."

Empress turned to me and asked, "What do they know?"

"About you?"

She nodded.

"Only that you're their Empress," I said. "Regardless of how you were...appointed, your new empire needs stability."

"Thank you," Empress said, patting my shoulder. "But my future is still questionable at best."

"All the more reason we need to get back to my time," I said. "Yseri and Jainon will understand, I'm sure."

"I can only hope."

"If not, you can stay with me," I said, nudging her with my shoulder. "We'll have a grand time together."

Jack came clomping over, ruining the bonding moment we were having. It was hard to be mad at him for that, though. He moved stiffly and winced more than once, and he undoubtedly was in more pain than he let on.

"I'm about ready to sell that thing for scrap," he said.

"We'll find a new one," I said.

"We better," he said. "Because now it's your turn."

"My turn?"

"To deliver," he said. "I risked life and limb trying to get spacetime to cooperate enough to snatch you from the fire. Now you need to make good on your promise."

Though he hadn't given any details, I didn't need them. Whatever had happened between the time he first jumped back in time and when he showed up with a Progenitor land speeder sporting a sweet cannon, a lot had taken place.

"I haven't forgotten," I said, realizing I needed to say something. "And I'll make good on my promise. We'll get Kevyn."

"Good," he said, releasing a puff of air. "I'm glad you're up for it, but there's still a glaring problem."

"There is?"

"Yes," he said. "You nuked our only way home."

I glanced down at the portal device. It was every bit as broken as TG2 had said it would be if I fired it one last time. "I know," I said. "But there are other ways to get back."

"Normally, I'd agree," he said. "But you also managed to destroy this webway with that wormhole you made."

I gave my best Cheshire grin. "And?"

"What?" he said, clearly taken aback by my cavalier attitude to it all.

287

"TG2 said they had spaceships that could jump spacetime," I said. "And since I need a new one anyway..."

Jack shook his head and laughed. "That's your plan? Find a lost time-traveling spaceship from an even more lost race?"

"Yup. Unless you have a better idea," I said.

"No," he replied. He mulled some thoughts over in his head, which he didn't share before giving a curt nod. "Fine. We'll figure it out. But I still have two other things we need to talk about."

"Which are?"

"First, I expected to be treated differently."

"You think I haven't treated you right?"

Jack threw a glance at Empress and hesitated with his reply. "We've had...conversations. I'm not saying I'm always right, but from here on out, I think it's only fair you trust me more. I did say a few things would happen that clearly did, despite your objections."

I folded my hands and rested my chin on them as I mulled his unspoken request. He wanted me to consider his points more without dismissing his concerns as coming from someone who only looked after himself.

"Fair enough," I said. "What's the other thing on your mind?"

The corners of his lips drew back, and his eyes sparkled. "I think for saving your life you should thank me now and kiss me later. Or you can kiss me now, too, if you'd really like to show your appreciation."

"How about I thank you now and I'll buy you a root beer later," I countered.

"Deal, but you'll still end up kissing me later," he said with an overly exaggerated, playful wink.

A soft hiss filled the air. Jack and I looked around, trying to find its source. The Kibnali did, too, Empress included, but confusion didn't fill their faces. Only elation.

Three talon-shaped aircraft flew overhead in a V formation, no more than a few hundred meters from the ground. As they passed over, the two in the rear split to either side and made lazy circles around while the third entered a tight loop before skimming the arena for a closer look.

"Praise to the gods!" Jainon shouted, grabbing her sister by the shoulders and squeezing tight. "Will you stop your incessant blasphemy now?"

Yseri, looking stupefied, cracked the smallest of grins, which I'm sure she was both reluctant and relieved to do. "Perhaps."

I stood and helped Empress to her feet. She leaned heavily on my frame, and I'm proud to say I didn't collapse under her bulk. She may have been the smallest of all the Kibnali I'd met thus far, but she still had a lot of meat to her.

Sensing I was missing something both obvious and important, I asked the only question on my mind and hoped I wasn't about to jinx us all. "Are those aircraft Kibnali?"

Tolby nodded and wrapped his arm around my back before squeezing me. "That they are, Dakota. That they are."

I gave my bud a playful bump with my hip. "So, you're going to get them to give us the full VIP treatment and what not, right? Because I could really go for a hot tub, chocolate strawberries, and a bottle of champagne right about now."

Tolby made a face...you know, *that* face that was equal parts cringe and worry.

"What?" I asked, but my shoulders fell as the answer came to me in a flash. "Oh, right. You guys aren't the most hospitable species on first contact."

Tolby grinned and gave a sheepish shrug of his shoulders. "Exactly. We're more of the conquer-and-enslave-first-and-ask-questions-probably-never sort."

I sent a shrug of my own right back at him. "Eh, we'll manage," I said. "We always do."

Though Tolby didn't argue that last point, there was still the look of worry in his eye, and if I'm being honest, I probably

should've heeded his warnings a little better because, well...
Spoilers: things get worse.

(PAGE LEFT INTENTIONALLY BLANK)

(EXCEPT FOR THAT LINE; AND THIS ONE, TOO)

SO CLOSE TO HOME
(DAKOTA ADAMS BOOK III)

Know what's great about a little black dress?
I can really rock it when it's time for some R&R.

Know what's not so great about it?
It's a pretty crappy outfit to have when Armageddon comes and your holiday goes belly up.

Which is exactly what just happened to me.

So now instead of sipping mimosas and playing with exotic wildlife, I'm trying to survive a cataclysm of biblical proportions. But hey, at least I'm getting my cardio in for the year.

And if somehow I can find Yet Another Wormhole™ and warp my butt back to Mars, I'll have one hell of a story to tell.

That said, always remember, if I die, I want a Viking funeral.

ACKNOWLEDGMENTS

As always, I have the usual crew to thank: My wife for putting up with a lot of bad writing over the years, my wonderful editor Crystal for turning slop into something decent, Katrina for proofing it one last time, and my kids for giving me endless ideas on what's fun and adventurous.

I'm also forever grateful to Katherine Littrell who breathed wonderful life into the characters and gave Dakota the voice she needs.

Of course, none of this would be possible without all my brilliant readers, new and old; so here's to hoping you enjoyed this book two and are off to see what book three has in store.

ABOUT THE AUTHOR

When not writing, Galen Surlak-Ramsey has been known to throw himself out of an airplane, teach others how to throw themselves out of an airplane, take pictures of the deep space, and wrangle his four children somewhere in Southwest Florida.

He also manages to pay the bills as a chaplain for a local hospice.

Be sure to drop by his website https://galensurlak.com/and sign up for his newsletter for free goodies, contests, and plenty of other fun stuff.